SHE'S STILL THE ONE

Kaci Rose

Five Little Roses Publishing

ISBN: 978-1954409019

Book Cover By: Coffin Print Designs
Editing By: Debbe @ On the Page, Author and PA Services
Proofread By: Nikki @ Southern Sweetheart Services

To all the best friends that turned into the best forever love.

CONTENTS

BLURB

Bro Code Rule #1 – You can't have your best friend's younger sister.

Austin

What is it that guys I date don't seem to understand what a causal relationship is?

That doesn't mean to propose to me. This is why I packed up everything into my car, and I'm now heading to my brother's home.

Only he's not there, but his best friend, Dallas, is.

Damnit, he's the reason none of my relationships have worked out. I compare them all to how he treats me.

When they go on tour and drag me along, it's hard to hide feelings in the small space of a tour bus. But my brother has made one thing very clear.

Dallas is no good for me, and we both risk losing my brother, if we go any further.

Dallas

It sucks when you can't have the one girl you love.

When the band I started, with Austin's brother, took off, girls were easy. It was less messy having flings, but it earned me a playboy reputation.

Then, she moves into the house with us.

Even when her brother has made it perfectly clear she's off limits, I can't seem to stay away.

She's still the only one who makes my heart race.

Can I convince them both I've changed, and I will be a one-woman man for the rest of my days, if she just chooses me?

GET FREE BOOKS!

CHAPTER 1

Austin

Why is it that the only guys I seem to attract are the weird ones? Seriously, how hard is it for guys to understand what a causal relationship means? Isn't that every guy's dream to find a girl who wants just casual? It must not be, because my now ex, Branden, proposed to me two nights after three months of what was supposed to be casual dating.

So, that's why everything I own is now loaded up in my car. Driving down the coast from Portland, Maine was fun, but now, I'm driving into Nashville from the north, and I get my favorite views of downtown, along the Cumberland River. The sun has just started to set and is throwing some amazing oranges and purples behind the downtown skyline. I roll my windows down and just soak it in.

I'm back in the south.

Once I pass downtown, I continue on to the Belle Meade neighborhood at the south end of Nashville. This is where all the top music guys in the city live, who don't want to buy a massive estate outside the city limits. This is also where my brother and his band mate and best friend, Dallas, live.

I try to think back over the last three months. Did I give Branden any signs that we were more than casual? I don't think so. We would go days without talking, and we saw each other once a week, if work allowed. The sex was pretty good, but I never stayed the night at his place, or even had a toothbrush there, so I'm not sure how he thought proposing was the next step.

I sigh. I hate that I left my roommate with such short notice, but she didn't seem to care, once I offered to pay my rent for the next month, before I left. Thank God, for my job as a graphic designer, because it means I can work anywhere.

I park my car and grab my overnight bag. I can bring the rest in tomorrow. The garage is large enough that we each have our spots. Plus, the guys have a few fun cars they don't take out much.

Walking in from the garage and listening, I hear the TV in one of the living rooms, but I'm not sure which one.

"Hello?" I yell out, as I set my bag on the kitchen counter.

A second later, I hear footsteps, and Dallas appears around the corner.

"Austin?" He asks, like he isn't sure it's me. His icy blue eyes still sparkle, and I know it's why he can get any girl he wants. Those eyes draw you in, and the sexy tan skin, abs, and ink keep you hooked.

"Yeah, is Landon here?"

"No, your brother is out of town. He's been working with a charity on our off time."

"Oh," I say and deflate. I really wanted to talk to him in person. Otherwise, I could have stayed in Portland and called, if I had wanted.

"Hey, what's wrong? You know you can talk to me, right?" He looks concerned.

"Yeah. I um... Well, I'm moving back in for a bit anyway, if that's okay?" I say uncertain if he even wants me here. I know my brother would be over the moon, but Dallas I'm always unsure of.

My brother and Dallas bought this house with the money from their first huge check, and the place has been my safe haven ever since. My room is always the way I left it the last time I was here, and the kitchen is to die for, so I'm always cooking, which the guys love, so it's a win.

"Of course, this is as much your home as it is mine or Landon's. You know that. When does your stuff get here?"

"Oh, it's in the car. I didn't have much. I can get it tomorrow, as I have what I need now." I place my hand on my bag.

"I'll unload it first thing in the morning," Dallas nods.

"Oh, I can do it. It's no big deal."

"Non-negotiable. Besides, your brother would have my ass letting you carry boxes up to your room. Come join me in the living room, it's just me and some snacks."

"Oh, I can go to my room. I didn't mean to interrupt your alone time."

"Don't make me throw you over my shoulder, Austin." His tone may be joking, but I know he would do it, because he has before.

Dallas has been my brother's best friend, since they were about ten, and I've had a crush on him for about as long, but he never asked me out, so I settled for being friends.

Since their band, *Highway 55*, made it big, he's known for his playboy reputation, but it's not as bad as the tabloids make it seem. Yeah, he doesn't do relationships, and he's had his share of one-night stands, but he's always upfront with the girls, so they know what to expect. He doesn't lead anyone on, and I respect that. He also treats me like gold, so I know when he decides to settle down that girl who captures his heart will be one lucky lady.

This fact makes spending time with him alone a little tricky, because I make sure I don't let my feelings show. I wasn't prepared for this tonight, and after the long drive, I really was planning to go to my room, but I also won't pass up time to spend with him either.

I follow him to the living room at the back of the house. This is the one we all use the most, because it's the most comfortable and not as fancy. They don't use it for entertaining, like the front living room.

We both sit down on the same couch facing the TV, but Dallas turns sideways to look at me.

"What happened?" He asks.

"I was ready for a change." I shrug.

"Austin..." His tone is a warning. He's always been able to read me just as well as my brother does.

"Branden proposed," I say, slumping back against the couch.

I must be more tired than I thought, because I swear I see hurt flash across his face for a brief second, as his eyes go wide. "What? I didn't know you were that serious."

"We weren't! It was casual, no titles. I didn't even have a toothbrush at his place. We saw each other maybe once a week, and we didn't even talk every day. Then, two nights ago, he takes me to dinner and says he has something to talk to me about. I thought he was going to want to be more serious, and I had planned to break up with him. He knew the score from the start, but no, he does this whole dramatic proposal with everyone in the restaurant watching and oohing and ahhing. So of course, they all thought I was this big bitch. when I said no, grabbed my things, and ran out. I packed my car, left that night, drove until I was tired, grabbed some sleep, and continued all day yesterday and today."

I enjoyed living in Portland, Maine. The views are breathtaking, and it's a very relaxed vibe. I rented a room, and the place was right downtown, so I could walk to just about anything. Though, I will miss that place, I'm looking forward to getting back to Nashville, too.

"Geeze, Austin. Why didn't you call? One of us would have flown up and driven back with you." He shoves some taco dip and chips at me, his silent demand that I eat something.

"I know, but I wanted to get out of there. So, I paid my room-mate for next month and left. I'm going to miss my days by the lighthouse, but I don't know, I just needed to be here."

I loved taking my laptop down to The Portland Head Light, the famous lighthouse on the rocks, and sitting at the picnic table, working on it with the water as my view. It's the biggest thing that sold me on living there.

"Well, I'm glad you're here," Dallas says, as his eyes sweep over me. If he was anyone else, I'd think he was checking me out. But I know Dallas, he's making sure I'm okay, so he can report to my brother that I'm all in one piece, safe and sound.

"Want to watch a movie?" He asks.

"Sure, you know what I like," I say, as I stand up and grab a bot-tle of water from the mini fridge in the corner of the room. I also grab my favorite blanket from the rack, before I take my shoes off and sit back down.

Dallas puts on an action comedy film, and we're both quiet, during the beginning. I see him texting on his phone but quickly forget it, as I get into the movie. Then, my phone goes off, and I see a text from my brother.

"Tattletale." I huff out, and Dallas just laughs.

Landon: You should have called. Anything could have hap-pened.

Me: Not like you were here anyway.

Landon: I'll be home in a few days.

Me: That's what D said.

Landon: I'm glad you're back. I missed you.

Me: Missed you, too. Go do your charity thing and get home soon.

Landon: Stay safe, and let D know if you need anything.

As we watch the movie, I glance Dallas's way a few times. He got some new ink on his arm that I can't fully see. I have always loved Dallas's tattoos. They have a deeper meaning for him, even though, he won't share what some of them are.

"You aren't watching the movie." He smirks, when he catches me looking at him.

"You have some new ink. Can I see it?"

Giving me that panty dropping, cocky half-smile America loves, he lifts his shirt sleeve to reveal what would look like a simple nature scene to anyone else, but I recognize it instantly. It's the field the guys would always take me to on picnics. It's where we spent lots of our time in the fall, because the changing leaves were breathtaking, and it's also where we were, when they got the call about their record deal the summer after I graduated high school.

"I miss that place. Life was so much simpler then," I sigh.

"Yeah, it was. Some of my best memories with you and Landon happened there. It's the one place that the rest of the world couldn't touch us."

We stay up well past midnight talking about some old memories, discussing the movie, catching up on some TV shows, and just catching up in general. Dallas has always been so easy to talk, too.

I don't remember falling asleep, until I'm jolted awake with a warm body cuddled with mine.

CHAPTER 2

Dallas

I'm fighting waking up, because there's a warm body pressed against me. Normally, I don't let a girl stay the night, and when they try to cuddle, it makes me want to bolt, only this girl pressed against me isn't making my skin crawl.

I crack open my eyes and see I fell asleep in the living room, and it all starts to come crashing back to me.

Austin.

She fell asleep watching the last movie. I decided to finish it then carry her to bed, but I guess I fell asleep, too. Then sometime in the middle of the night, we must have shifted to lying down on the couch. She's pressed between me and the back of the couch with a long, tan leg swung over my hips. She's using my shoulder as her pillow and has her arms flung across my stomach.

I let her warmth soak into me and try not to wake her, because I want to lie here just a bit longer.

I have had a crush on this girl, since high school, but you can't date your best friend's younger sister, right? In fact, Landon makes that perfectly clear any time he's caught me looking at her. Austin was off limits then, and I know she still is, especially because of my playboy days, once we got our record deal.

Her brother won't care that I'm tired of that lifestyle and

haven't been with anyone in over six months. It's the fact that I lived it at all. It was a way to forget everything. The fact that I couldn't have Austin, my mom dying, and dealing with sudden fame.

Landon's my best friend, and he's supported me through it all, never questioning or judging me, but I know I'm not what he wants for Austin. She deserves somebody respectable that you can't find lewd stories about online almost weekly. The press also doesn't care that I haven't been with anyone. They know how to take a photo just right to make it look like whatever they want it, too.

I sigh, pushing the thoughts out of my head and try to be in the moment with Austin, because I might not get this chance again, having her cuddling with me.

She didn't seem quite her normal self last night. Granted, she had been driving for over two days, but I think this thing with Branden shook her up more than she wants to admit. She's tried dating, but half the guys wanted to date her to get to Landon and me, or they didn't treat her as well as we did. We did set a pretty high bar.

Her last long-term relationship was about a year ago, and his excuse for breaking up with her was that she was too close to her brother and me. Do guys really get upset about that? So, she started this casual thing with a few guys, always breaking it off, when they wanted more. But this guy, proposing after three months? Not cool.

She stirs, and I'm disappointed that our snuggle time is coming to an end. I can tell the moment she's awake, because she freezes. I'm guessing like me, it takes her a few moments to remember where she is, and who she's with.

When she lifts her head, and her gray blue eyes meet mine, my heart starts racing. She rests her chin on my chest and gives me a soft, sleepy smile, and right here in this moment with her dark brown hair slightly a mess, I can't remember a time I have ever seen her more beautiful.

"Thank you for letting me talk last night. I think I needed to vent more than I realized," she says.

"Of course, I'm here anytime," I say.

Then, a slight pink tints her cheeks, and she sits up.

"Sorry, I didn't mean to fall asleep on you," she says.

I know I need to fix things and put that wall back between us to keep us both safe, even though I don't want, too.

"Don't worry, sweetheart, I'm used to having beautiful women throw themselves at me." I give her my famous cocky smirk.

"Ugh!" She wastes no time throwing a pillow at my head, causing me to laugh. There we go, back to our normal.

"Why don't you go get a shower and all? I'm going to take you out to brunch, and I have a surprise that might cheer you up," I tell her. The thought had been in my head last night that I needed to do something for her, like her brother would, to get her mind off Portland and everything she left behind.

As she heads upstairs, I snag her keys and go out to her car and start bringing her bags and boxes inside, setting them on the kitchen floor. She doesn't have as much stuff as I expected, about six boxes and four suitcases. Then again, she has a lot of clothes and items she keeps here regularly, too.

Once everything is out of her car, I start carrying them upstairs and leave them in the hallway by her bedroom door. If she's showering or changing, that's the last thing I need to walk in on, as much as my cock might like the idea. When I bring the last load in, I knock on her door.

"Yeah?" She calls but makes no move to open it.

"Your stuff is out here in the hall. I'm going to go get ready," I call back, and then head to my room across the hall from hers.

I take the quickest shower I ever have in my life, and then get dressed in dark jeans and one of my raglan shirts she loves, before going downstairs. I find her in the kitchen with coffee, and she already has a cup made for me just the way I like it. A dash of cream, as opposed to her several sugar packs and a lot of flavored creamers.

"I feel bad. Landon is cutting his trip short, and he'll be here tomorrow," she says.

I try to hide my disappointment, as I was looking forward to more time with her alone, but I know the whole reason she came was to see her brother.

"That's good, though. I know you want to talk to him, and he's worried and wants to make sure you're okay himself," I say.

"I know, but still. I'm a big girl and could have waited a few more days." She shakes her head, as we finish up our coffee.

"All right, hungry?" I ask, grabbing the keys to my 1969 Corvette Stingray I restored, after we got our record deal. This is my fun car that I only take out on special occasions, and getting a day alone with Austin, is very much a special occasion.

"We're taking the Vette?" She asks all giddy. She loves this car as much as I do. I try to tell myself that's the only reason I chose it, and not because it puts us in a small space together, or that when I put the top down, she can't stop smiling, as she tries to contain her hair.

"Got a hair tie?" I ask her. She holds up her arm, where she has one around her wrist, like a bracelet.

"Ready!" Her smile is infectious, as we head to the garage and get in.

"Oh, I love this car. You keep it in such great shape!" She runs her hands over the hood, and I feel the movement, as if she were running those hands across me. It's making my cock so hard I have to shift to hide it behind the door.

"Of course, I do. It's a classic. Get in, I'm starving." Just not for food, I add in my head. The moment she closes the door, her scent fills my car, and I almost hate the idea of putting the top down later. I want the car to smell like her--orange blossoms with a hint of coffee.

The smile never leaves her face, as I drive to our favorite place in all of Nashville. Well, all of Tennessee and the surrounding states, really. *Loveless Cafe.* Normally, the wait would be a good hour no matter what time of day, but I've helped the owners with some promotions, so I never have to wait for a table now.

As we pull into the parking lot, Austin groans. "I have missed this place. Don't get me wrong, I enjoyed the lobster, but I craved their biscuits and pecan pie something fierce!"

At least, she remembers to wait to get out of the car, until I come around to open her door. This is as much being a gentleman, as it is for her protection. Never know when crazy fans are around.

"Let's get a picture in front of the sign, before we go in," I suggest, and Austin practically drags me in front of the iconic neon sign for a photo, before we head inside.

"Well, if it isn't Dallas McIntyre!" Gigi calls from behind the counter. "Aren't you a sight for sore eyes? Oh, and you brought a woman. Did hell freeze over?"

I laugh. I don't bring girls here, and I don't take girls out for that matter. When I show up, I'm normally alone, but Landon has come with me a few times, too.

"This is Austin, Landon's sister. She just got back into town and is craving your biscuits." I tell her.

She grabs two menus, "Come, come, this girl is too skinny. We will feed her and plump her right up. Oh, Austin dear, you are just a doll. You should try our pulled pork barbeque omelet. I'll add a little extra pork fat in it to get some meat on your bones, yes I will." Gigi gushes.

Austin laughs but can't get a word in.

"Your Dallas here, has been such a blessing helping with some promotions, and he's had some great ideas to help us expand. A few new menu items are thanks to him, and his weird ordering, too! Let me get you some biscuits." She walks off, before either of us can say a word.

"Don't bother ordering. She'll just bring you something else, but whatever it is, it will be amazing. She's always having me try new things." I warn her.

"How long have you been working with them?" Austin asks.

"A few years now. They catered the food the night we did that Christmas special at the Grand Ole Opry, and we got to talking. She has so much energy and is such a great lady. I couldn't help but connect with her."

Austin smiles, as we start talking and catching up. She tells me about some of her recent graphic design work, and I talk about a few other local businesses I've been working with in town.

She congratulates me on another song, reaching number one. That's eight number one hits and a platinum album, which is still crazy to me.

Breakfast flies by, and the food is of course amazing, and when Gigi won't let me pay, I leave a tip that more than covers the meal.

"Home?" Austin asks.

"Actually, I have someplace else to go. It's a bit of a drive. Top up or down?" I ask.

"Down." Austin rolls her eyes at me, like it's the stupidest question she's ever heard. She's just so damn cute, when she rolls her eyes. She puts her hair up, as I put the top down, and we head south to Franklin, Tennessee.

"Where are we going?" Austin asks, as we enter the town.

"To The Carter House," I tell her. Austin loves historical homes, and I heard about this one recently and know she will love it.

We spend the next few hours touring the house, grounds, and visitor center. We learn a major Civil War battle took place right in the house's front yard, and it was described by one of the family members that you couldn't see the grass there were so many dead bodies, covering the ground.

Austin gets a chill with that comment, and I give myself permission to wrap my arm around her in comfort. I tell myself that it's just to comfort her from the creepy history. It's not so I can feel her warm body next to mine. When I pull her in for a hug, it's not to feel her tits against my chest. She doesn't stay in that hug with her head on my chest for anything more than comfort, as she listens to the tour guide.

Maybe, in a different world in another time, this could be more, but I have to be happy with this.

CHAPTER 3

Austin

I'm really glad I decided to stay here. I've already been more productive today, work-wise, than I have been in weeks. This house always has my inspiration flowing. I've always thought of this as home, but I have never really stayed here longer than it took to decide my next stop in life. It's been my layover point, safety net, and safe haven, since I graduated high school. Maybe this time, staying here in Nashville with my brother, is my next stop.

I'm working in the dining room today, which has great views of the amazing pool area and is far enough away that if Dallas decided to watch TV, it won't distract me. Though to be fair, Dallas is always considerate of me. When I'm working, he will watch TV in his room, rather than chance distracting me. I'm not sure what he's up to today, but he's been in and out of the house.

We had a great time yesterday taking the house tour, but I was up all night, thinking of the few minutes I spent in Dallas's arms. It was like instinct for him, when I felt that chill run through me, he was right there to comfort me. On the way home, we rode with the top down again and talked about some other places to visit. He even pulled over and let me drive the last few miles home. That was a close second to the highlight of the day.

I smile to myself, as I stretch and take in the space around me. This dining room is so comfortable, and it doesn't feel cold, like many in the large houses around here. One of the walls in this room is exposed brick. The reclaimed wood dining room table is large enough to sit twenty, if you put in the leaves, but they always keep them out, so it can sit ten right now. The table has matching wood chairs on one side, and on the other side, along the wall with the windows to the backyard, is a bench seat attached with pillows. It looks more like a long window seat than a dining room table bench.

The pillows are all done in gray and creams and pair good with the brick wall. It's homey and relaxing. Remove the pillows and add some fancy place settings, and you have a very formal space. The decorator the guys used knew her stuff.

I didn't sleep as well last night, as I did the first night pressed against Dallas. I try not to admit that to myself, because the reality is hard to handle. It isn't the first time we have fallen asleep together. I have crawled into his bed a few times, when the storms get too bad, or I've had a bad dream, but we never cuddled like that. We always stuck to our sides of the bed.

I push it all out of my mind and work on this brand kit for a lingerie boutique. They need a logo and a brand design of colors and fonts. From there, I will help design her website and social media graphics. I love her stuff and am having a lot of fun mixing the leather and lace theme she wants to go with.

I'm so into my work I don't hear Landon walking in, until he's right in front of me.

"How you have always been able to block us out so intently and work, I'll never know," Landon says.

I jump up and hug him, as my brother gives me my favorite bear hug. He isn't a hugger by nature, and I haven't seen anyone else get bear hugs from him, but I love them. They make me feel safe and always pull me out of a bad mood.

"I missed you so much," I whisper.

"Me too." He squeezes me again, before pulling away. "Where's your stuff? Do you need any help?" He asks.

He looks around, like he expects all my stuff to be piled nearby. His dark brown hair that matches mine is longer than the last time I saw him with a slight curl to it. His gray eyes land back on me.

"No, Dallas brought it all up from my car yesterday, and I unpacked most of it last night. Landon?" I ask hesitantly.

"Yeah?"

"I think I want to stay here a bit, not just pass through," I tell him, not sure if he will like his little sister here, cramping his style.

"I'd like that. I always hope you'll stay, when you visit, but I never want to pressure you."

Just like that, the decision is made.

I nod. "Done then. How was your trip?"

"Good, let me go get a shower and unpack, and we can talk, while I make dinner." He says.

The best thing about my brother is that he loves to cook just as much as I do. It relaxes him, and if you try to stop him from cooking, he gets upset. So, while normally I would tell him to go sit down, because he just got in, I'll cook. He wouldn't like that. So, I learned to stop fighting him over the years.

I turn to my computer and save what I've been working on and check my email to make sure everything can wait until tomorrow.

I'm closing my laptop, when my brother comes into the kitchen in his sweatpants and a t-shirt. His hair is slightly a mess and still damp from the shower. He and Dallas are about the same height, but Dallas works out more, so he has a bit more bulk to him than my brother.

Doesn't matter though, they both get girls throwing themselves at them. While Dallas has taken advantage of that fame, my brother hasn't really. He doesn't do flings, which seems to make him only more wanted by his female fans.

I walk into the kitchen, and before we even start talking, Landon wraps his hands around my waist and lifts me, setting me on the counter between the stove and the fridge. This has become our thing. I sit on the counter, while he cooks, and we talk. He doesn't want me helping, but he wants this time to catch up and just bond, his words not mine. It's also the perfect spot to sneak food and taste test, as he cooks.

"So, anyone special in your life?" I joke. This is always the first question I ask, when we have our cooking time like this.

He laughs. "We're getting ready to go on tour, so it wouldn't be fair to her, apparently." His square jaw ticks, as he grits his teeth.

Her. Oh, shit. My brother has his eye on someone. I can't remember the last time he was serious about a girl. Wait, yes, I can. It was that Shelia girl, who used him for her fifteen minutes of fame. I got my nice little revenge on her, spreading some rumors about her being pregnant and trying to stick my brother with the baby. I laughed, Landon got mad, we fought and didn't talk for a week, and then we got over it. Dallas thought it was funny, at least. No one has really heard from her since.

"Who is she?" I press.

"I don't want to ruin it, but yes, there is someone. I've asked her out. She said no, because of the tour. I think she has a problem with me being a rock star. So, I'm going to wait, until after the tour and try again." He sighs.

They're getting ready to go on tour again soon, and I'm looking forward to having the house to myself and some space to clear my head, even if the tour is just a small one up the east coast.

"What if she's dating someone else by then?" I push.

"Then, it wasn't meant to be. Now, tell me what happened with Branden."

I go over everything I told Dallas last night. When Landon starts laughing, I throw one of the nuts from the trail mix I was snacking on at him, which only makes him laugh harder.

"I think you dodged a bullet. I don't know of any sane guy who proposes after three months of a causal relationship." He says.

"Exactly! I mean, the sex wasn't even that good, he was just there." I joke at the same time Dallas walks into the kitchen and sits on a barstool at the island.

"Some conversation you have going on here." He says, but he's used to our weird talks. Nothing is off limits with my brother and me. We're the only family we have left, so we each play mom and dad to each other, and we decided long ago no secrets and nothing out of bounds. *Nothing can drive us apart.*

This is why my brother is my best friend, and why this place always feels like home.

"What? Sex is a topic you're very familiar with." I joke around, but something flashes over Dallas's face, but it's gone just as fast. I think I must have imagined it.

"So, what's for dinner?" Dallas changes the subject.

"Chicken Parmesan. Austin's favorite to welcome her home. She has decided to stay here, instead of moving on, and I couldn't be happier." Landon says, his face beaming.

"I agree, the house is just better, when you're here. And Landon cooks better food for you." Dallas jokes, as he gets up to set the table. My legs are in front of the silverware drawer, so he makes this big dramatic show of lifting my legs onto his shoulder, so they are out of his way to get in the drawer.

I have to brace myself, so I don't fall, because I can't stop laughing. Once he has what he needs, he puts my legs back down and pinches my hip.

"Besides, I like you in the kitchen here with Landon. It makes this place feel like home." He says and moves to the small table in the kitchen that seats four. We eat here, when it's just us.

"I agree," my brother says, unaware of the slight touch Dallas gave me on my hip. That is new. He normally just jokes, like picking my legs up, but the touch on my hip felt more intimate.

It sent shock waves up and down my back. I'm just overthinking this, right?

"Alright, let's eat!" Landon says, as he takes the food to the table, and Dallas comes over to help me off the counter.

"Man, a girl jumps from the counter once, sprains her ankle, and she never lives it down." I huff with a smile on my face. I love how protective these two are of me, even if it can get a tad bit annoying.

I sit across from my brother with Dallas between us, as Landon starts talking about his trip.

He's setting up a charity to raise money for music scholarships and to help keep music programs in schools. He's hoping to expand it in a few years to open up spaces, where kids can come in and practice, and even use the instruments there that they can't afford to buy on their own.

"I'm really proud of you, and I know Mom and Dad would be, too." We don't bring our parents up much. Not because they were bad parents, they were the best parents. When they died in that car accident, it devastated us both. Dallas was our rock through it all. It just hurts to talk about them still, but we do it, because we refuse to forget them.

I know it's still painful for Landon too, because his eyes mist over, and he leans back in his chair, looking at the ceiling. This is when Dallas glances at me and smiles. He turns back to his food, before my brother catches him.

We talk more about the charity and the work he has been doing, and I catch Dallas looking at me more and more, and so does my brother. When it happens the third time, my brother kicks Dallas under the table and doesn't even try to hide it.

I roll my eyes and change the subject. "This is really good, Landon. Thank you for making it. I was missing your cooking."

"Consider it an incentive to stay this time." He says.

"Done," I laugh.

"So, you know we have this tour coming up, right?" Landon asks.

"Yeah, I may be on your mailing list." I shrug.

"Well, what do you think of coming with us and singing a few songs?" Landon asks.

Wait, what?

CHAPTER 4

Dallas

"Well, what do you think of coming with us and singing a few songs?" Landon asks.

Oh, yeah! In my head, I'm doing fist pumps. Austin has an amazing voice, but she just isn't a fan of getting up on stage. She has sung some duets with us in the past, and the fans always love her.

Landon insisted, so she could get some of the royalties, and he could make sure she was taken care of. I insisted too for the same reason. She makes good money as a graphic designer and can support herself, but we both like to ensure she doesn't need anything. Though, I know the money goes into a savings account that she hasn't touched other than to invest it. But that's our secret from Landon, because he'd insist she go buy something silly just because she can, but that isn't Austin.

"I think it would be a good idea. You can earn some extra money, travel, and hang out with us. Plus, you can work anywhere," I say.

"Of course, you take his side." She sighs. "Tell me about the tour."

"Well, we just got off a big tour a few months ago for this album, and it did great. We sold out shows everywhere we played. So, our manager asked us to do a smaller tour up the east coast to give it another push. One of the stops is in Asheville, and we can spend a day at The Biltmore." I try to bribe her, because I can't admit that I'd love nothing more than to have her in the small space of the tour bus with us for weeks.

"How long is the tour?" She asks.

"About six weeks. Our manager is trying to get a few more stops added on at the end, but I don't see it happening. The record label wants us to get back and start working on songs for the next album. They want one more from us, before it's time to talk about renewing our contract." Landon says, and I nod my head, finishing up the food on my plate.

"You would be on the main bus with us. We have stops spaced, so we can go out and do stuff in between. I know you like to explore, and Dallas is right. You can work anywhere, so do it on travel days and between shows. You don't even have to sing at every stop, if you don't want to, maybe just the big ones," Landon says.

I see the wheels turning in Austin's head. She's running over the pros and cons, and if she can make it work with the clients, she has now. She always thinks things through, before committing to something big. Landon and I both know this, so we give her a few moments and shovel food in our faces.

"Okay, but I want to be able to go out and explore or else." She gives her brother the stink eye.

The last or else was her putting itching powder on his clothes, before a concert. This was years ago, before we were selling out the big places, but he hadn't broken a promise to her since.

"I swear, I will make it happen." Landon holds up his hands in surrender.

After dinner, Austin clears the table, "I got dishes, since you cooked."

"I'm actually going to go up and go to bed. It's been a long few days, and I'm beat." Landon pulls Austin in for a hug. He kisses the top of her head, and then turns to me. "Night, man. We can talk tomorrow about the tour details."

"Sure, I'll call Dave tonight and get him up-to-date with Austin coming with us."

Dave is our manager and is great at making things happen. I think he will be happy to promo Austin on tour with us.

Landon heads upstairs, and I join Austin at the sink. "You wash, and I'll dry?"

"Sounds good." She smiles at me. We have a dishwasher, but we all grew up washing dishes by hand, and I know for Austin it's therapeutic. I also knew she'd hand wash them, so she could start thinking through her plans for the tour.

I grab a towel and stand beside her. Bumping my shoulder into hers, I say, "I'm really glad you're coming with us."

We make quick work of the dishes, but neither of us says much else. There has always been a comfortable silence between us. Rarely is there a need to fill it, and it's one of my favorite things about our relationship.

"I'm going to head to my room and give Dave a call," I tell her, and she offers me a soft smile.

"I should start planning what I'm going to pack. I need to find everything anyway."

We walk upstairs together, and like a gentleman, I let her go first. It's not because I want to stare at her ass on the way up the stairs. Really, it's not, but I can't tear my eyes away. The way those yoga pants grip every curve of the heart-shaped mounds makes me want to grab hold of her.

Crap, I need to rein my thoughts in, or the next six to eight weeks on tour will be torture and just plain weird. This girl is my best friend's sister and not even interested in me.

It must be because I haven't gotten laid in the last six months. My normal meaningless hook ups just don't appeal anymore. I want to settle down, have a family, and kids. I want sex to be about connecting with someone on a deeper level, not just about chasing my release.

The problem is everyone around me wants the playboy. They want to fuck a rock star and have a story to tell. I used to not care, but now, it bothers me. I just don't know how to break the cycle and turn my image around, and I'm not ready to talk about it, because I don't know if I could even explain it to Landon.

I close my door and flop down on my bed, hitting Dave's number, but it's Mitch who answers. He's our assistant manager and takes over, whenever Dave isn't around.

"Hey, Dallas. Getting ready for this tour?" Mitch asks.

"Yeah, that's what I was hoping to talk to Dave about. Is he around?"

"No, he had to go out of town. Some family thing. You're stuck with me on the first leg of your tour, I'm afraid."

Huh. We have been with Dave for six years now, and never once, has he ever had a family thing or put anything. before the job. I hope everything is okay, but I know better than to pry.

"Listen, we were talking tonight, and Austin is back in town. Well, we were thinking of having her come on tour with us. Nothing big, but maybe a song or two, during the bigger shows. She's going to come either way to spend time with us, though, it might be something to advertise."

"Oh, I like that idea. She has her own little following. Fans love the brother and sister duet between her and Landon. They eat that up. We're pretty much sold out with the exception of a few venues. This might push the rest of the sales. I'll get on it. Only one song each show?"

"Yeah, somewhere in the middle. She won't want to open or close the show, you know her." She hates being on stage, but she would hate opening or closing even more, so it's not an option. "So no, we won't make her do it."

"Sounds good. I'll get a press release going and push it out on social media. Maybe, you guys could share some of the old videos of her on the tour a few years ago and get fans excited on your social media, too."

"Good idea."

"Alright, thanks for giving me more work. I was getting bored. Talk soon."

We hang up, and I go online and grab a link to the video I love the most of Austin. I have it bookmarked, because I watch it more than I should. It was taken two years ago, when she did a few tour stops near Washington, D.C. with us. This was the stop where Landon wasn't feeling very well, so I filled in on the duet, and the fans went crazy. So much so, that the record insisted she and I do a duet together.

The spark in her eyes as she looks at me. I know she was doing it for the fans, playing up to the mood, but even from this fan's video, you can see the emotion in her face, as she sings. At that moment, it was just her and I. The rest of the arena fell away, and I had never wanted to kiss her as badly as I did in that moment. I know after that I hurt her, because I had to put space between us. If she knew my thoughts, she'd have freaked out.

Those few moments on stage also made it impossible for me to be with another girl for months. I felt like I was cheating on her when I tried, which was crazy.

I share the link on my social media, and it gets comments immediately. Fans are so excited she's touring with us and are begging people who have tickets to record her song and share it.

I watch the video again, before tossing my phone aside on my bed. I'm thinking of different outings I can take Austin on, like spending a whole day at The Biltmore Estate.

I'm still making plans in my head, when there's a knock on my door.

"Yeah?" I call out, thinking it's Landon, asking if I called Dave, but when Austin steps in, I quickly sit up.

"I don't know what to wear on stage. What have you guys been wearing for this album?" She asks, but I notice a few dresses in her hand.

"Jeans and a button down shirt nothing too dressy."

"Can I try these on for you, and you tell me if it's too much? I'd ask Landon, but I'm sure he's asleep, and I don't want to bother him."

"Of course." She smiles and heads back across the hall.

In a few minutes, she's back and waiting for my opinion. She looks stunning in a simple black dress with a high neckline.

"I like that one with your cowboy boots." I tell her, while still running my eyes over her.

"Yeah, that's what I was thinking. I can add a jean jacket and switch up some accessories, and it would work for a few different shows. Okay, next one."

She goes back across the hall to change again, and when she walks in this time, the air is sucked from my lungs. Holy shit, where did she get that dress? It's a deep royal blue with a plunging neckline and ends several inches above her knee. Just above appropriate.

"No," I growl.

"No?" She looks almost disappointed.

I can't take my eyes off her; she looks so fucking hot in this dress. I grip the sheets and force myself to stay seated in the bed and not walk over to her and take her in my arms. Fuck, I need to get laid.

"If you wear that dress, we'll be fighting off every guy in the arena, who's trying to get to you. That dress is sexy as hell and good for a date night with someone you plan to get laid with, but not on stage for everyone to see." I'm honest with her, and her cheeks turn pink, as she ducks her head.

"Go change, Austin," I say in a stern voice. Seeing her flushed in that dress is too much. Thankfully, she turns and heads back to her room. I take a few deep breaths and will my cock to go down, before I scare her. She's been here for a few days, and I can't keep myself under control.

"Okay, last outfit. Are these shorts okay? I can pair them with a lot of shirts? Or I could wear some of your shirts you will be selling at the shows to help promote them." She says, as she steps back into the room.

Fuck. At least, her ass is covered. *Barely.*

"I think those will be fine, but nothing shorter. And no shirts that show your stomach off."

"Duh." She rolls her eyes. "No tank tops, and nothing where you can see my bra. I know the speech."

I nod, but I still look at her tan legs on display.

"Thank you, Dallas. I think my nerves are just getting to me." She whispers, but I hear it loudly, as if she was standing next to me.

I sigh. "You will do amazing. If you want to back out any time, you know you can, even last minute. We got your back."

"I know." She offers me a soft smile, before turning back to her room and closing my door behind her.

I look down at my hard cock. Fuck, I'm in so much trouble.

CHAPTER 5

Austin

I've been too many concerts, and it's always a high, when the crowd is feeling it and on their feet, cheering, singing, and dancing. It's a whole other experience, when you're at the side stage.

From the side stage, I can see Dallas and Landon, the band, and the crowd. It's doing nothing for my nerves.

We're on the first stop on the tour, and this is the first time in a few years that I have been able to see the guys live. Their fan base has grown, and now, they're singing to sold-out shows, even on small tours like this.

The guys feed off it, they always have. The louder the fans are, the better the concert. The lights are going over the stage, and the crowd is feeding into the hype.

Right now, they're singing one of their slower love ballads that make all the girls swoon. Then Dallas turns, almost like he's facing the side of the stage, but he faces me and our eyes lock. This is the experience every girl in the crowd is hoping for. For a brief moment in time, they can pretend he's singing to them.

I want to pretend he's singing to me. In an alternate universe, maybe he is. Maybe, we would be together. I need to lock these feelings away, or the next two months are going to be painful and horrible for both of us, making things just plain weird, since we are spending so much time in the cramped space of the tour bus.

After this song, I'm going on and should be preparing. But Dallas still hasn't taken his eyes off me, and they have gone from the playfulness they had, when he first looked my way to downright steamy.

I'm in the black lace dress he approved, along with a jean jacket, black and gray cowboy boots, and a long turquoise cross necklace. I did my hair in a crown braid with the help of the drummer's wife. She's so excited to have another girl around on this tour, and I can't blame her. It will be nice to get away from the guys now and then.

The music stops, but Dallas still doesn't take his eyes off me. My brother introduces me, and the crowd screams. It's then Dallas smiles and holds his hand out for me to join them on stage. Like a magnet that has no choice, I'm drawn to him and take his hand. Just like that, I'm not focused on the crowd, which would have made me nervous.

He leads me over to Landon, who wraps an arm over my shoulders and kisses my temple. We get set up for our song, and I stand so I can see Dallas, while I sing, because for some weird reason, he seems to calm me tonight.

The first strings of the duet play, and the crowd cheers, as Landon and I sing the song he wrote about me being the best thing in his life and his best friend. It wasn't written as a romantic song, but we have been told by several people it was the song they danced to at their wedding, because it's the type of relationship they want with their spouse. Those moments when fans relate to your songs make any unease about being on stage worth it.

"This next song was one Austin and I used to sing together. Then, the last time she was on tour I was sick, so Dallas filled in, so I could go backstage and puke my guts out." Landon pauses, and everyone laughs.

I smile, because I remember that night, like it was yesterday, and judging by the look on Dallas's face, he does, too.

"It seems you guys liked it better, when Dallas and Austin sang it, so that's what we'll do." The stadium roars, and I just shake my head and move to stand by Dallas in the center of the stage.

'You ready?' He mouths, and I nod.

He strums the first chord of the love song that hit number one a few years back. I never wanted the kind of fame that came with it, and I thank Landon and Dallas for taking the burden that came with that hit off me the best they could. It's allowed me to live a semi-normal life, as a rock star's sister.

Once again, as he starts singing, Dallas's eyes are focused on me, and I couldn't take my eyes off him if I tried. In my mind, I know he's doing this, so I have somewhere to focus that isn't the crowd, but my heart wants to think he's doing this for another reason.

The heat from the spotlight pours down on us, and the vibrations from the music fill my body. It's then, I get that little rush that makes me understand why the guys love what they do. My heart races with the words of love Dallas is singing, and that I get to return to him though only in this song, if he only knew.

As we wrap up the song, the crowd cheers, and only when I feel Dallas's hand on my lower back under my jacket, do I turn to face the crowd and look at them for the first time. Many are standing, couples are intertwined in each other's arms, and there are scattered signs all across the crowd.

I laugh at a few and make a note to tease the guys later. A few signs declare the girl wants to have their baby; there are a few proposals, and one asking to be Dallas's sugar baby. That's the one I plan to kid him about later. I hug both Landon and Dallas, and then wave at the crowd, before heading back off the stage.

"Glad to have that over with?" Ivy, the drummer's wife, asks.

"Very." I smile, as I hand the tech guy my mic.

"Let's get a drink and relax. I think they only have a few more songs, and then things back here get loud," Ivy says.

"Let's do it."

Backstage, there are several dressing rooms surrounding a large open area with couches and chairs, along with a snack and drink station. Ivy hands me a bottle of water, and I shrug out of my jacket. Note to self, no more jackets on stage. Those spotlights are no joke.

"So, I know how Dallas and my brother act on tour and the days off, but what is married life like on tour?" I ask her, as we curl up in one corner of the large u-shaped couch.

"Like a vacation that's interrupted by work. We make it a point to go out and explore the area, when we can, but I have a lot of downtime. I can only listen to so many sound checks. Dom doesn't mind me skipping them, as long as I'm at every show."

Dominic is a talented drummer and has been with the guys from the start. When they got married, they had such an awesome rock star themed wedding with lots of leather and lace. Landon was insistent that he could bring her on the road, if he didn't quit on them and would even hire a nanny, if they decided to have kids. That sold the deal, and I think it made Dom loyal to them for life.

They don't have kids yet, but they do have the master bedroom at the back of the bands' bus. Dallas, Landon, and I are on the main bus.

"I'm hoping to steal you away for a girl's day about halfway through. I will be so sick of my brother, and I'll need a break." I smile.

"Done, just name it. Oh, you have no idea how happy I am you're here. I love my husband and the band, but having another girl around, who isn't trying to get in the guys' pants is a breath of fresh air."

We hear the guys wrap up the show.

"Speaking of, get ready for groupie central," I sigh.

"My least favorite part of the night, too." She agrees, and we turn to watch the hallway from which the guys will come off stage. No sooner do they get off the stage, you can hear the girls, trying to get their attention. They walk into the room, heading straight for the drink table and both guzzle down a bottle of water, before coming up for air.

Then, they look around the room, and as soon as their eyes find mine, they nod at me, before turning their attention to the venue's assistants and the girls surrounding them.

One girl presses her boobs up on Dallas's arm and rubs on him, like she's in heat. I turn my eyes to Ivy, because I can't watch it.

"You going to be okay? There's Dom, and we normally head right back to the bus. The show makes him hot, if you know what I mean." She wiggles her eyebrows at me.

I laugh, "Oh, I know. I'm going to head back to the bus, too. It's just creepy watching girls rub on them like they're in heat."

"See you tomorrow!" Ivy says, and then jumps up and runs to Dom's arms. She leaps, and he catches her, as she wraps her legs around his waist. Dom is a pretty big guy. If I didn't know he was the drummer, I might think he was a bodyguard. I watch Dom carry Ivy out the back door, and I sigh. What a girl wouldn't give to have a guy like that.

I look back to where the guys are still surrounded. One of the girls from the guy's management team is there and flirting with my brother. He seems to be flirting back just a little. Maybe, it's a good thing the girl from the charity turned him down. Doesn't look like he's ready to settle down.

I try not to look, but my eyes move on their own to Dallas. The blonde is still rubbing her tits on his arm, some brunette has attached herself to his arm, and all while, he talks to a guy in front of him.

Fuck, I can't stay here and watch this. I stand up and without looking back I make my way out to the bus. One of the security guys from the back door walks with me to the bus door, since it's now dark out. I thank him, going in to grab my yoga pants and a t-shirt to change in the bathroom and clean off my makeup.

Was it my mind playing tricks on me that made it seem like Dallas was uncomfortable with the girls all over him? That's crazy, right? He lives for that sort of thing. He will pick one of them, head to his dressing room, bang the crap out of her, come back to the bus, and pass out.

Why does it hurt so much more now knowing that's what he's doing? It's been this way for years; nothing has changed. I need a distraction, since I know I will have the bus to myself for an hour, maybe more. Going to the living area, I grab a bag of pretzels and another water, before sitting down on the couch.

I love this bus. It's extra wide, so we aren't cramped. There are two couches facing each other and a dining room table booth across from the small kitchen. There are four large bunks, and each of us has our own TV in the bunk. But since no one else is here, I'll settle in on the couch, where it's more comfortable.

Turning the TV on, I pull up a sappy Hallmark movie, planning to get lost in someone else's happily ever after, since mine seems to have taken a wrong turn. The movie is just starting, when the bus door opens.

Great, there goes my relaxing evening. So, help me if one of the guys thinks they're bringing some random hookup into this bus, I will rip their balls off. They have never done that shit to me before, and I won't tolerate it now.

Imagine my surprise, when in walks Dallas.

Alone.

CHAPTER 6

Dallas

This used to be my favorite part of the night, when everyone wants your attention. People from the venue are always talking your ear off, and whatever girls are backstage swarm you.

I'm trying to talk to Mitch about the plans for the next few days, and there are two girls who aren't getting the hint that I don't want them hanging on me. I pull my arm away, but they just reattach themselves.

I turn to look at Austin, thinking maybe I can give her the come rescue me look, but she's standing up and hurt mixed with disappointment is all over her face. Shit, she's thinking I'm going to be taking one of these girls home.

Six months ago, yeah, I probably would have, but not now. I can't stand their touch, when the girl I've wanted for more than half my life, is walking out the door upset.

"Mitch, let's finish this in my dressing room," I say and yank my arms away from the girls a final time, before stalking across the room.

I slam the door and lock it, before turning back to Mitch.

"No more groupies. I'm done being pawed over. I'm done with that life. If you aren't going to help try to turn my image around, then you will at least keep them away from me backstage after shows, or the tabloids will be painting me the hulk, instead of

37

the playboy." I growl at Mitch.

His eyes go wide, and I take a deep breath and grab another bottle of water. This isn't his fault. He wasn't on the last tour. Hell, Dave wasn't even on the tour. He popped in at some of the key shows, and as long as the PAs he had on us gave good reports, he let us be.

"Shit, I'm sorry. Just no more. This is getting old fast, and I'm really over it."

"Uh oh, Dave's going to be pissed." Mitch looks almost scared.

"What does me wanting to turn my life around have to do with Dave?" I growl.

"That's not it. It has been our experience, when a band member says, 'This is getting old,' it's code for they are thinking of leaving the band."

"What? I'm not leaving. The playboy life is getting old. I want to settle down, have a family, and kids. I sure as hell don't want to quit."

He gives me a skeptical look. "If you say so, man." He pulls out his phone, and his fingers go flying across it, texting or emailing.

"We're done here, and I'm going to go to bed. The first stop always drains me." Not really, but any excuse to get out of here, I will use.

"Yeah, go, go. See you in Atlanta." He doesn't even look up from his phone.

I walk out careful to avoid the group now surrounding Landon, who has his back to me. One of the security guards walks with me to the bus, and I take a deep breath, before opening the door. I hope she's still awake. I don't want her going to bed thinking I was out all night with someone.

Walking into the bus, I find Austin on the couch. She's curled up with a blanket and some movie on. Though, she has washed off her makeup, her hair is still in the loose braid from the show. She looks more beautiful now than she did on stage earlier.

What puts a smile on my face is the look of pure shock on her face. I'm glad I can still surprise her after all these years.

"What are you doing here?" She asks me, as her eyebrows bunch together, like she's concentrating on what she wants to say next.

I shrug my shoulders and flop down on the couch next to her in the middle seat. I don't want too much space between us.

"You're here." Is all I say.

"I had my bets on you and the blonde." She tries to joke, but I can tell it bothers her.

"Nope." I pop the p, looking over at her. Then, I say the one thing I've had trouble voicing to Landon, but to Austin, it seems to flow right out. "It's been months, since I've been with anyone. That life just doesn't appeal to me anymore. I've actually been feeling a little lost. Landon still sees me as a playboy." I laugh bitterly.

"I mean, my best fucking friend can't even believe I want to change my ways. How am I going to get anyone else, too?" I lean my head on the back of the couch and stare at the ceiling unable to look at her. I can't take it if she gives me that same look Landon does. The look that says 'sure you do' without them actually having to say it.

When her soft hand touches my arm, I roll my head to look over at her.

"I believe you. I've watched you these past two weeks. You're home alone every night. Hell, if you hadn't changed your ways, you would have had a house full of girls the night I showed up, enjoying the fact that Landon was gone, and you could go at it anywhere in the house. If you ever used my room, I don't want to know. Lie to me and tell me your housekeeper Lysol's everything." She offers me a big smile.

"I'll tell you a secret." I grin, though I doubt she believes what I'm about to tell her.

"Hmm, I'll offer you one in return. You go first."

"I never slept with a girl anywhere in the house or on the property."

"What? Why?" She asks shocked. I pick my head up and turn my body to face her.

"It's your home and Landon's, and it never felt right. Plus, it's harder to kick a girl out than leave, because I didn't do the whole spend the night thing." I cringe at that. I want to be honest with her, and I can't change the past, but I know how it sounds now.

"You've never had a girl in your bed?" She asks.

"No one but you," I say, as I think of all the times she would crawl into bed with me over the years, when she was scared. A bad dream, or a bad storm, or the time Landon made her watch *Paranormal Activity*, and she couldn't sleep, much less sleep alone, for weeks. After that, we both agreed no more horror movies for her.

I expect her to go off on some tangent about not believing me, but instead, she shocks the hell out of me and smiles.

"I like that. A piece of you only I get."

Damn. It had been hard to hold my feelings back for her before, but this girl is making it impossible not to fall in love with her. Then, she reaches out and takes my hand and gives it a squeeze. When she goes to pull her hand back, I tighten my grip. I'm not ready to let go and give up the warmth this small touch gives me. It centers me as much as it's turning me on.

I clear my throat. "So, how was it on stage tonight?"

"Better than I expected thanks to you." She says, as she leans her head to the side and rests it on the back of the couch. Her eyes rake over me, but her expression is hard to read, it almost looks like she's holding back a smile.

"What did I do?" I ask her.

"You held my attention and made me forget about all the people in the crowd."

Damn, I hadn't done it on purpose. I just couldn't take my eyes off her. In that dress, she looked breathtaking, and getting to sing the song with her, even I forgot we were on stage in front of thousands of people. It felt like we were in our own little bubble, and she was singing to me, because I sure as hell meant every word I sang to her, even if I can't tell her that. But if I could tell her that, it would probably send her running scared.

So, I take the coward's way out and let her think that was exactly what I was doing.

"Happy to help. I know you don't like the crowds, but they loved you tonight, and I was glad you were there."

"I can see why you guys like it. It was a thrill, but it's still not my thing. So, don't get any bright ideas about me going on the next tour with you guys."

"What were you going to watch?" I ask her, changing the subject.

"Some Hallmark movie. We can watch something else." She hands me the remote.

"Nope, you were here first, so let's do it." I hit play, and we settle in to watch the movie about a girl returning home and falling for her high school boyfriend all over again, and how close to home it hits.

About twenty minutes in, she keeps shifting around. "You okay?"

"Yeah, this couch isn't as comfortable as it looks."

Nodding my head, I walk to my bunk and grab my pillow. The side of the couch is next to the booth from the dining room table, and there's an art to getting comfortable. Instead of letting Austin in on the secret, I decide to push my luck.

"Here scoot over," I tell her, and she gives me a weird look, then moves to the center of the couch, where I was just sitting. I put the pillow against the back of the booth and settle in, facing sideways. I put one leg up along the back of the couch and keep one rested on the floor.

Austin opens her mouth, no doubt to ask what I'm doing, but I just grab her hips and pull her to me, until her back is resting against my chest. The TV is on the wall at about the driver's seat, and now, neither of us has to turn our neck to watch it.

"Better?" I ask her, even though I can feel her whole body is tense.

She takes a deep breath and leans all the way back against me a little more. Then, she finally relaxes and pulls the blanket up over herself.

"Yes, thank you." She whispers, her voice uneven. I'm glad I affect her at least some. If I don't want my cock getting rock hard and digging into her back, I can't even think about her body leaning on me.

She's still a bit tense, so without thinking too much, I start running my fingers up her arm slightly. She shivers and pulls the blanket tighter, but she finally relaxes.

The movie is almost over, when the door opens, and we both jump apart, as Landon walks in. He sees me and stops dead in his tracks.

"Man, I didn't expect to see you here." Then, he looks over at Austin. "What's wrong?"

"Nothing. Just was watching a movie and got into it, when the door opening scared me." She says.

She's a fast thinker. Plus, it really is the truth; she's just leaving out the fact that we were cuddling on the couch.

He looks over at me again. "You going back out?"

I have to fight not to roll my eyes. How can his sister believe me, but he can't?

"No." Is all I say. I don't want to have this conversation in front of Austin.

"Well, let me text Tony, and we can head out early then." He says.

Tony is our bus driver, who we picked up about three years ago. He's a big guy and has doubled as a bodyguard a few times. Tony is a good guy, doesn't put up with shit even from us, and has been great at keeping us in line. He's a big part of the reason I want to turn my life around.

On the last tour, there were many nights I couldn't sleep. When he would be driving, I'd come up and sit with him, and we'd talk. He was like me, running around, a new girl every night, until he met his wife, and she made him want to change. They were married for ten years, before she passed away from cancer.

I confessed to him about Austin, because I knew he wouldn't tell anyone. He's seen and heard plenty around here, so he could have leaked to the press for some nice money. But he hasn't, so we trust him and pay him well for it.

I was up all night with him, telling him everything. From that night on, there hasn't been another girl. He made me realize I was using the girls to push Austin away and make sure I had no chance with her or any decent girl.

Tony walks in a few minutes later. He looks like a biker with his gray hair pulled back in a low ponytail and long gray beard. His jeans have holes around the knees, and he always wears a shirt supporting our troops, police, or firefighters.

Today's shirt says, 'Stomp my flag, and I'll stomp your ass.' That pretty much sums up Tony in one shirt.

The moment he's in the door, Austin's face lights up.

"Hey, Tony. What's on your to-do list in Atlanta this time?" Austin asks.

Tony always picks one thing to see or do, while we're at each location, before he comes back to the bus and sleeps. Both Landon and I can drive the bus if he ever needs a break, but he's never once taken one, and he always has us to locations early.

"Georgia Aquarium. I want to see those whale sharks again."

Tony winks at me, and then does a quick walkthrough of the bus, before getting ready to head out.

"Well, I'm going to bed. I'm beat." Landon says and makes his way towards his bunk.

Turning to Austin, I run a finger lightly up her arm, like I was doing before. I'm quickly becoming addicted to touching her. "I really enjoyed watching the movie with you."

She offers me a soft smile. "Me too."

I glance over my shoulder and see Landon is in the bathroom, so I lean down and kiss her cheek. "Go get some sleep, baby girl. We have a long day tomorrow." I don't know why I just called her that, and I wait for her to call me out on it, but instead, her cheeks flush, and she ducks her head and goes to her bunk.

I settle into the passenger's seat next to Tony and sigh.

"Going to be a fun tour, huh Dallas?" I know exactly what he means. Being so close to Austin, it's not going to be easy to hide my feelings. Day one, and I've failed miserably.

I have a feeling this tour is either going to make us or break us in more ways than one.

CHAPTER 7

Austin

I'm excited today is a down day. We have a few concerts under our belt now, and tomorrow night, we play in Asheville, North Carolina. So today, Dallas and I are going to visit The Biltmore Estate. Landon is doing some food tour that sounded really fun, too. But having a day of Dallas to myself, as we explore this mansion, holds a little more appeal.

Landon headed out about thirty minutes ago, saying he was going to start the day coffee shop hopping. More like getting mobbed by fans, as he tries to drink coffee. Pass.

I take one last look at myself in the mirror. I have on jeans, tennis shoes, and a long blue flannel shirt. I braided my hair over my shoulder, and I have sunglasses to use that will hopefully stop anyone from realizing it's me, not that I'm as recognizable as the guys.

I'm finishing my hair, as the bus door opens, and Dallas steps in. He runs his eyes over me, and it feels more intimate than it has in the past. Things have shifted, since our night of watching the movie on the couch. It's more intense. He flirts and chooses to spend time with me over the crowd, like Landon is.

"You look beautiful." He looks me over again, and then clears his throat. "I rented us a car for the day." He nods his head towards the door.

I smile and grab my purse, as we head out. When I see the car, I just laugh.

"They didn't have an older one, I tried." He says, as I take in the brand-new Corvette. I shake my head and look over at him.

"This is perfect."

Dallas opens my door for me, before moving to his side and getting in.

"Top up or down?" He asks.

"Up on the way there; down on the way home."

He nods and revs the car, before heading out. I take in Asheville, as we go. Dallas drives a bit slower, almost like he knows I want to see everything. As we pull into The Biltmore gate, it's like being transported back in time. The long winding driveway pulls you away from town and down into the rolling countryside. I can imagine horse-drawn carriages making this drive and later the cars from the 1920's.

I look over, and Dallas's smile is as big as mine. We skip the visitor center, because he bought our tickets online and head in scoring a parking spot that's close enough to walk.

The views of the front of the house with the large fountain are exactly like the pictures.

"We have to get a picture," I say. We turn our backs to the house, as I pull out my phone to take a selfie with the massive house in the background. Dallas wraps his arm around my waist and pulls me to his side. He leans his head to the side on top of mine, and we both have huge smiles.

"This is my new favorite picture," I tell him.

"Don't post it online, until after we leave, or we'll be mobbed." He says.

"Yeah, I'll wait until tomorrow to post it, but I'll send it to Landon to show him what he's missing," I say, as I send a quick message to him.

Me: You could be here, but no, you're too busy stuffing your face right now.

I send a winking emoji with it, and instantly, those three dots pop up, letting me know he's typing back.

Landon: Have fun, and it's not just any food.

A photo comes in of him at a table with coffee, a donut, French toast, and some egg dish.

Me: Minute in the lips a lifetime on the hips. Got to keep your figure, until you land a sugar mama and get a ring on it. Then, you can let yourself go.

I laugh out loud at my own joke. Dallas leans over my shoulder and reads the text and laughs, too.

All I get back from Landon is a middle finger emoji, so I put my phone away and turn back to Dallas.

"Let's do this."

We make it all the way into the house without being stopped once for Dallas being asked for an autograph. We walk the main floor, which is an indoor winter garden, the dining rooms, a sitting room, the back porch, and my favorite room, the library.

I stand in awe, looking at the huge two-story library with a massive fireplace.

"I love the look on your face," Dallas whispers next to my ear.

"What look?" I glance over at him.

"The look of pure wonder. I knew you'd love this room."

"Someday, I want a library like this. More shelves than I can fill with classics, rare books, and all the dirty romance novels I can get my hands on. Complete with a huge fireplace and the most comfortable couches."

"I'll make sure you get it." He whispers, almost like he doesn't want me to hear. I don't push it, because I want to hold on to the dream. *Maybe someday.*

Before we move on to the second floor, we head out to what used to be the stables, but they're now shops and a few places to eat. We go sit down for lunch at the restaurant, which has all the family's recipes, so I'm really excited about trying some of them.

We get seated at a booth, and Dallas sits beside me, instead of across me.

"Oh, you're Dallas McIntire!" The hostess squeals.

Great.

"Yeah, listen, we want to have a low key lunch. I'm happy to sign something on our way out, if we can eat in without being bothered." Dallas flashes her his smile all the magazines have dubbed his 'pantie dropping smile,' and she melts.

"Oh, of course. I'll keep the girls away. You got it."

She gives me a once over, and must decide I'm not a threat, and places her hand on his arm, before walking away.

"Well, she seems fun." I laugh, as I open the menu.

"Hey, we've been lucky all day. It was only a matter of time, before someone recognized us." He says.

"You. She has no clue who I am. You're the one every woman in here is drooling over." I nod towards the dining room, where more than a few heads are turned our way.

This used to bother me in the beginning, but over the years, I realized they truly are looking at Dallas and don't even see me. Fine by me, I just go about my business and let them deal with it.

When our food comes, I can't take the first bite, before two guys stop at the table.

"No way! You really are Austin Anderson!" The first one says. "We saw you across the room and didn't think it could really be you. My sister is a huge fan of your brother's band, but I really enjoy the songs where you sing, too."

I shift uncomfortably in my seat. It's rare someone recognizes me, so I smile and whisper for only Dallas to hear.

"I'm sorry for this."

Then, I turn back to the guy who was just talking. "Thank you, hear that, Dallas? He likes my stuff better."

The guy's eyes shoot over to Dallas.

"Oh, no way! My sister is going to be so upset she ditched us today."

I pull a pen and a notebook out of my purse and hand them to Dallas and smile at the look he gives me. I learned a long time ago to carry some pens and paper, when I'm out with them. It just makes life easier.

"Dallas would be happy to sign an autograph for her. You can hold it over her head for a few weeks."

He laughs, "Only if I can get yours with it and a photo? I know you're trying to eat. We'll make it quick, and then leave you alone."

I know they will, but the problem is they have now drawn attention to us, and people will keep coming by the table.

We sign the paper, and a waiter takes a photo of the four of us.

"If you post it online, tag Dallas please," I ask them. Despite the interruption, I still want a copy of the photo.

"Oh, you bet. Thanks again!" They say and head out.

"I know you don't like the attention, and you don't have to apologize for shifting it like that." He says and nudges my shoulder with his. We eat fast and are only stopped two more times.

"Never fails. I need to start asking for male servers." Dallas says, when he opens the check to find his waitresses name and number scrawled across the receipt with a bunch of hearts.

"Let me," I say.

"No way am I letting you pay." He's always been like this. No matter if it's a day out like this, or something as simple as an ice cream cone. If I'm with him, he never lets me pay for anything.

"Fine, do you have cash?" I ask.

"Yeah." He hands me enough to cover the bill with a tip and puts it on top of the receipt. I hand it back to her with a smile on my face.

"Thanks, but I don't swing that way." Then, I take Dallas's hand, as we leave, only stopping, so he can sign an autograph for the hostess.

I go to let go of Dallas's hand once back outside, but he doesn't let me, and I don't fight it.

We spend the rest of the day finishing the house tour and the gardens, before going down to the village green, where there are more shops, a winery, and a few restaurants, along with a small museum.

The whole day is perfect, and we are only stopped a few more times for autographs, so Dallas is really relaxed. He's constantly touching me, holding my hand, or has his arm around my waist, pulling me close. I know he's doing it to protect me, as we walk around, but it's so easy to let my heart hope it's more.

As we leave, he puts the top down and takes the long way back to the bus, and we crank up the radio, when one of the band's songs comes on. I can't remember the last time I laughed so hard.

We stumble into the bus still laughing and find my brother, leaning against the kitchen counter, giving us a strange look.

I clear my throat.

"I'm going to take a shower, before you two hog all the hot water." I head in, grab my clothes, and take a fast shower, the smile never leaving my face. When I turn the water off, I can hear them talking, as the wall is so thin.

"You've changed, man." My brother says.

"I have, you didn't believe me, but I told you I'm tired of the playboy life. I haven't been with a girl in months. I want more. I want to be a better person, even if the media won't change their mind. It's hard when even you won't believe me." Dallas says.

I'm glad they're talking about it. I slowly start getting dressed, making sure I'm quiet enough that I can still listen to them. If they didn't want me to hear, they could have stepped outside after all.

"I'm proud of you. I also knew you'd wake up one day and want more." Landon says. He pauses, and then continues, "Just no Austin. I see it in her eyes she likes you, she always has, and she doesn't need to be hurt like that."

What the actual fuck, Landon? I'm pissed. I finish getting dressed with the intention of going out there and giving him a piece of my mind, when Dallas snaps.

"So, you're proud I'm doing good. Yet, I'm just not good enough for your sister, but I'm good enough to be your friend?" Whoa, Dallas is pissed. His heavy footsteps rock the bus followed by the slamming of the bus door.

Great.

I step out of the bathroom.

"You're an asshole, Landon. He's been trying to prove to you for weeks he's changed, and the only thing you can say is great, but you still aren't good enough for my sister? Since when do you get a say on who I do, or don't date, or even sleep with?"

I turn and grab a pair of jeans and a shirt and slip back into the bathroom to change out of my PJs to go after Dallas.

"Austin, you know Dallas's past as well as I do."

"I also know some shitty things in your past that you've done. Do you want me to only judge you on those moments? Maybe I should, then moments like this wouldn't be a huge disappointment." I grab my phone and head out.

I know Dallas, and I know he won't go far. I pull up a map and see there's a local dive bar about a block away. I'll bet anything that's where he is.

I'm going to prove to him my brother is wrong, if it's the last thing I do.

CHAPTER 8

Dallas

What the hell was I thinking? That I could spend a day with Austin and let my guard down, and maybe, her brother would see I've finally changed? How can he be proud of me, but still think I'm such a bad person that I have to stay away from Austin?

I rub my hand over my chest. Fuck, it hurts more than I thought it would. Getting so close, and then losing it like that. Losing what, I'm not sure. This is all assuming Austin would even give me a chance, but it sucks to not even be able to find out.

I walk into this dive bar and not one person even turns my way. Perfect. I head straight to the bar and order a whiskey. There's a hint of recognition in the bartender's eye, as he nods and pours my drink, but he doesn't say a word. I'm grateful for that.

I stare into my drink and replay the day in my head. It was perfect. I almost felt like she was staking her claim with the waitress, and after that, it was just fun. I couldn't keep my hands off her, and she couldn't keep her hands off me. I can't remember that last time I laughed so hard.

It was just easy. I wasn't Dallas McIntire, rock star. I was Dallas, the kid she grew up with. I didn't realize how much I missed that side of myself until today. But no matter what I do, and how much I make amends for my past, her brother will never see me as more than a playboy, when it comes to his sister. He'll never approve, and if he won't approve, there's no shot for Austin and me.

Either way, I lose someone, and there's a chance Austin could lose Landon, if she did go out with me. Not that she would want, too. Why would she want to date me with my past?

Maybe, Tony was right. I was using my playboy lifestyle to push her away, so I didn't get hurt, because now, it's what will keep me from her, so I will never know.

I finish my drink and hold it up to the bartender, and without a word, he pours me another one and goes off to help another customer.

I don't think I will find another girl like Austin. I've met a lot of people and not one has compared to her. So, I guess that means I'm destined to be alone for the rest of my life, having to watch Austin fall in love, get married, and have babies. I will have to put on a happy face and be content with being Uncle Dallas.

It feels like a vice is tightening around my heart at just the thought of it. How will I handle it in real life?

I'm so deep in my own head I don't realize someone sat down next to me, until they place a hand on my arm. When I turn my head and find the pair of gray blue eyes, looking at me that I know so well, all the tension leaves my body.

"Landon is an asshole, and he doesn't get to dictate my life," Austin says.

"You heard all that?" I ask, a bit shocked. I thought she was in the shower. I know the bus walls are thin, but I guess, I assumed the water would drown out the sound of us talking.

"Yes, and he's wrong, you know."

"No, he isn't. He's right. My life's a mess." I say, looking back down into my drink. I don't think I can handle a look of pity on her face.

"Your life *was* a mess, Dallas. Even then, was it really? You were happy, you were dedicated to the people important in your life, and you have an amazing career. You weren't an asshole, you were honest and upfront. Yes, maybe a little reckless, but aren't we all? When it was no longer working, you realized it and did something about it."

I have no idea what to say to that, so I keep my eyes on my drink, until I feel her hand on my arm again. I slowly turn to meet her gaze.

"I told him he wouldn't want people to judge him for things he did in his past, so what gives him the right to do it to you? He isn't a saint either, and that's just the stuff I know about." She gives me a small grin.

I shake my head, "Still you deserve better."

She laughs. Full on throws her head back and laughs.

"I don't see how that's funny," I say. Has she lost her mind?

"Dallas, you're the reason all my relationships have failed."

"What?"

"You treat me so well that I compare every guy to you. Every date I'm on in my head, it's been, 'Oh, Dallas would have opened the door,' or 'Oh, Dallas never would have picked this restaurant.' And 'Dallas wouldn't have said that, or he would have said this.' Finally, I just gave up and went for casual, and then the freaking guy proposes after three months. I mean, come on. The dating pool isn't that great out there from this end either."

"I can't get between you and your brother." It's a simple statement, and one she really can't argue with.

"Dallas, my brother is a big boy. Regardless of how he's handling things right now, all he wants is for me to be happy, and a guy who treats me right. Now, if you plan to go run and cheat on me every chance you get, then yeah, it will cause problems."

"I may have been a playboy and didn't do relationships, but I don't cheat. I can commit and be a one-woman man." I interrupt her. Her thinking I'd cheat on her doesn't sit right with me.

"Can you be a one-woman man? From where I'm sitting, that's the only thing holding me back. I haven't seen you do it, and I'm not sure my heart could take it, if you can't be." She whispers the last part, making my heart race.

I stand up and hold out my hand.

"Enough with the heavy, let's dance," I say, desperate to change the subject. All this has to be hypothetical, because there's no way this perfect girl is thinking of giving me a chance. It's nice for her to stick up for me, but I can't give myself that kind of hope. So, I will take what I can get. Tonight, that's holding her in my arms, while we dance.

She takes my hand, and I lead her on to the dance floor. I wrap one hand around her waist and hold her other hand in mine. Pulling her close, so I can feel her body next to mine, I rest my head next to hers.

"Remember the last time we danced together like this?" She asks me.

"Your prom," I tell her.

Like I could forget that night. She had been dating one of the guys from the football team, but she caught him cheating on her a week before prom. The guy lashed out and grabbed her arm, before she ran off. She had called Landon in tears. We were recording our first album, and he was about to drop everything and head home to kick the guy's ass and be there for her.

I stopped him, and said if I went, I could take her to prom. She deserved the experience, and she wouldn't go with him, and we both couldn't leave at the time. He agreed, and I was excited to go. I went all out and gave her the full prom experience. I rented a limo and spoiled her with a spa day before prom, the works.

She didn't even ask why Jimmy had a black eye at prom, though, I'm think she knew why. I made sure it was the best damn night of her life. Ignored everyone but her. We danced, until she couldn't dance anymore, and then ended the night out on our field. The one I have tattooed on my arm.

We lay on a blanket out there, and for hours, we talked and cuddled. I wish more than anything I could have completed her prom experience and taken her to a hotel room and spent the night making love to her, and in my fantasies, we did. But I had to leave the next day and get back to Nashville, and I couldn't do that to her. I had no idea where the future would take us then.

This is a huge part of why Landon is so protective of her. I know since then he's had a hard time letting her go and do her own thing, and even had people check up on her, when she isn't here.

"It was the best night of my high school life, anyway. It meant so much to me you coming to my rescue like that." She says. "Even back then, you set the bar really high."

She sighs and rests her head on my shoulder. I pull her hand up to my chest and rest it right over my heart. Right where she has been all this time. Right where I will always keep her.

"This is my favorite side of you." She says and lifts her head to look up at me.

"Oh, yeah? What side is that?"

"This sweet, caring side. It seems I'm the only one who gets to see it. I want to keep it that way, but I know that's just me being selfish." She rests her head back on my shoulder, and this time, I rest my head on top of hers.

"You're the only one who gets this side of me, and there's a very good chance you will be the only one who sees this side of me. It's not being selfish, if it's the truth."

Thankfully, another slow song starts, and we just keep moving.

"How do you do it?" She asks.

"Do what?"

"Make me feel so safe and like the world can't touch me right now."

I smile, loving I can make her feel safe. If that's my only job in my life, I will make sure she always feels safe. I take a deep breath.

"I don't know. Maybe, it's because you know you're always safe with me. No matter what, I will always be here for you."

She lifts her head and looks into my eyes then. We don't say anything, but I can't help but look at her lips. The lips I want nothing more to kiss and taste. When her tongue darts out and wets them, I know in this moment she'd let me. She wants this as much as I do.

My heart races, and my head lowers closer to her without even realizing I'm moving. The need to kiss her is overwhelming. Our noses brush, and I'm so close I can feel her breath mix with mine, before the music changes, and everyone starts yelling and singing and moving around us. A couple bumps into us laughing and dancing, and just like that, the spell is broken, and we step apart.

Austin smiles and grabs my hand and pulls us into the dance, and the rest of the night is light and fun. We smile and laugh. Sitting down in a back booth, we have some cheese fries and a drink, before heading back to the bus.

She lets me hold her hand on the way there. I do it as much for me as I do for her safety. It's dark out, and we're in a town we don't know. She's quiet, and I think she's dreading going in to face her brother, as much as I am. I send up a silent prayer that he is already in bed, but I know Landon, he will wait up, until Austin is back to make sure she's okay.

We turn the corner, and the bus is in front of us, as I sigh.

"Thank you for coming after me tonight. I had a really good time." I tell her.

"I did too, and I meant what I said. You're good enough. Don't let him tell you otherwise. He's just being an asshole, when he says that."

I squeeze her hand. "Well, your opinion is the one that's important anyway, so it doesn't matter."

I open the bus door and step aside to let her in before me. We get inside, and Austin stops dead in her tracks in the living room. I step around her to find her brother standing up.

He looks at her, and back to me, but doesn't say anything.

"Dallas, why don't you go to bed? I think Landon and I need to talk." She says without taking her eyes off her brother. Her tone is one we have both heard before, when she's really, really, really mad at us, and she has only used it a few times before.

I nod, but whisper in her ear, "It's nothing worth fighting with him about."

She doesn't say anything, but she looks at me like I'm crazy. I know there's no changing her mind, so I head back to my bunk, grab some clothes to change into, and go into the bathroom.

"You can't just go off and not answer my texts. I have to know you're okay." Landon says.

"I was fine. I was with Dallas."

"But I didn't know that. Do you have any idea what was going through my head?"

"I have an idea *Dad,* and I really don't care. How dare you stick your nose in my love life? You have no right."

Love life? Does that mean she wants a relationship with me? Do I stand a chance? I'd give anything for a chance with her. I know I'd do anything to prove I'm the guy for her and make her mine.

But her brother is right to an extent, she deserves someone better and who doesn't have my past. If I'm going to have even a slight chance, I need to get the rest of my life in order and stay the course.

I can be that guy. I will be that guy.

CHAPTER 9

Austin

It's been a week, since I was dancing with Dallas in the bar. A week, since I've been in his arms. A week, since our almost kiss. I miss him something fierce. He's up and gone, before I get up in the morning, and he spends most of his time at the venues with Landon or with their team. No more movie nights and no more going out. At least, he and Landon seem to be okay and talking, even if it feels like he chose my brother over me. Though, what did I expect? Landon is his best friend, and Landon is the band.

It's hard to be ignored. I didn't even want to come on this tour, it wasn't in my plans, but they talked me into it. I've been trying to figure out my next steps, because if they think I'm going to be staying at the house after this, they are dead wrong. I've thought about a cabin in The Rocky Mountains. That's far enough away, and the possibility of no cell phone service sounds good to me right now.

Every show, it hurts singing with him and putting on an act like nothing is wrong, when everything is wrong. He's very good at making it seem like he's singing to me. The look in his eyes was too much tonight, and I couldn't look at him. For the first time on the tour, I sang to the crowd. I prefer the thousands of nameless people, instead of looking into Dallas's eyes for another night.

Being on stage with them, takes everything out of me. I normally bolt, before they finish the show. But tonight, Ivy caught me and wanted some girl time, and I couldn't tell her no. That is why I'm currently sitting backstage with drink number, well, I lost count. But it feels good to laugh about them getting lost yesterday and having to call Tony to come get them. Tony gave them a lecture the whole way back to the bus. It feels great to talk to someone, since Landon and Dallas have been ignoring me. Assholes.

"Can you believe there are only two more weeks of this tour left? I'm so glad the last week of shows fell through. I'm ready to be home and have some downtime." Ivy says.

"Yeah, I'm over it, too. It's like the guys don't even want me here anymore. I could probably blow off the last few stops, and they wouldn't even care."

"Oh, sweetheart, you know they would. Especially Dallas, I see how he looks at you."

"Better get your eyes checked. He goes out of his way to avoid me lately." I shake my head and take another sip.

"When you aren't looking, his eyes are always on you. He's watching you and knows your every move almost before you do. He's always sending people over with water or food. You didn't think those people did that just to be nice, did you?"

Damn, I did think that. I thought it's what they did for all the performers at each venue. I had no idea Dallas was behind it.

"Why would he care? He's been ignoring me for over a week now. I thought there was something there, but I guess I was wrong. My asshole brother stuck his nose in where it doesn't belong, and ever since, Dallas has been going out of his way to avoid me."

Ivy watches me but doesn't say anything.

"What?" I ask her.

"Your brother has been going out of his way to avoid you, yes, but not Dallas. You know he asked me the other day to stay with you backstage, while they were performing, so you weren't alone?"

"What when?" I'm confused, why would he do that?

"A week or so ago."

That was after our night at the bar, and when he started ignoring me.

"It doesn't make sense," I say more to myself.

"Oh, honey, guys don't make sense. My guess is if your brother was all up in arms, Dallas is trying to prove to him he's worthy of you, before he makes a move. He's going to want your brother on his side for your sake, for his sake, and the sake of the band. He and Landon go their separate ways, and then everyone here is out of a job."

I sigh. I know she's right to an extent.

"Then, why ignore me altogether and push me away? Why not talk to me instead? I'd have understood that."

"I don't know. You need to talk to him about that."

I nod and finish my drink and signal for another one.

"Maybe, you should slow down on the drinks. I've never seen you drink so much."

"We have an off day tomorrow, and I plan to spend it in bed. Watch some Hallmark movies, or read some kinky romance books, and ignore everything for a day."

"Dom and I plan to head out and explore a bit, and you're welcome to join us." Ivy offers.

"Nah, I don't want to be your third wheel. It'll just remind me of everything I can't have, because my brother prefers I be alone and miserable."

Ivy's face goes soft, and I look down into my drink, because I don't want to see pity or God knows what else there. It is what it is. I will move on after the tour and find another causal relationship. Preferably one that doesn't propose after three months.

The concert wraps up, and I roll my eyes. Ivy knows the basics of what's going on with Dallas, Landon, and me, but she doesn't push, and that's why I like her. I don't want to talk about this anymore, and she doesn't force me, too.

I brace myself, because I know the guys will be here soon. Then, Ivy will be with her sexy husband, and I will need to decide my best course of action. I should get up and let Dom and Ivy walk me to the bus, but I'm frozen in place, when Dallas walks into the room. Why does he have to be devastatingly handsome?

When they enter the room, Ivy leaps into Dom's arms, and they head off to the bus just like every night. I'm so happy for them, but I want that, and it seems like Landon is making damn sure I'm not going to get it. *Fuck him.*

When I look over at them, that same girl is flirting with Landon again, and he's soaking it up. I can't stand her, and even more so after talking to some people on the tour with us the last few days. When my brother busts out laughing, good ole liquid courage mixed with some truth serum hits me and mixes with my anger that I've been stewing on for a week now. I'm up and across the room pushing people out of the way, until I'm standing right in front of the girl, whose name is some flower I can't remember right now.

"Hello, Landon," I say, as sweetly as I can.

He cocks his head to the side and studies me. "Austin."

"Oh, you do remember me. Huh, never would have known."

"What are you talking about?" He asks.

"You asked me to do this tour remember?"

"Of course, I remember." He shifts on his feet, looking a bit annoyed.

I'm proud of myself for resisting the urge to punch him in the face just like Dallas taught me. Let him explain a black eye to the press.

"Then why have you been ignoring me for the last week?"

His eyes go wide for a fraction of a second. "I haven't been ignoring you."

"Come on, Landon, when was the last time we lied to each other? Other people have even noticed you've been going out of your way to avoid me."

"Well, if you treat him like this, I can understand why." Flower girl says, and I turn to her.

"Oh, and you need to stay away from my brother. You aren't good enough for him. He doesn't need some whore like you. I'm not allowed to date anyone, then neither can he. He wants to stick his nose in where it doesn't belong, then I will, too." I look back at Landon. "What happened to that sweet girl at the charity you wanted to ask out? Oh, now I get why she said no, because you wanted to whore it up on tour. Good job. I'll make sure she knows that, too. I hope she's dating someone else by the time the tour is over for her sake." When I finish my rant, the entire room is silent, and Landon's eyes are wide.

The next thing I know, Dallas is in front of me.

"Come on, let's head back to the bus." Dallas tries to take my hand, but I yank it away.

"Oh, now you want to talk to me. Fuck off. Both of you." I turn to leave, but in one quick motion, Dallas grabs my arm, flips me over his shoulder, and starts walking.

"What the hell are you doing? Put me down, asshole!" I start beating as hard as I can on his back, but I'm easily distracted by his ass, which is right in front of my face.

"I'll set you down, when we get to my dressing room. Looks like we need to have a chat."

"You have had a whole week to 'have a chat,' but no, you ignored me too, so fuck you. I want to go home. I'm done with this tour, and I'm done with both of you." I start pounding on his back again.

"Too bad, because I'm not done with you," Dallas says, and then a door closes, as he sets me on my feet.

Oh, shit. The smoldering look in his eyes says I'm in a whole lot more trouble than I thought.

CHAPTER 10

Dallas

"Come on, let's go back to the bus." I try to take her hand, after she gets finished yelling at Landon and the girl next to him.

She yanks her hand away from me. Crap. Everyone in the room is watching, and Landon is shooting me his pathetic 'please help me' eyes.

"Oh, now you want to talk to me. Fuck off. Both of you."

"Damnit, Austin. It looks like we need to have a talk." I say.

So, when she turns to storm off, I do the first thing that comes to mind. I bring her back to me, which is pretty easy with her being drunk, and then I flip her over my shoulder and storm out of the backstage area towards my dressing room. I send up a silent prayer that she doesn't puke all over me, before I get there.

"What the hell are you doing? Put me down, asshole!" She starts beating on my back, and I smile even though, I know it would piss her off even more. She has some fire in her.

"I'll set you down, when we get to my dressing room. Looks like we need to have a chat." I tell her.

"You have had a whole week to 'have a chat,' but no, you ignored me too, so fuck you. I want to go home. I'm done with this tour, and I'm done with both of you." She starts pounding on my back again.

Oh yeah, we need to talk. There's no way I'm letting her leave the tour early. Because I know if she goes home now, she will pack up and be gone, before we get home. Not an option.

"Too bad, because I'm not done with you," I say, as I enter my dressing room and close the door behind me.

I put her down on her feet with her back to the door. Staring into her eyes, I reach past her and lock the door.

Then, in order to get my emotions under control, I turn my back to her for just a moment. Carrying her like that; having her so close, was such a turn on, even when she was yelling at me and cursing at me. After a few deep breaths, I can get my cock to go down enough that I can turn and face her again. She hasn't moved one inch.

"You've been drinking, baby girl?" I ask her, even though, I already know she has. Making a note to myself to remember to say something to Ivy about not letting her drink like that. I know she's her friend, but it could get her in serious trouble, if the wrong person noticed and tried to take advantage of her.

"Yes, so what? Why do you even care?" I can hear the irritation in her voice, but there's also underlying hurt.

I hated our show tonight. She wouldn't look at me, when we sang. She'd rather look out at the crowd, and that's when I knew I was losing her. I hadn't realized Landon had been avoiding her all week as well. I thought giving her space would let the two of them work things out. No wonder she's all worked up and hurt.

"What was that outburst about?" I ask, keeping my voice soft, because I don't want to give her another reason to go off on me. Not until I have my answers.

"He thinks he has a say in my life and can drive you away, so why can't I have a say in his life? Besides, I can't stand that girl."

Can't blame her there. She tried to attach herself to me at the beginning of the tour, and when I told her to keep away, she latched on to Landon. That's his business, and I figured he was using her for some fun, but she's been around him at every stop. But that's not the issue I need to address right now.

"Drive me away?" I ask her. I need to know what's going through her head. I've given her space, yeah, but Landon hasn't driven me away.

"You have avoided me all week. You're out of the bus, before I get up and come home late. You won't talk to me or even look at me."

Damn, I really thought she and Landon were working things out. I didn't realize he has been avoiding her too, or I wouldn't have stayed away, but I was never far away. I knew where she was, and what she was doing. I was always right here in case she needed me, like tonight.

I've spent the last week trying to get my life in order, so I can be the man she deserves. At some point, I will need her brother to be on board with this, and it's going to take time. So, I want to lay the groundwork now and get everything in order, because staying away isn't an option anymore. I plan to make her mine, but I want to do it the right way.

"I just need some time, baby girl. I need to make sure I do this right, and that I'm good for you. Will you give me some time?" I ask her, trying to beg her to understand with my eyes, but it doesn't work.

She rolls her eyes "Getting some last action in?" She turns to try to leave, but I'm on her, before her hand reaches the door.

I pin her to the door with my body and rest my arms on either side of her, caging her in.

"There's no one but you. There hasn't been anyone, since you've been back, and even a few months before that. There won't be anyone but you. You got me?" I make it perfectly clear and lay it on the line for her.

With her being drunk, I know we will have to have another talk tomorrow, but I don't want her going to bed and stewing on this making it into something it isn't.

She looks up at me unsure, almost fearful to believe me, but I stay strong for us both. She's scared and has been hurt before. I'm not backing down and plan to prove to her that I can be the man she needs.

Finally, her eyes drop, and she nods.

"Good, now let's get you back to the bus, so you can sleep this off," I tell her.

I pull my phone out and shoot a text off to Landon.

Me: Hey, I have Austin. I'm going to take her to the bus. Maybe wait an hour, before coming in? She's still really mad at you, and I think it's best to just let her get to sleep.

Landon: Okay. I'll hang out here and do some damage control. I'll talk to her in the morning.

Me: Go easy on her. She's hurt, even if she went about it the wrong way. I'll text you, once she's asleep.

I put my phone back in my pocket and look back at Austin. She has been watching me with this questioning look on her face.

"You good to walk?" I ask her.

She just nods, but I put my arm around her waist anyway and head out to the bus with her. The security guy walks out with us, and then opens the bus door for me, while I help get her inside.

"Need help getting ready for bed?" I ask her.

She looks like she's considering it, before she shakes her head no and goes to her bunk.

Sitting on the couch, gives me the best view of the bathroom door, and I wait for her to come out.

What a mess. It's been hell this last week staying away from her, and it looks like it did no good. In fact, if anything, it made it all worse. It's not like I enjoyed myself this week. I've spent the last week contacting the girls I used to just call up for a quickie any time I wanted. I didn't owe them anything, but I wanted to end it and tell them I was seeing someone.

Austin deserves that, so no one thinks they have a claim on me but her. There were about eight different girls that I used to call, a few from our popular stops, and two more back in Nashville. Most of them didn't care; a few asked me why I even bothered.

One seemed upset and said she had no problem being my side piece and could keep things under wraps. Sadly, she was also one of the ones in Nashville. I wasn't so nice to her, making it very clear I wanted nothing more to do with her. She never seemed clingy or attached before, but she was also the one I'd take as a date, if I needed to have one for a record event. I guess, she read too much into it.

It took me three days to call them all, and it really drained me. After that, I just felt dirty. Austin didn't seem to care about my past, but at some point, we'd have to sit down and talk about it. It needs to happen, before I ever get her to bed. If I ever get that chance.

When she comes out of the bathroom, she walks towards me.

"Can we cuddle just until I fall asleep? I'm still mad at you, but I missed you." She asks, as she looks down at her feet. Her voice is tiny, and she looks so vulnerable right now.

There's no way I'd tell her no. Any time I can get with her, I'll take. I won't stay away anymore. Not if it hurts her like this.

"Of course," I tell her and sit back on the couch. I grab the TV remote, put on one of the mountain men TV shows, and then lay down on the couch.

She grabs a blanket and lays down facing me and buries her face into my chest. I cover us both up with the blanket and tuck her head under my chin. I wrap one arm under her and run my hand through her hair. I know this is the easiest way to calm her. It always has been, since we were kids. I rest my other hand on her hip and hold her close.

No words are spoken; we just lay there, soaking each other in. Being this close to her, is making my cock hard, and I don't try to hide it. I want her to know what she does to me. Though, I won't let anything happen tonight, not while she has been drinking. I hope tomorrow in the light of day she still wants to give us a chance. If it's the last thing I do, I'll make this up to her.

Austin relaxes in my arms and her breathing gets even, so I know she's asleep, but I still lie there and soak her in. My phone goes off in my pocket, and I carefully pull it out without waking her.

Landon: You guys make it to the bus okay? She still mad?

Me: We made it. She's almost asleep and seems to have calmed down. I think she's more hurt than anything. I pulled back, because I wanted you guys to work it out, but I hadn't realized you pulled back, too.

Landon: Shit. So, now she thinks we both have been ignoring her all week?

Me: Pretty much.

Landon doesn't know about the real reason I pulled back. He doesn't know about me calling the girls and ending it, and my plans to move forward with Austin. I've thought about this a lot, and I think the best thing I can do is prove to him how well I will treat her by actually doing it. He might get mad at first, but when he sees it with his own eyes, I'm sure he will come around.

Me: Listen, I'll get up early and leave you two to have the bus tomorrow, so you can work it out. Then, I'll talk to her later in the afternoon. We'll make this right. We have to, or if she goes home early, you know she won't be there, when we get back.

Landon: Yeah, that's not happening. We'll fix this.

I wait a few more minutes and enjoy her cuddles and her being pressed against me, before I carry her to her bunk and tuck her in. She snuggles right into her bed and looks so peaceful. I kiss her forehead, and then send Landon a quick text that she's asleep.

I will fix this, because losing her now that I've decided to make her mine just isn't an option.

CHAPTER 11

Austin

You would think the threat of a hangover would be enough to deter me not to drink like that anymore, but no. Here I am, head pounding, and I know if I were to do it all over again, I'd still pick up that drink.

Flashes of the night come back to me. Talking with Ivy, and then yelling at my brother and that girl. That makes me cringe, because there were so many people around, and I can only imagine how it went down. If it's not the front page on some gossip rag right now, I will be shocked.

Then, there was Dallas, carrying me over his shoulder to his dressing room. Did he really ask me to wait for him? There really hasn't been anyone, since I've been back? All the questions make my head hurt more. We need to talk later, but right now, I plan to follow the smell of coffee and bacon out to the main living area and kiss whoever is cooking.

I didn't expect it to be my brother. I was thinking maybe Tony, as he's good at making sure we eat in the morning, after we drink. Then, he lectures us to death about not drinking again.

"Hey, this is almost done, but coffee is ready." He looks at me almost shyly.

Damn, I don't think I'm ready for the conversation. The last thing I need with my head pounding is my brother lecturing me.

I hesitantly make myself a cup of coffee and go sit down at the booth across from the small kitchen.

I sip my coffee, as Landon plates our breakfast and sets it down on the table. Omelets, and bacon, and biscuits. This is a suck up breakfast. He slides in to the booth across from me and gives me an unsure smile.

I glare at him and pick up my fork and start eating. No point in letting good food go to waste, when I have to sit through a big brother knows best lecture, right?

"So last night?" He starts.

I just shrug and keep eating.

"We have to talk about this, Austin."

"Why? No one has wanted to talk to me for a week. Why start now?"

"That wasn't on purpose. I assumed you didn't want to talk to me and would talk to Dallas, and he assumed you were trying to work things out with me and took a step back."

"And all week neither of you talked about it and realized it?"

He ducks his head to look at his hands in his lap. "No, we avoided the topic. I did it, because I didn't want to fight, and I assume it was the same for him."

"Can't say I blame him. Hell, I'm surprised he talked to you at all, after you basically shit on everything he's been doing to get his life in order."

"I did not! I told him I was proud of him."

"Then, in the next sentence, said he wasn't good enough." I huff.

"For you. Come on, do you really want to be with a former player? Do you know how many girls he's been with? I doubt even he knows."

"Wow, great words of praise for your best friend. Does he know what a backstabbing asshole you are?"

That seems to shake him enough that he shuts up and thinks

about his next words.

"I won't apologize for being protective of you." He levels me with his 'I mean business' gaze.

"Well, I won't apologize for being protective of you either." I lean back and cross my arms over my chest. He tilts his head to the side and looks at me but doesn't say anything.

"That girl..." I start.

"Daisy." Ha! I knew it was a flower name.

"Fine, Daisy. She has been bragging to people of 'nailing you,' and how she'll make a great trophy wife and knows just how to spend your money."

His eyes darken, and I can tell he isn't happy. He hates gold diggers, even if it's just something casual. When he's in a relationship, he likes to spoil his girl and has no problems spending money on them, but the parasites that are there just because of his money are a deal breaker for him. He's been burned by them one too many times.

Finally, he sighs, and I know he's letting his guard down. "Thank you for having my back."

"Always. I just wish you would trust me," I say.

"Of course, I trust you."

I shake my head. "No, you don't. Not in the way you expect me to trust you. Thank you for breakfast." I go to stand up and take a shower, but he reaches for my hand.

"Hey, there are two more weeks of the tour. You'll stay, right?" He asks.

"I don't know. I can't do two more weeks like how this last week has been."

"I swear it won't be. I'll be stuck to you like glue, if that's what it takes."

I just shake my head and stare out of the front bus windows.

"We'll see. I still need to talk to Dallas. I may have been drunk last night, but I wasn't drunk enough to realize you really fucked with his head, and now, he has this notion he isn't good enough for anything. You're his best friend, and if you don't believe in him, who will? That's where his head is, and it's fucked up. If nothing else, I'll stay for him and be his cheerleader, so at least someone is supporting him."

When I finally look back at my brother, hurt is written all over his face. But he needs to deal with this, and I won't hold his hand to do it. I turn and go gather my stuff to take a shower. Once in the bathroom, I send a text off to Dallas.

Me: So, I just talked with my brother. Now it's your turn. You free later?

Then, I hop in the shower and let the hot water soothe my muscles in my neck and shoulders. When the water starts to turn cold, I smile and get out. Landon deserves two more weeks of cold showers for all this, so I don't even feel guilty.

I check my phone and nothing from Dallas. I get dressed, taking my time to do my hair and put on a little bit of makeup and still nothing from Dallas.

Me: You don't get to ignore me. I will track you down.

I grab my stuff and go to the arena we'll be singing at tomorrow. Tony drove us all night to get here. It's weird falling asleep in one place and waking up in another, but that's the life on the road.

As I walk into the backstage area, it takes me a minute to get my bearings. I've been here with the guys a few years ago and not much has changed. I check the dressing rooms and nothing. Finding one of the security guys, he tells me Dallas was here earlier this morning and left.

So, I text Ivy.

Me: Any idea where Dallas is? He and I need to talk.

Ivy: No. I haven't seen him all morning. Did you talk to Landon?

Me: Yes, we talked. I don't know how productive it was, because I wasn't ready to forgive him, but we talked.

Ivy: I asked Dom. He said last he knew Dallas was talking to some of the band guys, but that was an hour ago.

Me: Damn, he's good at this avoiding me thing. He isn't even answering my texts.

Ivy: You feeling okay? I haven't seen you drink like that before.

Me: Yeah. Landon force fed me, and I've been drinking water. I will be fine.

Ivy: Well, my offer stands, if you want to join us!

Me: Thanks. I guess, I'm just going to go nap in the bus. He has to come back at some point.

Disappointed, I head back to the bus. I thought we had made progress yesterday, but if he's going to go back to avoiding me, then I guess not. By the time I get back to the bus Landon is gone, thank God for small favors, so I sit on the couch and go through my emails, when Dallas finally texts.

Dallas: Sorry, I was dealing with a fight between a few band members. I hate playing referee.

Me: Fun.

Dallas: I swear I wasn't ignoring you.

Me: It's fine.

Dallas: No, it's not. Let me make it up to you. I was told about an amazing taco place a few blocks from here. Meet me for lunch in an hour?

Damnit. I love tacos, and he knows it.

Me: Fine, see you then, but so help me, if you stand me up...
Dallas: I. Will. Be. There.

He sends me the restaurant info, and I see it's within walking distance, and there's a mini shopping mall on the way, so I decide to go walk around there, as I wait for him.

We are in Jacksonville, Florida getting ready to do our Florida loop, before hitting the Gulf Coast states. So of course, everything here is beach related.

I pick up some beautiful glass floats that will go great in my bathroom, and a beautiful starfish wall decor piece that's on driftwood with some saying. My bathroom is beach themed with blues, so it will fit right in.

Afterward, I make my way down to the restaurant and find Dallas at a back table already waiting for me.

"You're early," I say, as I sit down.

"Didn't want you to think I wasn't coming." He smiles and nods towards my bags. "What have you got there?"

"There was a super cute little shopping area on the way here, so I just picked up a few decorations." I smile.

"Beach stuff for your bathroom?" He asks.

"You know me so well."

He smirks, because it's the truth. I'm pretty sure he even knows me better than Landon does. Mostly because, he pays more attention.

"So, best tacos in the area?" I ask.

"Yep, all the locals say we have to try this place, so I figure it's a good place to grab lunch and talk away from everyone."

The server comes over, a guy thankfully, and takes our drink and food order, before we get a chance to talk again.

"So, let's rip off the Band-Aid. If you're going to chew me out, just get it over with, so I can eat my tacos and still have time to meet up with Ivy and Dom and be the pathetic third wheel." I say.

If this is another talk like I had with my brother this morning, I'd like to get it behind us.

He cocks his head to the side. "Your talk with Landon didn't go well?"

"You can say that. He basically expects blind trust in him, but he won't give it in return. I love him, but I can't wait for him to go on his trip, when we get home. I need space from him."

"If I had known Landon was avoiding you, I would have been right by your side. I really thought you two were working things out." His voice is sincere, but all it does is make me want to cry, and I won't cry in front of him. I was such a mess last night, but I'll keep myself together now at all costs.

"Sounds like you were busy anyway, so it is what it is."

"No, baby girl, you know what I was doing? Do you really want to know?" I'm thrown off by the baby girl nickname. Again, I really like it, but I thought maybe it was just a fluke last night.

"It doesn't matter."

"Apparently, it does. I spent the last week calling every girl I had an open understanding with and telling them not to expect to hear from me again, because I was in a relationship. I wanted to make sure to close every door of my past, before we walked down this road." He leans forward on the table and takes one of my hands in both of his.

"We?"

"Yes, we. Your brother has always been stubborn. He doesn't take words at face value; he expects them to be backed up with actions. So, I can tell him, until I'm blue in the face that I've changed, and that I'll treat you right, or I can do it and prove it with my actions."

My mouth literally falls open, because this is so not how I expected this conversation to go. I thought I'd get a lecture about drinking and not making a scene on their tour. I go off on him for ignoring me, and we'd move on.

Our food comes, and it gives me a welcome break to gather my thoughts, but Dallas beats me to it.

"After the tour, we can talk more, okay? Now, I don't like the idea of you being a third wheel. Tell me you have better plans than that, after we leave here."

"I guess, it's back to plan A. I'll head back to the bus and watch some TV, or maybe, work on a client website I hadn't planned to start, until we got home. Can't hurt to get a head start. What are your plans?"

"I have a meeting at two with Mitch, and then maybe, I'll join you. Downtime sounds really good right now."

For the rest of lunch, we talk and catch up from the last week, and just like that, it's all behind us, and suddenly, I can't wait for this tour to be over for an entirely different reason.

CHAPTER 12

Dallas

Today, is the last show of the tour. I am ready for it to be over, because that means we go home, and then Landon heads out for his sponsorship deal and the meeting with the charity he's helping. He will be gone for two weeks. That's two weeks I get Austin to myself. It's all I've been able to think about. Making plans, things I want to do with her, and places I want to take her.

Our last stop on the tour is Memphis, Tennessee, and this show is an earlier one than normal, so it's before dinner. It's still a packed show and judging by the sound check, it will be a great one.

We're all getting ready for the show, and Austin has been chatting with Ivy a bit, but her eyes always find mine every so often, and when she finds me watching her too, her face lights up with a huge smile.

The last few weeks of the tour we found ourselves falling into an easy routine. Landon would get up and make all three of us breakfast. We'd all sit and talk and use that as our catch-up time from the day before. Then, we'd go our separate ways.

If it was an off day, Austin and I would go with Ivy and Dom and explore. If it was show day, I'd go with Landon and oversee everything and get ready. Then, I'd meet up with Austin again for sound check. After each show, we'd head back to the bus and watch TV, until Landon got back, or until she started to fall asleep.

As much as I love the routine, I'm ready to be home and start a real routine and relationship. I want to have something solid with us, so by the time her brother gets back, I can show him, instead of telling him.

Showtime.

We head out on stage, and the screams and cheers are deafening, and I know my smile is as big as Landon's. I don't even have to look over at him. He starts hyping up the crowd, which he's really good at it, and we start singing.

As with every show, every song I'm singing is to Austin. I guess, it's been that way on all the tours, even if I never admitted it to myself.

The first part of the show passes so fast, and before I know it, it's time for Austin to come on stage. Landon introduces her, and the crowd cheers. As she steps out on stage, I'm frozen in place.

She's in a light blue off the shoulder dress with long flowy lace sleeves. She has on brown cowboy boots and a large brown belt at the waist of the dress. Her long, dark brown hair is falling down in waves over her shoulders, and I don't think I've seen her this dressed up since prom.

She walks over and hugs me, like she has every show. This time I pull out one of her earpieces, so I can talk to her.

"You look absolutely beautiful, baby girl," I tell her and watch the pink coat her cheeks. I love that I can still make her blush.

I don't want to let her go, but I know she's heading over to give Landon a hug too, before we start singing. Like it does every time she's on stage, the crowd falls away and we sing to each other. Her eyes focus on me and mine on her.

Landon asked me why we stare at each other, when she's singing. I told him she needed someone to focus on, so the nerves from the crowd didn't get to her, and it would be plain creepy for her to sing to him. He agreed and let it go. While it's the truth, it wasn't the whole truth, and I felt like I was lying to my best friend.

Her set ends, and she hugs us both again, before walking off stage. I watch her go, and when she hits the edge of the stage out of sight of the crowd, she turns and winks at me, and I feel like I've won the lottery.

As we finish the show, all I can think about is getting to Austin, as I make my way backstage. She has changed into more casual clothes, shorts and a shirt, but she still looks as beautiful as, when she walked out on stage.

I walk over to her and grab her hands, swinging her around.

"Let's go celebrate," I say.

She giggles, as I spin her, and I swear it's my favorite sound in the world.

"Sure, where did you have in mind?"

"Your pick. Tacos or BBQ, I know a good spot for both."

"We're in Memphis we have to do BBQ!" She says.

"Give me ten minutes for a quick shower and to change."

Dom walks up beside Ivy, and after their kiss, he turns to me, "We'll wait with her." He gives me a nod. We haven't talked about it, but with the time we have spent with them lately, I'm sure he knows my feelings for her.

I give him a nod of thanks and rush off to my dressing room for the quickest shower of my life.

I walk back out and take her hand.

"It's a few blocks, you don't mind walking, do you?" I ask her.

"No, I like to see the city."

We walk hand in hand, talking about the show, and before we know it, we're at the BBQ place I was told about.

"This place has won several awards, and the guy at sound check swears it's the best in town," I tell her, as I open the door for her. The hostess recognizes me, but she keeps her cool and seats us in the back, where we will be least bothered.

One of our security guys, who tagged along with us, sits down at the bar with a clear view of us. He's in plain clothes, and unless you know him, you'd never know he was security. Our team does well at blending in. For the first time in a long time, I'm thankful to have him around, knowing he will keep Austin safe as well.

The conversation flows easily, as we eat and taste each other's meals. There are several long stares, but as much as I want to reach across the table and take her hand, I don't. I know people have seen us, and the last thing we need are photos circulating, making this look like a date. Us out to dinner is easily explained to Landon. Hell, he knows we go out to eat at these stops, so he won't give it a second glance.

I hate having to hide things, but for now, I think it's for the best. I just need to prove myself to her, to him, and to myself.

After dinner, we head outside again, but I'm not ready for the night to be over.

"Want to walk the shops?" I tilt my head towards the sidewalk.

"Yeah, I love window shopping, because each city is so different." She says, and I push my luck just a bit and take her hand. I can wave this off, as making a protective thing, if needed, right? Keeping her close, as we walk a busy downtown, that justifies holding her hand.

We barely get two stores down from the restaurant, before we're stopped by fans.

"Oh, my God! It's Dallas McIntire. We are such huge fans!" The blonde waves over her shoulder at her two friends, who are with her.

Austin has let go of my hand and stepped off to the side out of the way, but when I look over at her, she's all smiles and winks at me. So, I paste on my rock star smile and sign autographs.

"Please, take a photo with us. My sister will never believe me otherwise!" The blonde says, and I agree. They arrange themselves around me, and the blonde is on one side, pushing her tits against my arm, as she gets ready to take a picture. Austin's lips purse, and my smile almost slips.

The second she takes the photo, her hand that was on my back slips to my ass, and I jump from the group, like I'd just been burned.

"Okay, ladies, enjoy your night." I keep the fake smile in place and put an end to it. This is also my bodyguard's sign that I'm done and to move them along. He steps in, as the blonde starts to pout and says something I block out, as I walk over to Austin, who is fighting a laugh.

"What happened?" She asked.

"The blonde grabbed my ass," I say irritated, and that's when Austin busts out laughing, and I stand there in shock. "What the hell is so funny about another woman grabbing my ass, and then rubbing her tits all over me so much that I need a shower to get rid of her perfume?"

She laughs even harder, holding her stomach, as I just stand there in awe. I love her laugh, but I still don't get what's so funny.

"No one would believe me." She wheezes out.

I take her hand again, as we start walking.

"Believe what?"

"The rock star playboy running away from a woman grabbing his ass." She says and bursts into a giggle again.

I shake my head and give a dry laugh. "Yeah, some playboy."

"Oh, Dallas, I'm sorry. I know you've changed really, I do, but it also takes some getting used, too. A year ago, you would have soaked it up. Hell, maybe even gotten her phone number. That's the Dallas I'm used, too. But this Dallas, I like him much better, and it will just take some time to get accustomed, too."

"I wish the fans and the media would believe I've changed."

"I don't think your managers will let it happen." She says sadly.

"Why not?"

"Because you as a playboy makes money. They can sell out an arena with girls who think they have a shot at one night with you. They can use it to sell stories and hype the band. You fed into it good, and I'm pretty sure you didn't care, but they used it to their advantage, and they still will. But they won't like the thought of you settling down." She shrugs.

What the fuck? I think over the last few years, and damn, she's right. They did play up the playboy status, didn't they? It was splashed on front covers, when I'd do photo shoots and on websites.

"And you're okay with this?" I ask her.

She shrugs, "I don't have a choice. If you change your image, there's a really good chance the band's popularity will go down. How could I be that selfish and do that to you and my brother? Do I like it? No way."

"We'll figure it out. Landon and I have been tossing around the idea of starting our own label. It would give us so much more freedom, and we'd be able to help new talent."

We walk for a bit in comfortable silence just checking out the store windows, when she sighs.

"What's wrong?" I ask her.

She holds up our hands. "This feels like a date."

I smile at that. I'd like it to be a date, and I've never been more comfortable on one.

"It does feel like a date, huh? What if it was?" I ask. I want to know where her head is.

She gets quiet and turns her head to look at the store window we are slowly passing.

"I'd like that." She says barely above a whisper.

There's a little side alley in front of us, so I pull her with me down the alley just enough, so we're out of lights from the street. I push her up against the wall, my body against her. She's so warm and soft.

"Then to make it a date, there needs to be a kiss," I say, as I slowly lower my head to hers.

If she doesn't want this, she can turn her head, or even push me away, but her eyes fall to my lips, and in that moment, I know she wants this kiss as much as I do. My lips crash into hers, and every teenage fantasy I had of kissing Austin is shattered. The reality is so much better.

She melts into me and wraps her arms around my neck, pulling me in closer. I kiss her like this might be our last kiss, with all the passion and need built up over the last ten years of wanting her, but not being able to have her.

I want to own her and possess her with this kiss, stake my claim. This amazing, sexy, and beautiful girl is mine. When I lightly nip her bottom lip, she lets out a groan that goes straight to my cock. I know she can feel how hard I am, and I don't try to hide it.

I never want to stop kissing her, but a car horn reminds me we're still very much in public, even if we can't be seen very well. I slowly pull away, leaving a soft kiss on the corner of her mouth, before I rest my forehead on hers. We both catch our breath, still wrapped in each other's arms.

"Wow, baby girl. I've never had a kiss like that." I say, as I run my hand over her arm and put her hand over my heart. I want her to feel what she's doing to me. I want her to know only she has ever made me feel this way.

"That was a pretty damn good kiss." She says breathlessly.

"It's getting late. Let's get to the bus, so we can go home," I say, even though, the bus with her brother is the last place I want to be.

We take our time walking back hand in hand, smiling and soaking up each other's company.

The second we walk into the bus together, Landon is glaring

at me, but I just shrug at him and smile. I doubt he will go off on me again, where Austin can hear.

The next morning, we're finally home, and all head into the house. I'm unpacking, when Landon steps into my room. He leaves tomorrow, and yeah, I will miss him, but I can't wait to have two weeks alone with Austin.

"You know I'm gone for two weeks. That leaves you with a few meetings on your own. Will you call me after and let me know how they go?" Landon asks, talking about the meetings at the label.

"Of course."

"Also, watch over Austin. Make sure she adjusts after the tour okay. We're used to it, but she isn't."

"You don't have to ask me, you know I wouldn't let anything happen to her."

"Do it while keeping your hands off of her." He growls, and then turns and heads out of the door.

Austin is standing in her door across the hall, and she narrows her eyes at Landon. He grunts and goes downstairs.

Austin and I don't move. We just stare at each other. Then, she steps into my room and gets close enough to whisper, but not close enough for me to reach out and touch her.

"You better not keep your hands off." She says.

"Didn't plan on it, baby girl," I smirk.

CHAPTER 13

Austin

Landon left this morning, and I feel no guilt that I'm relieved he's gone. I felt like I would look at Dallas the wrong way, and he'd just know. Or that we'd avoid each other a little too much, and he'd know something was up.

Thankfully, we passed with flying colors, and Landon is now on a plane to the other side of the country for two weeks.

Now, I'm trying to work with the sexiest man in rock and roll, sitting at the other end of the dining room table, shirtless and answering emails on his computer. He seems to be looking at me a whole lot less than I'm looking at him.

Thankfully, after the tour, I don't have to worry too much about work. I made some good money and was able to stick to a few of my favorite clients, and right now, I'm working on the graphics for the lingerie store's website.

"You seem awfully distracted over there." He grins at me.

"That's what happens, when you have a sexy man sitting across from you shirtless, and you're working on a lingerie web-site," I smirk back at him.

"Christ." He says under his breath and closes his laptop. Then, he's up and stalking towards me, before I can think twice. He turns my chair with me in it to the side and leans down, until we're face to face.

"Show me." His voice is hoarse, so I do as he asks and show him the website I've been working on.

A minute later he leans in and rubs his nose up my neck, before kissing across my jawline and giving me a chaste kiss on my lips. I don't even realize I whimper, until he smiles.

"Later, right now, I need to feed you dinner." He says.

"Nope, I'm cooking for you, already have it planned," I tell him and steer him to one of the bar stools at the island.

We talk, as I make lasagna roll ups. I thought this would make a good dinner, because I'll make double, and then we can have them for lunch a day or two later.

After dinner, Dallas pulls me into the living room.

"I loved watching TV with you that first night you were here, and when we watched movies on the road. So, that's what I want, to snuggle and watch some shows with you." He says a little unsure. It's such a simple thing, but then my brother normally wedges himself between us, so it's a big deal to watch TV without him.

"Sounds perfect," I say, as I sit down and cuddle up to his side. He pulls a blanket over us and wraps his arms around me. Every so often, I look up at him and manage to get a quick kiss in, but he pulls back, before it goes any further.

After the fourth time, he must read the frustration on my face, because he chuckles.

"We're going to take this nice and slow, baby girl. That doesn't mean I don't want you, because I do, but I want to make sure we do this right."

With a sigh, I agree and snuggle into him.

* * *

It's been almost a week of the most perfect routine I could

have asked for. Every morning, Dallas wakes me up with breakfast and coffee. Then, I work, while he works on new lyrics for the next album. A few times we both exercised out by the pool, instead of inside. Then after lunch, we took some downtime to clean the house or read in the library. Then, we'd work some more.

I'd make dinner every night, and after dinner, we end up on the couch watching TV. I've fallen asleep twice and woken up to Dallas carrying me to bed. He always lays me down with a kiss on the forehead, before heading off to his room.

Dallas wasn't kidding about taking things slow. We haven't taken things past kissing. Mind blowing sexy kissing. The best kisses of my life kissing. I can only imagine how things will be, when we take it to the next step. That's what I'm thinking about, as I come downstairs for breakfast.

Dallas is just setting food on the table, when I make it to the kitchen.

"Morning." He says, kissing my cheek and directing me to the table, where he already has a cup of coffee waiting for me.

Once we sit down, he looks up at me.

"Would you like to go out on a date with me today?" He asks, and he seems a little nervous.

I perk right up.

"Of course, I would. Where are we going?"

"It's a surprise. But we have to stop at the label first, because our manager is insisting on talking to me. Then, I'm all yours for the rest of the day."

I quickly finish breakfast, and then head upstairs to get ready. I dress casually, because if I needed to dress up, I know Dallas would have told me. I'm in black skinny jeans and a dark burgundy dressy loose top. I leave my hair down but put some waves in it and a touch of makeup.

I go downstairs and find Dallas waiting for me, leaning against the kitchen counter in dark jeans and a button down shirt, making my mouth go dry. He can be in the most casual clothes and still look so damn sexy.

He catches me checking him out, and I don't even try to hide it. Grinning at me, his eyes run over my body, and I can feel them, as if it were his hands on me. He pushes off the counter and stalks towards me.

"God, you're beautiful. I almost don't want to take you out and share you." He wraps his hands around my waist and kisses the top of my head.

"Let's get this meeting over with, so I can have you all to myself." He takes my hand and leads me to his truck.

"No convertible today?" I joke.

"No, this will be more practical for what I had in mind."

"Am I dressed okay?" I ask, suddenly nervous.

His eyes run over me again with such heat in them on my skin.

"You're perfect." He whispers, before starting up the truck.

He takes my hand and holds it the entire way to the label. I always love driving down music row here in Nashville. All the labels are set up in old historic homes, and they put banners out in the front yard, bragging about their new number one hits.

"Oh, look Brantley Gilbert has another number one." I sigh. "Why couldn't you get signed with him?" I joke.

This earns me a glare from Dallas.

"What? Can't I have guys that I wouldn't mind being a notch on their bedpost?" I roll my eyes and try to hide my smile. He pulls into the parking area, and before I even realize what's going on, he has my seatbelt undone, and he's pulling me into his lap.

He doesn't say anything, as he just stares into my eyes, like he's trying to tell me something he can't find the words to say.

"You're too good to be a notch on anyone's bedpost. It's why I kept you at arm's length for so long. How you can forgive my past and be here with me today, I will never know, but I'm so grateful you are."

Then, his lips are on mine, and it's a gentle kiss full of promises. When I try deepening the kiss, he pulls away. That small, short kiss has me already on edge. All these sexy kisses leading to nothing are driving me crazy.

"Let's get this meeting over with." He opens his door, carries me out his side, and then sets me on my feet. Then, he gives me a pained look.

"I will proudly hold your hand in there, but I think it's best they don't know about it, before Landon does." He says.

"I agree. And just so you know, I'd proudly hold your hand in there and anywhere." I don't just say the words; I mean them with everything in me.

We walk in checking in with the receptionist, and then sit in the waiting room.

"What's this meeting about?" I ask.

"The new album they want us to start working on. I'm sure this will be their 'suggestions' of the direction we should go." He says.

"Don't let them bully you. You guys are good, and your fans love you. They'd be good to remember that." I tell him honestly.

He grins, but Mitch comes out, before he can reply.

"Dallas, we're ready." He stands and looks at me.

"Go do your thing." I hold up my phone. "I have a book to read."

"I won't be long." He says and heads back.

The receptionist looks at me and smiles. "What are you reading?" She asks.

I pull the romance book I'm reading, as she comes to sit beside me, and we talk books and swap titles. Turns out, we love to read the same dirty romance novels, and she gave me some good suggestions.

"I've never met anyone who reads the same things I do." She

says almost shyly.

"Me either." I smile. "I'm Austin," I say.

"Deanna." She smiles. "How do you know Dallas?" She asks, her shyness showing again.

"Oh, his band mate Landon is my brother. Landon's out of town, and he's nice enough to let me tag along today, because I needed to get out of the house." I shrug.

"You're Landon's sister?" Her eyes go wide, and she chuckles.

"Yeah, guilty. Please, don't hold it against me." I laugh.

She looks back down the hallway Dallas disappeared, too.

"I have been working here two years and both of them are always nice, when they come in. Once, I was carrying some boxes from my car, and Landon stepped in to help me. I mean, a famous rock star helped me carry file boxes. Who would believe me?"

"Good, I'm glad he helped, or I'd have kicked his ass, and he knows it. Same with Dallas. I made sure they had manners. They can go to parties and do whatever, but they will treat a lady with respect or answer to me." I say.

"Yeah, I learned that one the hard way." Dallas grins, as he walks back into the room.

Deanna jumps up. "Sorry, Mr. McIntire." She says and runs back to her desk.

He looks at me with a questioning look, before turning to her. "You can call me Dallas, and there's nothing to be sorry about. I appreciate you keeping Austin company for me."

Deanna smiles and ducks her head. You would think working at the label she'd be used to getting attention from the musicians in and out of here each day.

I stand up and walk over to her desk.

"So, feel free to say no, but I'd love to talk books again with you and have someone to discuss them, as we read them. Would you want to exchange phone numbers? I'm going to read that sugar daddy one you recommended next." I say.

"Oh, I'd love that. I'm going to read the one you're reading now, when I get home." She hands me her phone, and I put in my number and send myself a quick text.

As I'm handing her phone back to her, Dave walks out.

"Oh, Dallas, I'm glad I caught you. One more thing..." Dave says, but stops dead in his tracks, when he sees me.

The look he gives me creeps me out and kind of makes me want to rip his eyes out. It's leery and causes me to do something I haven't done in years. I move to stand behind Dallas and use him as a shield.

"What the fuck?" Dallas growls.

CHAPTER 14

Dallas

The look he's giving Austin pisses me off more than I can ever remember. But when it makes her so uncomfortable, she slips behind me to get out of his line of sight, and then it's time for me to step in.

"What the fuck?" I growl.

"I... um... I just thought she was in Maine. I didn't expect to her here." Dave stumbles over his words.

Austin rests her head against my back, and I know she can feel how tense I am. It's taking everything in me not to launch at this guy. I know Landon would have my back with this, whatever the consequences are.

"What the fuck does it matter? You don't look at her, and you don't fucking breathe in her direction again. You fucking got it?" I growl.

Dave's eyes go wide, and he just nods.

"Good, now whatever you came out here to say, you can shove it." I turn and wrap my arm around Austin's shoulders and drag her from the building away from his view. I don't stop, until we are back in my truck and the doors are locked.

I finally look over at Austin, and she's studying me.

"Are you okay?" I ask.

She doesn't answer, instead she leans over the console and kisses me. It's a deep kiss full of more meaning than just a thank you. Her lips on mine soothe the anger that was coursing through me. When she pulls back, she's a bit flushed, and it's sexy as hell.

"Okay, I have to call Landon, because he'll be pissed if I don't. Then, I'm taking you out and making you forget all this."

She nods, as I pull out my phone and dial Landon.

"Hey, man. How'd the meeting go?" He asks.

"Good, until the end," I growl.

"What do you mean?" He's instantly stone cold serious.

"Well, I brought Austin with me, because she's been working all week and needed to get out of the house. We were going to do lunch after. Anyway, the meeting went fine. Austin was hanging out in the waiting room, and when we were leaving, Dave came out and saw Austin."

I describe his look, and how Austin even moved behind me.

"Well, I don't know about you, but this settles it. I want to be done and start our own label. We have one more year on our contract. You with me?" He asks.

"You don't even have to ask. If Austin wasn't there, I'd have laid him on his ass. If I never have to see that fucker again, it will be too soon."

"Agreed. How was the meeting before that?" He asks.

I reach over and grab Austin's hand and hold it in mine, as I recap the meeting, and how they want to put out another record, before our contract is up and want to start negotiating a new contract, even though, we've mentioned going out on our own before. We both agree we aren't giving them another record after this. We will deal with it, when he gets home.

I bring Austin's hand to my mouth and place kisses on the back of her hand, while her brother talks about his trip out there. Austin's breathing picks up, and I know she's just as affected by me, as I am of her.

We hang up, and I look over at Austin.

"Ready to get out of town for a while?" I asked her.

"More than you know." She forces a smile.

I check my phone and make sure the food I ordered for us is ready for pickup and make my way there.

"Stay here. I'll be right back," I tell her, once I park.

"We aren't eating inside?" She asks.

"No, baby girl. I have bigger plans. I'll be just a minute. Lock the doors." I tell her.

I close the door behind me and wait, until she locks them, before heading into the deli to grab our lunches. I've eaten here before, and the staff is pretty good at not making a big deal about who I am, so I'm in and out pretty fast.

When I climb back into the truck, I pull her in for a quick kiss, before getting on our way.

"So, do I get a hint? Like how long, before I can eat this food that smells so good?" She asks. She seems back to her normal self, and any traces of the mood from earlier are gone.

"Not too long," I tell her, as I drive out of town. About fifteen minutes later, I'm pulling on to a dirt road, and she just gives me a weird look.

"A friend of mine owns this property and lets me come back here to write songs or do whatever I want. I thought we could have a picnic here, because it kind of reminds me of our spot." I tell her.

She smiles, and her hand reaches for my tattoo of the field we spent prom night in.

"Sounds perfect."

I get to the field that has some beautiful purple wildflowers, and it's at the base of a large hill, not quite big enough to be a mountain. I pull out the large blanket I packed in the back of the truck earlier and set it out, and then grab the food and her hand, as we settle on the blanket.

"I love this little deli. They make the best sandwiches, but they're always packed. The staff doesn't make a big deal, when I'm there, but other customers always do. One day, once we are public, I'll take you there and show you off, but for now, this is the second-best option." I tell her.

"I love this, because I don't have to share you with anyone. Your fans are important, and I would never stop you from interacting with them, but it kinda sucks, when they insert themselves into our time, when we're out."

"Like the lunch at Biltmore?" I say.

"Exactly like that. So, I'll take a date like this any day." She leans in and kisses me in what I'm sure she meant to be a light, fun kiss, but it instantly turns steamy.

She wraps her arms around my neck and pulls me close. I wrap an arm around her waist and gently lean her back, until she's laying on the blanket with me over her. I refuse to take it beyond a kiss. Not here. I want her to know that I want her, because she's different, and not just for sex. All I wanted from the other girls was sex, none of this. I want everything from her.

After a few minutes of kissing, I pull back.

"Let me feed you, baby girl," I whisper against her lips.

She nods, and I help her sit up. I start pulling out the fried chicken sandwiches and bottles of water with their homemade chips.

She digs in, her whole face lights up, after she takes the first bite.

"This is really good, Dallas." She says.

"So, how's work going?" I ask her.

"Good, I slowed down, since the tour, only working with a few of my favorite clients. I like not having to take every little thing to just pay bills, but to be honest, I feel like such a freeloader not paying my share." She says.

"As if we would let you." I smile at her. "Plus, you'll get money from the records and the tour. Really, you don't have to work." I remind her.

"I know, but..." She hesitates.

"But what?"

"I don't touch that money. It goes into a savings account that I leave alone. It gets invested per your insistence, but that's it. I've always paid my bills with the money from my job."

"Building a nice retirement fund?" I ask her.

"Not really."

I look at her, and she seems a little hesitant to continue. I can't have that.

"No walls up, Austin. We aren't doing this halfway." I tell her.

She nods and takes a deep breath.

"I guess, I always planned for that to be my family money."

"What do you mean?" I ask.

"Someday, I want a family. I started doing these casual relationships, and I guess, I saw the dream of getting married and starting a family begin to slip away. So, I planned that money to be for my family. When I was ready, I'd be a single mom, have children, and that money would support my kids and be passed down to them, when the time came." She shrugs.

"You don't want to get married?"

"I do, but I guess the more I dated, the more I lost hope in finding a guy. Well, you set the bar pretty damn high. I was always waiting for a guy that treated me like you always have. He hasn't shown up yet."

A pang of jealousy hits me, when she talks about marrying another man. But I'm also happy in a way that she has compared the other guys to me. It means I was doing something right all these years, even when I didn't think I could have her.

"Well, get ready to be blown away, because if you liked how I treated you, when we weren't dating, then I'm going to step it up now that we are."

She gives me this unsure look and my gut twists. She does want to date me, right?

"What is it?" I ask her softly.

"Are we dating?" She asks.

"Oh, baby girl. We're so much more than dating. You are mine, and I'm yours. Titles the whole nine yards." I tell her, pulling her against my side.

"I just... You haven't dated anyone before, I didn't want to assume."

"When it comes to you, assume away. I was slow to jump into this, because I wanted to do it right. I'm 100% in. Do you want this?" I ask her. I want to hear her words and not just assume them.

"Yes, I'm scared by how much I want this." She says.

"This isn't going to be casual. I want all of you." I tell her.

"As long as I get all of you, and I don't share." Her voice is stern.

"I'm only yours. I don't share either."

"Good." She says.

I lie down on the blanket and pull her down to lay with me, and we talk for a few hours about everything and anything.

"So, if we're going to do this, let's get the awkward stuff out of the way." She says.

"Okay, hit me with it. I won't keep anything from you, but I expect the same from you."

"All right then, what's your number?" She asks.

My number? She has my phone number, what number? Then, it dawns on me. Shit.

"More than I want to admit," I say, tensing up. I know Austin, and she's going to push this.

"Dallas..."

"Honestly, I don't know if you want an answer. I can sit down tonight and try to give you my best guess, but I wouldn't be stretching it to say over fifty." I cringe now. I didn't care then, because the number of hookups I had meant nothing. But now that I want to start a real relationship, that number seems like a hurdle, we might not be able to get over.

She sighs and nods her head. "Okay."

"Same question," I tell her, not sure I want to know.

"Six. How old were you your first time?"

"Ugh, you won't believe me."

"Dallas..."

"I was nineteen just after your prom. It was on our first tour, and women were throwing themselves at us. I never admitted to her it was my first time, and I also never saw her again."

I won't admit to Dallas that the entire time I was imagining it was her. Every girl I have been with didn't matter, because in my head it was always her.

"Same question." I urge her on.

"Eighteen, a few weeks after prom. A few friends were hanging out at a guy's lake house for the weekend. We spent the weekend together, and that was it. I moved a month later and haven't talked to him since."

Fuck, we could have been each other's first at her prom. How much different would life have been, if I had taken her then? I don't think I was the guy she needed then, and there's a very real chance it could have destroyed us.

"On to safer topics. Tell me about your first tour." She says and cuddles up to me.

She isn't running, so I hold her tighter and start talking. I tell her about our crappy bus, where twelve of us slept in it, and the fans that would try to sneak on it. If it kept her in my arms like this, I'd tell her every little detail.

As the sun starts to set, we pack up and get back in the truck.

I take the long way home, rolling down the windows and crank up the music, as we sing along loudly just like we used to do in high school.

I knew back then this girl was something special, and she finds ways to prove it to me again and again.

CHAPTER 15

Austin

By the time we get home that night, I have forgotten all about the creepy manager, until Landon calls.

"Hey, how's your trip?" I ask.

"Fine. I wanted to check on you and see how you're doing. Dallas called." He says.

"Yeah, I was sitting right next to him. Honestly, I'm fine. Dallas distracted me with food, and a day out was just what I needed. On the flip side, I made a new friend."

"Yeah, who?" He asks.

"Deanna, the receptionist at the label. We got to talking about books, and we read the same things, so we exchanged numbers and books to read. It will be nice to have someone local to talk to, especially about books."

"I'm glad. I haven't talked much to her, but she seems like a nice girl. Just be careful. You know people will try to use you, so just be guarded, okay?"

"I know, Landon. You give me this speech several times a year. It's why I stopped telling people I know you and Dallas, and many times, even deny being related to you."

"Which I hate, by the way, but I get why you do it."

"I'm fine, really. I was just about to make some dinner. We'll talk more later?"

I love my brother and all, but right now, I'm a little worried he's going to press about the day, and I don't want to slip up about me and Dallas. I want this chance with Dallas, and I don't want Landon to mess that up.

"Yeah, we'll talk later. Love you." He says.

"Love you too, big brother."

I head into the kitchen and find Dallas poking around in the fridge. He hasn't seen me yet, so I lean against the wall and just watch. How is this my life? This sexy man, who so many women want and would have loved to tame, is mine. But for how long?

I have known him my entire life, and as my friend, I trust him completely. But as my boyfriend? I'm worried I won't be enough. He's used to sex whenever with whoever, and he won't let us move past kissing. Can he be a one-woman man? I'm scared to give my heart completely over to him, but if I'm truthful, he's always owned my heart. It's just been easier, when he didn't want me.

Dallas realizes I'm there and smirks at me.

"You just going to stand there?" He asks.

"I was enjoying the view."

He stalks over to me and wraps his arms around my waist, pulling me in for a chaste kiss.

"What are you thinking for dinner?" He asks.

"Well, I was on this amazing date, and the food was really good, so I'm not that hungry. Maybe, breakfast for dinner?"

"Amazing date, huh? Good guy?" He asks. His hands are still on my waist, so I wrap my arms around his neck.

"The best. He just needs to see himself that way." I look him right in the eyes and watch a flood of emotions, as his eyes go stormy. They flash by so fast it's hard to read them, but I know he doubts himself.

"Pancakes or French toast?" I ask.

Then, his whole face lights up. "Will you make that French Toast Bake? I haven't had it in so long."

"Of course."

"I'm going to go change into something more comfortable." He says and kisses my cheek, before pulling away.

"Mmmm, maybe some gray sweatpants?" I suggest.

"Woman, it isn't sweatpants season!" He laughs.

"I will crank the air down in the house, so it is!" I yell back.

I start dinner with a smile on my face. I'm just putting it in the oven, when Dallas walks into the kitchen, wearing gray sweatpants and nothing else. He leans against the wall just like I was earlier and watches me.

I let my eyes wander over his sexy as hell body. Dallas has a beautiful body with chiseled abs, amazing ink, and the perfect tan, but he doesn't show it off very often. He doesn't take his shirt off at shows or pose with it off for photo shoots. I have seen him shirtless around the pool, but right now in the gray sweatpants, it's a whole new level.

He stalks towards me without a word and uses his thumb to pull my bottom lip from between my teeth. I didn't even realize I was biting it.

"Like what you see?" He asks.

All I can do is nod, because like doesn't even begin to cover it.

"Good, now it's your turn to go change. Put on those sexy cotton shorts, and one of those tank tops you like to wear around the tour bus and torment me with." He growls.

I shoot him a smile over my shoulder, before running upstairs and changing into the clothes he asked for. I run a brush through my hair and retouch my makeup, before heading back downstairs.

Tonight, I want to move things along from more than just kisses, so it's time to push some of his buttons. Seeing him shirtless sent me over the edge, and I'm going to have to break out my vibrator tonight, if he isn't willing to touch me. I will make sure he knows it, too.

As soon as I walk into the kitchen, his eyes are on me.

"Fuck." He whispers under his breath, as his eyes roam over me.

I walk over to the oven and open it to check on the casserole that I know isn't ready yet, and slowly bend down to look at it. He groans behind me, and I smile.

"Not quite ready yet," I tell him.

Then, turning to get plates to set the table, I open the cabinet and reach for the plates, which causes my shorts to ride up and give him a nice view of the bottom of my ass. I put on the shortest pair I own for this reason.

Only this time, when he groans, it's followed by him pressing his body to mine from behind.

"What are you trying to do to me?" He whispers, pressings his cock into me.

"You started this, when you walked out here with no shirt on," I say and slowly lower myself back to the flats of my feet. I enjoy the glide down his length, and when he leans forward and grips the counter surrounding me, I place the plates on the counter and turn to face him.

"You have been teasing me all week, Dallas, and then you walk out here like this tonight. It's time to even the playing field." I run a hand up his arm, over his shoulder, and down his chest.

This is the first time I get to see his ink up close. Over his heart is a tattoo of the state of Texas with a heart just to the right of the center. It has to hold some meaning, but being we aren't from Texas, I'm not sure what.

I run my finger over it to the crossed guitars on the other side with the quote, 'Because your mine, I walk the line' from one of our favorite Johnny Cash songs.

I'm distracted from my exploring, when the oven timer goes

off. Neither of us moves, but I meet his eyes. They're heated, as he's been watching me.

"Dinner time," I whisper. He moves and takes the plates to finish setting the table, as I pull the food out.

Dinner is intense. Neither of us says anything, but I swear Dallas is undressing me with his eyes. His gaze is just as fiery as when I was tracing his tattoos.

"Eat up, baby girl." He says breaking me from his gaze, as I realize I had stopped eating just to watch him.

I turn my eyes back to my plate and finish eating. Once I'm done, I stand to clean up the kitchen, when his hands take mine.

"Leave it." He says, and without letting go of my hand, heads to the living room. He turns the TV on to some cooking show and pulls me onto the couch next to him.

My ass barely hits the couch, when his lips are on mine. It's a deep, heated kiss that matches the intensity of his gaze earlier. He keeps pulling me closer, like he can't get me close enough.

Without realizing how it happened, I'm straddling his lap all without breaking the kiss. He starts trailing kisses across my jaw, as he tangles a hand in my hair and pulls my head back to start kissing down my neck.

"More," I gasp.

His hands leave my hair, and I look back at him.

"Are you wet for me?" He whispers, as his hand snakes up my thigh and into my shorts.

He runs his finger over my panties, making me moan.

"Yeah, you are. Damn, Austin, knowing I can do this to you." He shakes his head and keeps rubbing me lightly over my panties.

"Dallas," I groan.

"What do you need?"

"Your mouth." I want him to kiss me again, but he gives me a devilish smile.

"You want my mouth on you down here?" He rubs a bit harder, making me cry out.

"Yes!"

Then, an unsure look crosses over his face, and he pulls his hand from my shorts.

"What is it?" I ask.

He shakes his head. "You wouldn't believe me."

"Try me."

He studies my face for a minute, before he throws his head against the back of the couch and looks at the ceiling. Both his hands grip my hips, but neither of us moves.

"I haven't done that before, gone down on a girl. There are a lot of things I haven't done. I was very much a one-trick pony." His confession shocks me.

"What do you mean?" I ask, needing to know more.

He shakes his head, "This is totally going to kill the mood."

"Then, we will have just as much fun getting it back." I urge him on.

"I may have been a playboy, but it was always on my terms. I didn't kiss a lot and never in public. I only did it in one position ever, never took my shirt off, never went down on a girl, and never let them go down on me."

"You've never had a blow job?" I ask shocked.

His eyes find mine, as he shakes his head.

"What position?" I ask.

He gives me a dry laugh. "From behind, I never wanted to see their faces."

"Why?" I ask.

"I promise to tell you just not now. It's a little too deep for us tonight." His eyes plead with me to let it go.

"This is why you haven't let us go beyond kissing?" I ask him.

He slowly nods with that uncertain look back on his face.

"Do you realize you admitting this to me turns me on even more?"

Confusion clouds his face. "What?"

I laugh, "Dallas, I didn't care when I thought you had done more things with these women than I would ever want to try. But knowing you might at some point trust me with some of your firsts? That is a huge turn on."

He pulls my face to his and kisses me slowly, like he has all the time in the world.

"There's no might. You will be the one getting my firsts. All of them. I hope maybe we'll find some you can give me."

I laugh. "Trust me, I can name a few off the top of my head."

"Such as?"

"Well, I've never let a guy go down on me. I've never let a guy come in my mouth, I've never gone bareback, or had sex outside the bedroom." I shrug. "And when you decide to give me your reasons, I'll give you mine."

"Deal. Would you be up for checking off one of those firsts for both of us?" He asks.

"What did you have in mind?"

"I want you to come on my tongue. Ever since you stepped out in these tiny shorts earlier, I've been thinking about it. I want to know what you taste like. I want to know what you look like, when you let go and what drives you wild. Will you let me?"

I nod, a bit shy, but I want to do this with him. Only with him. He lifts me off him and lays me on the couch. His hands shake a little, and in some weird way knowing he's nervous, eases my nerves, too.

He slides my shorts off and tosses them on the floor and runs his hands back up my legs, spreading me wide.

"These panties are soaked. Do you have any idea how hot that is?" He asks.

I nod, as he smiles and leans down to kiss me just below my

belly button.

"Will you take your shirt off?" He asks.

I hesitate for only a minute, before I sit up just enough to pull the tank top off. I wasn't wearing a bra under it, so now, I lay completely naked in front of him with the exception of my barely there lace panties.

"So perfect." He mumbles against my skin.

He runs his hands down my side, until he gets to my hips, and he sees the tattoo there. It's a guitar with *Highway 55* written next to it, the band's name. On the guitar, are the orange wild-flowers that were always filling our field in the summer, when we were growing up.

Dallas stares at it and runs his finger over it, before looking back at me.

"When did you get this?" He asks.

"When you had your first platinum album." I see him doing the calculations in his head. That was several years ago.

"How have I not seen it?" He asks.

I shrug, "Because I wear mostly one-piece bathing suits around you guys, per Landon's orders." I smile.

After he caught so many guys blatantly staring at me, when I would swim in a bikini, he demanded I wear a bathing suit that covered more. So, I got a few of those cute vintage 1950s one-piece halter swimsuits with the shorts.

"I might have put that bug in his ear. I hate how they stared at you." He says, his eyes still on the tattoo.

"Any other tattoos I should know about?" He asks.

"If I told you, it would take the fun out of it."

He leans over and places a feather-light kiss over the tattoo, before kissing across the top of my panties to my hips, and then slowly pulling them down and kissing one leg and slowly back up the other.

He spreads my legs, and his eyes travel up my body to my

breasts, which he hasn't even touched yet. Leaning up, he takes one into his mouth, giving it a light nip, before moving over to the other, and then slowly kissing down my belly, before landing on my clit.

His tongue circles my clit, and he raises his eyes to me. Our eyes lock, as he continues the assault on my clit, and the sensations that take over my body are indescribable.

When his mouth moves further down, and his tongue slides into me, my hips buck trying to get closer. He rests an arm over my hips to hold me in place and rubs his thumb over my clit.

"Oh God, don't stop," I swear I can feel him smile against me, before he picks up the pace with his tongue, keeping slow firm strokes on my clit. The mixed sensations overwhelm me, and my climax hits hard. I cum harder than I ever have in my life, screaming his name.

Once my body relaxes, I open my eyes, and Dallas is staring at me in wonder.

"Mmmm, what is it?" I ask.

He shakes his head, "I think I just realized..." He stops and shakes his head again and grabs the blanket from the back of the couch, pulling it over us, as he lies down beside me.

"Honesty. I want all of you, Dallas."

"Probably not something to talk about after what we just did."

"Yet, I'm going to insist you do."

"I just realized how many women faked it with me. Watching you let go like that for me? I've never seen anything like it."

"So, you got two firsts tonight." I smile and kiss his chest. I trail my hand over his hard cock. "We can go for three."

"Mmmm, you can feel how bad I want you, but tonight was about you. My pace may not make sense to you, but I want to do this right. Though, I'll always make sure you're taken care of, okay?"

I snuggle into him and hum my agreement. Neither one of us is in a hurry to head upstairs.

CHAPTER 16

Dallas

I wake up around three a.m. and having a naked Austin pressed against me has me hard, but this isn't about me. She gave me the most wonderful gift last night. Knowing I made her cum is so powerful and very addicting. After one night, I'm addicted to making my girl cum and I'm already planning, when I can do it again.

I run my hand up and down her back, enjoying her smooth, soft skin. We both fell asleep on the couch last night after I made her cum. Holy hell, that was the most erotic experience of my life, making my girl scream my name from just my tongue. The bulge in my pants grows, and I didn't think it was possible.

I need to get relief, if I'm going to be able to sleep. I start to shift, thinking I can go to the bathroom and take care of it and come back, before she even wakes up but, I'm not so lucky. Her arm tightens around me.

"Trying to sneak away?" She asks, her voice laced with sleep.

"No, baby girl." I kiss the top of her head, and she shifts her leg over my hips, and it rubs against my cock. I can't stop the groan that comes from me, even this slight touch of her leg feels good.

"Please, Dallas. Let me." She whispers, as her hand trails down towards my pants.

Before her hand reaches my cock, I grab her waist, pulling her, so she's straddling me. Her breasts are on full display, and there's enough light from the moonlight coming in from the windows to see her. She's perfect.

As she starts grinding on me, my hands travel up her side and gently grab her breasts and run my thumbs over their peaks. This makes her gasp, so I do it again and earn a moan.

Her grinding on me feels so good I know I won't last long. I lean up and take one of her perfect tits into my mouth and suck it hard, and then do the same to the other. Gripping her waist again, I stroke her clit. She needs to cum soon, because I'm not going to last.

"Oh, Dallas. Oh, God." She starts to moan.

"Cum for me, baby girl. Let me watch you fall apart again."

She shifts again falling forward, resting on my shoulders, as her body locks up, and she screams my name. I hold out as long as I can to watch her, but less than two more stokes, and I'm cumming harder than I've ever done before.

"Fuck, baby, I needed that. Watching you, I just don't have the words. Though, we need to practice you being quiet, because we won't always have the place to ourselves."

She gives a light chuckle but doesn't move.

"Baby, I need to go get cleaned up."

"I don't think I can move. I feel like jello all over." She says.

With a little tricky maneuvering, I lay her down and run up to my room and clean up and change into clean sweatpants, before I head back downstairs. I find Austin already asleep again, so I crawl in beside her.

"Took you long enough." She says, and she attaches herself to my side. Maybe, she wasn't quite asleep yet.

"Want to go to bed?" I ask her. Her bed is more comfortable than this couch is any day.

"Nope, not moving and neither are you." She snuggles into me even more.

"Nowhere else I'd rather be," I tell her.

The doorbell going off wakes me up. I have Austin in my arms, and I sure as hell don't want to move. I don't remember falling asleep, but it was one of the best nights of sleep I can remember having in a long time.

What we did last night floats to the front of my mind, and the memories alone get me hard, but it doesn't last long, as the doorbell rings again. I sigh and start to get up.

"Are you expecting anyone?" Austin murmurs.

"No, baby girl. Get dressed. I'll go get it." I say getting up.

I watch Austin stretch her bare breasts on full display, and before I go, I lean down and give them each a kiss and forget all about the door, when she groans. I'm getting ready to settle back on the couch and give them more attention, when the doorbell rings again. By the time I get to the door, I'm getting really irritated. It's barely eight a.m.

Landon and I rarely close and lock the gate, because this neighborhood is gated and is really safe, but after this and while Landon is gone, I will be making sure it's closed. I don't want any more of my time with Austin interrupted.

I open the door to find a guy in expensive jeans and an old t-shirt with dark hair, standing on the porch. He looks me over, I'm still shirtless in the sweatpants I changed into early this morning, after round two of making my girl cum.

"What the hell do you want so damn early?" I ask, not even trying to be nice.

"Is Austin here?" He asks.

Jealousy, like I've never felt, surges through my body. Some guy coming and asking for my girl after last night? Fuck, I need to calm down. I don't get the chance to respond, before Austin is at my side.

"Branden? What the fuck are you doing here?" She says clearly not happy to see him at the door.

Branden, her ex, who proposed after three months. I don't move from my spot. Though, I know Austin can take care of herself, I'm here if she needs me. I'd love the chance to punch this guy in the face.

He doesn't answer right away and just looks her up and down.

"What are you doing here?" Austin demands.

"I wanted to talk we had a fight and..."

"We did not fight. I ended it, because you proposed after three months of a causal relationship. Now, how did you find me?"

She doesn't invite him in, and for that, I'm happy, because it means she has no intention of letting him stay.

Branden, or as I've been calling him in my head, sir who I want to punch in the face, shoves his hands into his pockets and looks at the ground. His body language just seems... off. I can't put my finger on it.

"I went to your apartment to try to talk to you, and your roommate gave me some of your mail that didn't get forwarded. One had this return address on it. Remembering your brother was here, I took a shot."

He looked at me, when he said, brother. Yeah, aren't you going to shit your pants, when you realize I'm not her brother?

"Branden, you need to go. I don't want you here, and I don't want you to come back. Set foot on this property again, and it will be trespassing. I don't know how you got in here, but I'm guessing the cops won't have a hard time figuring it out."

"Austin, come on. I love you, and I just want to talk. I get that it was too much too soon."

I growl, when I hear that, and his eyes shoot to me. He looks a little worried, as he should be.

"That's the problem, I feel nothing for you. It was a casual arrangement. It wasn't a relationship, and I'm starting to realize sex with you wasn't even that great. Goodbye."

She slams the door in his face and locks it, before turning

around and hesitantly looking up at me. I see a slight tremble go through her, and before I can say anything, I'm pulling her into my arms.

"I'm here, Austin. I'm right here. Not going anywhere."

She clings to me, like I'm her lifeline, and maybe, I am, but in this moment, I know I need her just as much. I run my hands down to her ass.

"Hold on," I whisper in her ear and lift her up. She instantly wraps her legs around me and buries her face in my neck. I carry her back to the living room, where we spent the night and sink down on to the couch, holding her tight. She makes no move to let go of me, and I don't want her, too.

I rub her back, and slowly, she stops trembling. Even once she's calm, neither of us moves. I will give her all the strength she needs always. I will sit here all day with her if that's what she needs.

"It doesn't make sense." She finally says.

"What doesn't?" I ask, not sure if I want to know the answer.

"How he got this address. You guys never mailed me anything. Did you send something, before I moved?"

"No, I didn't, but you'll have to call and ask your brother. He needs to know about this, too."

She nods, still lost in thought.

"Also, my roommate hated him. I doubt she'd just hand over my mail to him, especially since she knew what he did, and I was pissed and leaving."

"I don't know then. Maybe, he lied and told her you were back together?"

"It's been over two months. If he was so heartbroken, wouldn't he have tried to reach out to me before now?"

"Well, we were on tour. Does he know about the band?"

"I didn't tell him that Landon was my brother, but I didn't hide it either. He could have put the pieces together." She says, biting her lip, lost in thought.

I gently pull her lip from between her teeth.

"If he did, then he could have known we were on tour and waited, until we got home."

She shakes her head. "I don't want to think about this anymore. I'm sorry he ruined what I had planned to be a perfect morning." She says, leaning down to kiss me.

"Yeah, what did you have planned?" I ask her, as I run my hands up the side of her body.

"Maybe, a little of this." She grinds herself on my cock, which has been hard, since she wrapped her legs around me.

It doesn't take long, before we're both cumming again. I don't want to move. I want to spend the rest of the day right here making this girl scream my name over and over again, but there are things to do.

"Why don't we head up, get cleaned and changed, you call your brother, and then we'll have breakfast, and see where the day leads. Maybe, some pool time?"

She flashes me a smile.

"Sounds good." She climbs off me, and I watch her walk away, as she goes upstairs.

Then, all the dirty stuff we can do flashes in my head, and I'm hard again, like I didn't just come so hard I almost blacked out.

CHAPTER 17

Austin

I head upstairs to take a shower and get cleaned up. The hot water washes over my body and relaxes the muscles I didn't even realize were sore from sleeping on the couch. We probably should have moved to our beds, when we had the chance, but I didn't want to sleep without him, and I was afraid he'd insist on us going to our own beds.

I think about the events of last night, and it has me all turned on again. To say sex with anyone else was dull is an understatement. No one has made me cum like that before. It's already the best sex of my life, and we haven't even had actual sex yet.

I can only imagine, when we do, because it's going to be explosive. Getting out of the shower, I put on a swimsuit, since he mentioned spending some time by the pool. I grab a bikini and not the one-pieces Landon normally makes me wear, while I'm here. I also make sure it's the skimpiest one I have, since it will just be the two of us. This is the bikini I would wear, when it was just me, and I was lying out tanning. It's not one I would wear out in public. I throw on a cover-up and look at my phone.

Then, I sit on my bed and take a deep breath. I feel only a little bad that I'll be waking my brother up early, since he's two hours behind us, but I want to get this over with, so I can enjoy my day with Dallas.

I call my brother, and instantly, can tell I woke him up.

"Who's dead?" He asks in his groggy voice.

"No one yet anyway." I try to joke. I hear the rustle of sheets, so I know he's sitting up and trying to awaken.

"Austin, what's wrong?"

"Why does something have to be wrong?" I tease, but really I'm just procrastinating. I know I need to talk to him, but that doesn't mean I want, too.

"Because you're never up this early."

I sigh. Just rip off the Band-Aid and get it over with, right?

"I was woken up by Branden at the door."

"Your ex? What the hell did he want?"

"He loves me, wants me back, and all that bullshit, but that's only part of the reason why I called. Did you send me any mail right before I moved?" I ask.

He pauses for a moment, "What? Austin, I don't remember the last time I mailed you anything. We don't even do Christmas cards. I'm too busy, and we talk on the phone all time."

"I thought so. Well, I have no clue how he got this address then. He says it's because he went to talk to me, and my roommate gave him some of my mail, and one had this return address. He said he remembered my brother living in Nashville, so he took a chance."

"Did you ask Dallas if he sent anything?"

"Yep, he said no and to ask you."

"So, he lied," Landon says, talking about my ex.

"Yeah, looks like it. My roommate hated him, so I don't think she'd have given him the mail, even if there was any."

"Okay, hang on." He says, and there's some more rustling and the sound of a drawer closing.

"Now, tell me everything you know. I'll get this to our security team, and they'll look into him. I'm going to come home early, until they figure it out."

"Landon, no. Dallas is here, and he didn't leave my side the whole time. We just need to start locking the driveway gate. I told him not to come back, and I promise not to leave Dallas's side, but I don't want you cutting your trip short over this."

I also don't want to cut the time I have with Dallas short. It's only four more days, but that's four days where don't have to hide anything. With my brother on edge, now really isn't the time to tell him about Dallas. I need to make a mental note to tell that to Dallas, too.

"Fine, but I'm still giving his info to security. What's his full name?"

"Branden Lewis. He said he had been in Portland for a few years, and moved for his job. Never really said where he was from."

"That wasn't a red flag?"

"Landon, you won't like my answer."

"I need the details, Austin."

Well, this is an awkward conversation to have with your brother.

"Fine. It wasn't a relationship, it was sex, just something casual. It was nothing to go a whole week and not talk. So, when he proposed at three months, of course, I freaked and left. He said he was a network specialist, but I never asked the details or where he worked. He rented a small apartment above a coffee shop in downtown Portland, and you get to say nothing about the relationship, because you're worse than me!"

He grunts, and I know he's writing it down. But I also know he won't go into it, because this just isn't a conversation he wants to have. I remember after Mom and Dad died, he asked if they had given me the birds and the bees talk, and then he tried to give me an updated version. It was very awkward.

"Okay, do you have his address, phone number, or the kind of car he was driving?"

"Yeah, he drove an older Mercedes convertible, and it was red. I hated that car. And let me text you his number."

I pull the phone away from my ear and find his contact info and copy it and text it to Landon.

"Any social media profiles?"

"Yep." I grab the links and text them to him as well.

"I will get this to our security, and they'll check him out. It could be something as simple as a crazy fan who was trying to get to us via you."

"I never told him about you, but I didn't hide it, and he never asked. He might have put two and two together. Dallas suggested that too, when I asked why he waited over two months to talk to me."

"Because of the tour."

"Yeah. That's our thoughts, too."

"Promise you won't leave Dallas's side, until I get home, and we hear back from security?"

"I promise, Landon."

He's quiet for a moment before speaking.

"You're a trouble magnet lately, aren't you?"

"Want me to leave?" I ask and roll my eyes, because I already know the answer.

"Hell no. With all this, that's the last thing I want. I'll always take care of you, Aust always. No matter what."

"Okay, I'm sorry for waking you up."

"I'm glad you did. Now, I have some calls to make."

"Bye. Love you, Land."

"Love you too, Aust."

I hang up and feel a bit better that he's looking into Branden, because it's still not sitting right with me, though I can't put my finger on it. He lied about where he got the address. It could be a stalker fan thing. I'm sure it's not hard to get the address from public records, but that would mean he'd have to know who I was and who my brother was.

I flop down on my bed and think about last night. I don't want to be one of those clingy girls, but I do feel so much closer to Dallas, after last night. Knowing we were a first together, there's just something so erotic about it.

In a strange way, knowing things were almost mechanical with the other girls makes me feel better about it. He's already treating me differently, and I really like it. He's always made me feel special, but somehow, he's stepped up his game.

The morning light fills my bedroom and brightens my mood, as it lightens my room.

I'm about the get up and head downstairs, when my phone goes off.

Deanna: So, I just finished that book you were reading. OMG! It's so hot, and I just bought the rest of the series.

Me: I knew you'd like it! I love all that author's books; they are the perfect sweet and steamy!

Deanna: Yes, I plan to read all her books. I couldn't put this one down. I was up all night reading it. Thank God, I have today off work!

Me: Yes, I plan to start the one you told me about today. I'm going to spend a lazy pool day with my e-reader!

Deanna: Great minds think alike! I planned to lie out in the backyard. It's the perfect day for it!

Me: I'd invite you over, but my brother won't let me invite anyone over, until he gets home. Insert eye roll here.

Deanna: He's that protective?

Me: I guess, there's some stuff going on. Their fans are crazy.

I don't like to lie to her, but it's easier to explain this to her than going into the details of Dave and now Branden. I don't know her well enough.

Deanna: Yes, I've heard some crazy stories from other people at the label. Fans do some weird things.

Deanna: So, question. With your brother being a rock star and all, do you read any rock star romance books?

Me: From time to time, yes. I like to see how close they get it.

Deanna: I have a good series you'll love. I'll send it over to you.

Me: Thanks. I need to go make breakfast before Dallas burns the place down.

Deanna: He can't cook?

Me: Ahhh, he's a grill master, but him and ovens have a rocky history.

Deanna: Go feed that man, and we'll talk later.

It was really good to hear from her. She follows right away with the links to the books she was talking about, so I go to the website and download them to read, before heading downstairs.

I don't even make it to my door, when the doorbell goes off again.

Fuck. Is Branden back? Please, don't let it be Branden. Dallas will have him arrested, after he beats the shit out of him. I saw the look on his face earlier. I don't want to have to make that call to Landon.

I make my way down the hall, wanting to stay out of sight, until I know what's going on. What I find at the door is not one of the many options that went through my head.

Dallas has answered the door, and there's a very beautiful woman standing there smiling at him with her hands on his shoulders. His back is to me, so I can't get a read on him. She's in a skintight short dress, and her blonde hair is done is loose waves.

From here, I can tell her makeup is done perfectly, and so are her nails.

She looks just like the type of girls Dallas used to pick up.

What the fuck is going on?

CHAPTER 18

Dallas

What the fuck is going on today? I feel like I'm in the twilight zone! First Austin's ex shows up, now Beth? And all before breakfast. Does the universe really hate me this much? I can only imagine how this is going to play out in Austin's head. This has to be my punishment for being a playboy. Now that I want to change my life, I have to suffer for it.

Austin and I had such an amazing night together, and now, the universe is throwing everything it can at us to destroy that. Well, I won't let it and will fight for us no matter how long it takes.

I look at the woman in front of me. Beth was only ever a casual fling here in town. She filled in as a fake date at a few events over the last year, but we saw each other maybe once a month. It was quick sex at her place, and I'd leave. We barely even talked. Why she thought she had any right to show up here now is beyond me. We haven't been together in over six months.

"You hadn't called, since you've been back from tour. You always do." She purrs and rests her hand on my shoulder, while pushing her tits out. Good Lord, what did I ever see in her? Wait, I know. She was the exact opposite of Austin. That was my type, wasn't it?

I glare at her, which she ignores. Of course, this is the moment

Austin comes back downstairs. She couldn't have missed the doorbell, because she was in the shower. No, the universe hates me that much.

"Oh, is your friend staying for breakfast?" Austin says in a tone that could be mistaken for sweet as sugar, if I didn't know any better. But I know it's a tone that says I'm in a ton of trouble. It's filled with hurt she's trying to cover up.

"Of course!" Beth says and tries to step into the house.

I put my hand on her shoulder and start moving her outside.

"No," I growl, as I move us both on to the front porch and close the door behind me.

"I didn't call, because I had said I wouldn't be calling anymore. It was a fling and now it's over. Leave me alone." I growl.

"Come on, I don't care if you have other girls, you know that." She waves her hand at me.

"I'm done with that life. I don't have other girls, I have a girl. *The* girl, and I wouldn't fuck that up with you or anyone else. It's always been her, and by the grace of God, she has given me a chance. Now fuck off and don't step foot on my property again!" I roar.

Once I see shock cover her face, I don't bother with another word. Turning, I head back inside, making sure I lock the door behind me.

I didn't mean to lose control like that, but the thought of keeping someone on the side, while I have Austin didn't sit well with me. Austin is everything I didn't know I needed, and even in this short time, I know there's no one else for me.

If things don't work out with us, I know right now I'd never be able to go back to living the life I did before. The touch of Beth's hand just on my shoulder made my skin crawl. If I can't have Austin, I know I won't have anyone. Not that anyone would believe me right now, but I will show her and Landon in time I'm here to stay.

I take a deep breath and go into the kitchen. I finally get a good look at Austin, and she's wearing her bathing suit cover-up. The blue floral one that I like on her, because it makes her eyes pop. I can't wait to spend time with her in the pool later.

The fantasies I've had of her and me in that pool with no one else is around are so dirty I should feel guilty, but I don't. All I feel is excitement that we might get to try out a few of them today, but first, I have to get us back on track. I can only imagine what's going on in her head right now.

"What a day." I joke, but Austin just rolls her eyes and gives me a pointed look, before going back to making breakfast. She puts something in the oven, as her phone rings.

She sighs and answers it.

"Hey."

I can't hear the other end of the conversation, but I sit down on a barstool and wait her out. We're going to talk about this. If I've learned one thing from Landon's parents, it's that you never just assume something will work it's self out in a relationship. You talk about it, bring it to the forefront, and fix it.

It's the stuff you let stew and simmer that will end things in a blink of an eye. Austin's mom told me that. I think she knew how I felt about Austin, and how Landon wanted to keep me at a distance. It wasn't too long after that conversation they passed in the car crash.

"They got back to you already?" She slowly walks over towards the large window that looks out over the backyard and the pool. I try to stay in the moment and focus on my girl.

"But it could be nothing. I told you I don't have a lot of information."

Another pause, before she sighs. Her hand not holding the phone rubs her forehead just above her eyebrows.

"I know, I promised. I won't leave Dallas's side, as long as you don't come home early."

Ahhh, she's talking to Landon. It must be about Branden. Speaking of, I head to the gate panel by the front door and make sure it's closed, turn the locks on, and make sure the security cameras around the property are working along with the security system on the house. I set the alarm and check they're set to chime anytime a window or door is opened.

By the time I get back to the kitchen, she's off the phone.

"What did Landon have to say?" I ask.

"Well, I didn't have a lot of info on Branden, but they couldn't find a Branden Lewis in Portland. It's making Landon nervous, but seriously, we were casual. I don't even know his address. I just know he lived in an apartment above a coffee shop downtown."

"You should be more careful with the people in your life." I frown, and she drops the spoon in her hand.

"Do you even know the names of all the girls you slept with, much less their phone numbers, addresses, and place of work?" She snaps.

My gut twists, because she has a point. There were a few I didn't even know their names. I want to say it was different, but I've been around her long enough to know that is exactly what *not* to say right now.

"He wasn't a one-night stand, Austin. You were seeing him for three months." I try to calm myself, because being angry at her won't help the situation.

"Doesn't matter since you're still keeping someone on the side, apparently." She growls and tries to walk off.

Oh, hell no. Does she really think I'd do that to her? I'm new to this relationship thing, but I'm not a cheater and would never cheat on Austin. I've been waiting too long to get a chance with her, and I'm not fucking this up like that. If she only knew how long I wanted her, she wouldn't question me like this, but I don't think she's ready to hear it, it would just scare her off.

I follow her and wrap both my arms around her waist, before she even makes it out of the kitchen.

"Hey, remember on tour I said I had things to do, before you could be mine?"

"What like her?" She snaps back.

I step back just enough and smack her ass. This seems to stun her into silence.

"No. I had flings, and they knew the score, all of them. It wasn't a relationship. On tour, I called them all, including Beth, and told her it was over. I didn't even owe them that, Austin, but I did owe *you* that. I wanted to do right by you."

"How many women have been in your bed?" She asks, as I smack her ass again.

"Stop trying to put more walls up. Only you have ever been in my bed, all those times you didn't want to be alone. Only you." I whisper next to her ear.

"But she has been here before?" She says confused.

"Yes. She was my stand in date for a few events hosted by the label, one of which was held here a year ago, but we never slept together here. I've always thought of this as your house, too. So, I never brought anyone back here, I never could."

Her body loses some of its tension, and she relaxes into me.

"Why not?" She says.

Ahhh, the million-dollar question. How do I tell her, because it felt like I was cheating on her? Because I didn't want any of them in a space, I consider ours and is filled with her memories. I wanted to keep this space strictly hers and mine. There's no way to tell her that, so I go with a cop out.

"It just didn't feel right." I turn her in my arms to face me. "Let's have some breakfast, put this morning behind us, and not let it ruin our day, okay?"

She nods, and I kiss her forehead, before letting her go back to the kitchen to finish up breakfast.

Over breakfast, she tells me how the receptionist from the label had texted earlier, and they were talking books. Her face lights up over how much she loves having someone with her taste in books.

I make myself a note to get a hold of her tablet and check out the books she's reading. I can make it a point to look some up and send some to her, or maybe, get some signed copies for her to add to the library.

After we finish eating, we do the dishes from today and last night as well, before I turn to her.

"Ready to go swimming?" I ask.

CHAPTER 19

Austin

Am I ready to go swimming? I think we both need some cool water and to take a step back. It's been a crazy morning. First Branden, and then that Beth girl. I don't like how I felt, when I saw her hands on him.

"Yeah, I'll meet you out there. I just need a minute," I tell him.

He leans in and kisses my cheek, "Don't be long."

Once he goes outside, I take a deep breath and head to the downstairs bathroom. It's almost as big as the bathroom upstairs with one wall of mirrors. These would make for some interesting angles to fool around with. I stand there looking at my flush cheeks and think of Dallas, slapping my ass, twice.

The blush on my face deepens. I shouldn't have liked that as much as I did. Did he really say he hasn't been with anyone in this house, much less his bed? Damn. Why is that such a turn on?

I fix my hair and pull it up, so it won't get wet, while I'm in the pool or be in my way, while I'm tanning. I grab the sunscreen, a towel, and go out to the pool.

I stop dead in my tracks, because I find Dallas already in the pool swimming laps. His tan skin and muscles on full display, as he glides through the water. My legs carry me closer to the pool, and I just watch him mesmerized.

At the other end of the pool, he flips and heads back towards me. As he nears the wall, he slows and stands, wiping the water from his face, before looking up at me.

"You going to stand there all day, or are you joining me?" He asks.

I clear my throat and try to form words.

"I'll join you in a bit. I need to put on some sunscreen." I hold up the sunscreen in my hand.

"Need some help?" He asks.

I smirk, him putting sunscreen on me is just the start of the many fantasies I've had of him in this pool. But it seems like a good place to start.

"Sure," I say and head back towards one of the lounge chairs. Hearing the water dripping on the concrete, I know he isn't far behind me. I set my stuff down on the chair and turn back to find his eyes on me, as he dries off with his towel.

Without breaking eye contact, I grab the hem of my cover-up dress and slowly pull it over my head, leaving me in just the skimpy bikini I put on earlier. His eyes heat, as he looks over every inch of my body.

"Fuck, you're beautiful." He says, as he places his hands on my hips. I look up at him, as his lips land on mine. It's a short, sweet kiss, before he's turning me around, so my back is to his chest. His hands pull me against him, and his cock rests against my ass.

His hands slowly slide up my stomach towards my chest, before he grabs my breasts and kisses my neck. I reach up and wrap a hand around his neck.

"God, you're perfect. Sexy, beautiful, and mine." He lightly grazes his teeth over my ear lobe, before taking a step back. "Let's get that sunscreen on you. We don't want you to burn."

I sit down on the lounge chair, trying to regain some self-control, as he sits behind me, and he starts rubbing sunscreen on my neck, shoulders, and back. He takes it slow, rubbing circles and smoothing it in well. His touch is just firm enough to massage some of the tension from my shoulders, and I can't stop the moan that slips out.

His sharp intake of breath lets me know he's feeling this too, as he rubs further down my body.

"Lay down on your back." He says, his voice laced with lust.

I do as he says, wanting to see how far he will take this. His eyes roam my body again, before he squeezes more sunscreen on to his hands and starts on my arm, but his eyes never leave mine. When the sunscreen is all rubbed in, he moves to the other arm. It's such an innocent touch, but with the intensity of his eyes, the sensations filling me from just his touch, it's already so much more.

After both arms are done, he starts on my shoulders and rubs down my chest. He pays more attention than necessary to my breasts, and his hands slip under the triangle of fabric and pushes it to the side.

"Need to make sure I get every inch of skin." He murmurs, seconds before he leans down and takes my nipple into his mouth. He groans, and I can feel the vibrations to my core.

He pulls back and sensually rubs my breasts, before moving the fabric back into place and moving to the other to repeat the motion.

He continues rubbing lotion on my stomach and down to my bikini bottoms. He moves along the top, like he's teasing me, before dipping under the fabric. I raise my hips, encouraging him on to touch me where I need him most, but he doesn't. He scoots back and starts rubbing lotion on to my foot, and then slowly moves up my leg.

His eyes on me are intense, as he works the lotion into my skin. Smoothing the lotion into my thighs, each slow stoke gets closer and closer to my center, where I need him. His fingers ghost over my slit, before he moves to put lotion on my other foot.

He repeats the process of slowly moving up my leg. I'm so

turned on I'm aching for him, and if he doesn't touch me soon, I might combust. As he gets closer to my pussy, his fingers tease me over the fabric, spreading my legs and moving to kneel on the lounge chair. He runs both hands up my thighs and massages them right against the edge of the fabric.

When his eyes meet mine again, we lock on each other, and he unties the bottom of my suit.

"Have to make sure we get lotion everywhere." He says.

Without taking his eyes off me, he lowers his mouth and takes a long, slow lick up my slit. The sensation of having his tongue on me after all the teasing is almost too much, as my body trembles. I throw my head back and close my eyes, arching my hips.

He throws an arm over my hips to hold me in place, as he continues his slow, steady movements.

"Dallas," I moan.

"What do you need, baby girl? Tell me."

"More. Harder. Faster." I gasp out, unable to complete full sentences.

With a few more light, short strokes with his tongue, before sucking hard on my clit, he does as I ask, as two fingers slip inside me, and his tongue works my clit in ways I didn't know were possible.

"Oh, God. Oh, God." Is all I can manage, as I toss my head back.

"Dallas!" I scream, as my thighs lock around his head, and my climax washes over me. As I relax, Dallas starts kissing up my body with a huge smile on his face.

"Good thing the neighbors aren't nearby." He chuckles, and I throw my hands over my face embarrassed.

He grabs my hands with his.

"No, there's nothing to be embarrassed about. That was so damn sexy." He kisses me, and then leans down and ties my bathing suit back together.

"Now, let's go swimming." He says.

The rest of the day is filled with time in the pool, lots of kissing, petting, and teasing, but he never once lets me take care of him, even though, he's hard almost all day.

That night we go to bed in our own rooms, and I can't get our time on the lounge chair out of my head. No one has driven me so absolutely crazy with need like that before. I don't think I've ever been so wet or cum so hard in my life.

As I'm lying in bed, rain starts hitting the window followed by some lightning and thunder loud enough to make me jump.

I try to pull a pillow over my head, but it does nothing to drown out the noise. I have hated thunderstorms for years. My parent's car crash happened on a night like this. Finally, I give in and slowly make my way to my door.

When I look out into the hallway, I'm happy to find Dallas's door is cracked open. It's all the invitation I need to slip into his room and tiptoe over to his bed. The moment I start climbing into bed, he turns towards me.

"I was wondering how long, before you'd be in here." He says, pulling me close.

"I was debating it, even before the storm," I admit.

"You're welcome here anytime for any reason." He kisses the top of my head and holds me tight.

There have been many nights like this, when the storms get bad; I don't want to be alone. The first time I slipped into Dallas's bed was because my brother wasn't here, and I was nearly in tears, the storm was so bad. He held me and said he would always be here for me, and I could stay with him, during any storm.

It slowly became our ritual after that. I know Landon doesn't like storms either, but they don't seem to affect him, like they do me. Dallas has always understood and always been there. A few times, when I didn't live here, and a bad storm came in, I'd call him, and he'd stay on the phone with me, until I fell asleep.

"I'll be here for you, Austin, even more so now. You're my girl. Plus, I don't think I would have been able to sleep in my bed alone tonight. One night, and I'm already used to you being in my arms too damn much."

"Me too," I admit, but then wonder what the hell we're going to do when Landon comes home.

CHAPTER 20

Dallas

Waking up with Austin in my arms, and in my bed, is something I don't think I can live without again. It will be impossible to do, when her brother is home, until we tell him about us.

This isn't like any other time Austin has been in my bed. Normally, she would be on her side and me on mine, wishing I could wake her up with my hands on her.

Right now, her body is pressed against mine, her leg swung over my hips, and her head on my shoulder. I'm hard as nails, and this time I can do something about it.

I slowly roll her over on to her back and lean on my elbow and just watch my girl sleep. She's perfect in every way. So beautiful, but seeing her like this, has always been my favorite. Her walls are down.

She's in her classic summer sleeping clothes, a tank top, no bra, and short cotton shorts. If she were naked, I'd wake her up with my mouth on her, but I don't want to take my eyes off her, so my hand will have to do.

I lightly cup my hand over her breast and rub my thumb over the nipple and watch it form a stiff peak. I do the same to the other one, before slowly trailing my hand down her stomach to the edge of her shorts.

I hesitate for only a moment, before I slip below the hemline and rub my hand over her panties. They are wet, and I hope she's dreaming about me. I touch her lightly, before pulling the panties to the side and rubbing her clit skin to skin. A light moan escapes her, but she's still sleeping, eyes still closed.

I keep stroking and slowly slide my finger into her. She's so drenched it slides in easily. Her hips start to move to, as I add a second finger, and this time she gasps.

"Dallas." Her eyes open and fly to mine.

"You didn't waste any time getting good at this." She moans, and her hips move again.

"Making you cum is my new addiction," I whisper, as I kiss her neck and keep finger fucking her. I increase the pressure on her clit, and she moans again.

"Do not cum. You understand me?" I say in a firm voice.

She nods, as she gasps for air and squeezes her eyes shut.

"Baby girl, look at me," I say, and her eyes pop open and lock on mine.

I keep my strokes even and my eyes on her, but only a few more touches, and her hips buck again.

"Dallas, I need..." She moans and grips the sheets so tight, I think she might rip the fabric.

"I know what you need. This is going to be nice and slow. I have wanted to wake you up like this every time you've crawled into my bed. Every time I wake up with you next to me, I'm so damn hard, and all I can think about is making you cum. It's why I could never be here, when you woke up; I was always out the door soon, as the sun was up." I suck on one of her nipples over her tank top.

"Not this time. This time I get to make you cum. I get to hear you moan my name and watch you give yourself to me. So, you see, baby girl, I'll be taking my time and enjoying every moment of it."

I slow my strokes on her clit, and she growls in protest. I

smirk, as my eyes roam over her.

"Pull your tank top down, let me see those magnificent tits."

She quickly does, as I ask, and this time, I'm the one to groan, as I lean down and take one into my mouth then the other.

"Dallas, please. I'm so close." She moans.

I pull my hand from her shorts completely.

"Dallas!" She whines.

I remove her shorts and panties and position myself between her legs.

"You will come on my face, you hear me?" I tell her, and she nods, watching me.

I give her a slow lick, before I suck on her clit. Her back arches, and one of her hands starts pulling at my hair, like she's desperate to keep me there. There's no way I'm moving from this spot any time soon.

I suck harder, and it's all she needs to fall over the edge, screaming my name. I lick up every drop of the moisture she gives me long after her orgasm has receded. I love the little tremors that go through her body, as I lick her oversensitive clit.

When her whole body finally calms, I kiss my way back up slowly, because we have all day.

"Good morning, beautiful," I say, kissing her neck.

"That is one hell of a way to wake up." She has a satisfied smile on her face, and knowing I put it there, is a powerful feeling.

"Care to take a shower with me?" I ask, as I kiss her shoulder.

"Mmm, that sounds perfect, once I can move again."

Laughing, I stand and pick her up, carrying her to the bathroom. I set her down on the counter and the cold granite on her naked butt makes her squeal. I smirk, as I start the shower and get the water warm.

I remove her tank top, leaving her naked in front of me. I touch every inch of her. I've never wanted a girl so badly. Austin is different. She's perfect and incredible. I'll take my time, proving to her she's special.

"This is another first for me," I tell her.

"What is?" She asks, and she tangles her hands in my hair and pulls me closer.

"I've never showered with anyone before," I admit.

"Really?" She asks shocked.

"Told you I was a one-trick pony."

"Well, I can give you another of my firsts, too." She says with a devilish smile on her face, as she jumps off the counter and quickly pulls my pants and boxers down, before pulling me into the water.

"What first is that?" I finally ask her.

She smiles, as she falls to her knees under the water.

"I've never gone down on a guy in the shower." She looks up at me, as she strokes my cock. I have to brace myself on the shower wall.

When she takes me into her mouth, and those pink lips swallow me, I almost cum instantly. The water running down her skin, between her breasts. The feel of her warm mouth on me, as she runs her tongue on the bottom side of cock is beyond anything my imagination could have dug up. She starts working me in and out of her mouth, sucking hard and taking a bit more each time.

"Baby, I'm close." I give her a warning, and then she does the unexpected. She pulls off me completely.

"Austin, fuck." I moan.

Her eyes flick up to me. "Don't cum yet." She says, and all I can do is moan. She runs her hand up the sides of my legs, watching me.

She takes me back into her mouth and my toes curl. All my nerves are pulling tight at my lower back, and it's taking every ounce of control I have to not let go and fuck her mouth.

This time she uses slow and shallow strokes that drive me crazy, before taking me to the back of her throat, and then pulling off me completely.

"Austin," I whisper.

She gives me an evil smile.

This time when she takes me into her mouth, she's using the fast stokes she used before.

"Austin, shit." I squeeze my eyes shut, as I try to get myself under control. "I'm so close." I grit out.

When she moans with my cock in her mouth, I couldn't stop from cumming if my life depended on it. I brace my arms on the shower wall to help hold myself up.

I grit out her name, as the first spurts of cum roll down her throat, and she swallows every drop. When I'm finally spent, she slowly starts kissing her way up my chest, until she's right in front of my face.

"You..." Is all I get to say, before she's kissing me hard then pulling away.

"Let's get cleaned up." She says, as she reaches for my body wash and takes a little in her hands and starts rubbing it over every inch of my body. Beginning with my shoulders, working her way down my arms, she goes slowly over my chest, and then around to my back.

She pays special attention to my ass with a lot more grabbing than needed. Not that I'm complaining. She washes each leg, before giving my cock special attention. I start to get hard again, before she shakes her head.

"Don't need you getting all worked up again, do we?"

"My turn." I grab my body wash, loving the idea of her smelling like me.

I take the same path she did and start at her shoulders and down her arms. Gently pulling each breast into my mouth, before washing over them and down her stomach. Then, moving to wash her back and give her ass the same attention she gave mine.

As I wash both her legs, I take special care of her pussy, getting her just riled up, before stopping, like she did to me.

She smiles, as I help her wash her hair, before washing mine. I get out first and grab a towel to help dry her off, before reaching for mine.

"What are the chances I could keep you from putting clothes on today?" I ask her.

She laughs, "Slim to none."

"Can't blame a guy for trying. Can I interest you in a lazy day instead?"

"Maybe, a movie day?" She asks.

"Sold. Meet me in the theater room in ten minutes."

I hurry and get dressed in sweatpants and a t-shirt, and then head to the theater room. This is the room that sold both Landon and me on the house. Even though, there is a huge window in the room, there's a blackout curtain, which I now make sure is closed. I turn on the massive screen, and then start the popcorn machine.

Recently, I had ordered a few movies Austin had talked about wanting to watch, so I grab one and get it ready, as Austin walks in wearing another pair of cotton shorts and one of my shirts.

"I knew you took my AC/DC shirt!"

She laughs, "Guilty as charged. I took it with me, so I had a part of home. Wearing Landon's shirts was just weird."

"Well, in all fairness, it looks better on you than it ever did on me."

We settle into the large couch and spend a perfect day watching movies, snuggling, and making out. Everything feels right, and I know I'm not giving this up. I couldn't if I tried.

CHAPTER 21

Austin

I'm supposed to be working, but Dallas keeps finding ways to distract me. He was working out back right by my window. Then, he had to hang a photo on the other side of the dining room I'm trying to work in. Next, he randomly walked through the room with no shirt on twice, and now, he's sitting at the other end of the table, typing on his phone.

Thankful for the break when my phone rings, I'm surprised to see it's Belle. She's a pretty popular singer also at Landon and Dallas's record company. She started out about the same time as them and was on one of their tours, and the only other female at that time. So, we bonded and have kept in contact ever since.

"Belle, hey." I answer, when Dallas gives me the 'who is it?' look.

"Austin! Is it true? Are you in Nashville?"

"I am."

"Oh, please tell me you'll meet me for lunch. I know it's short notice, but we haven't seen each other in forever! We have so much to catch up on."

"Hang on, let me check." I pull the phone away and put it on mute.

"Belle wants me to meet up with her for lunch. You okay with that?" I ask Dallas.

He looks out the window for a minute, before looking back at me.

"Yes, as long as you take my security guy. He can be here in an hour. You stay with him, and he'll blend in, so you'll barely know he's there." He says in a firm tone.

"Promise."

I unmute the phone.

"I can get together with you. I'll need at least an hour, but we can meet at that southern buffet place we went to last time?" I ask.

"Of course, see you there soon!"

I hang up and save what I was working on. Then, I walk over to Dallas and kiss him on the cheek.

"I promise I'll stay safe. Plus, Belle has her own security. You have the tracker on my phone, and I'll be fine."

"It's scary, Aust. I want to keep you safe in this bubble and not let the outside world touch you, but at the same time, I don't want to be that guy that keeps you from your life and your friends. You mean everything to me, and I just need you safe. Not to mention, Landon will kick my ass."

"Why don't you come help me get ready?"

"Baby, if I come upstairs you won't be going anywhere for lunch." He growls, and I laugh.

I head up to my room to get ready. I keep it simple, but I also know this lunch will be photographed. Belle can't go anywhere without her fans posting about it and guys hitting on her. We actually find it kind of funny now. She was like me and a bit of an outcast in school and couldn't get dates to save her life.

I pull on Dallas's favorite jeans. The ones he says make my ass look great. I pick a dressy top with a high neckline and pull my hair back in a crown braid, before tossing on a bit of makeup.

By the time I get back downstairs, a guy who looks like he could be the hulk if he was only green, is standing with Dallas in the kitchen.

"Yeah, he won't stand out at all." I roll my eyes.

"Austin, this is Mason, and he'll be your security today."

I sigh, "Thank you, Mason, for indulging Dallas's overprotective side. I promise to not make your life difficult. I'm having lunch with a friend, and I'll even feed you."

"Not necessary, ma'am." He says.

"Very much so, because this place has kick ass food, so you will let me feed you, or I won't agree to this." I glare at Dallas, as I say this, but I notice Mason's mouth tilts up slightly.

"If you insist." He says, but my eyes still haven't come off Dallas, who is glaring at me.

"Don't make this difficult, or I'll keep you prisoner here," Dallas says.

"Plan to tie me to your bed?" I raise an eyebrow at him.

"Yes." He says.

"Explain that one to my brother." I kiss his cheek and head out the door.

Once in the garage, I turn to Mason. "You driving, big guy?"

"Yep." One word answers, great.

"Which one we are taking?" I'm referring to the car collection here. The boys love their cars.

He tilts his head to the SUV with tinted windows at the far end, so I follow him. At least, he's a gentleman, opening my door and all.

The ride to the restaurant is quiet, and as we pull into the parking lot, I get a text from Belle telling me she got a table in the back.

Before Mason can climb out of the car, I place a hand on his arm, and his eyes shoot to me.

"So, I don't want to forget to say thank you for doing this. I know you were hired on for Dallas and Landon, not me."

"You're Landon's sister, and our contract covers you. Always has, but never had a need to use it, until now. Stay there, and I'll come around."

I'm a bit shocked. He's always had me covered in his security contract? I guess it makes sense, especially after our parents died, and it was just us, but Landon never told me. Add it to the list of things to talk to him about, when he gets home. Maybe, I will open with this one.

Mason helps me out of the car, and we head inside. The waitress seems annoyed, when I try to walk past her, saying I know where I'm going, and the manager tries to stop me from getting to Belle's table, until she runs up and hugs me.

Her hair is done up in some fancy twist and is blonde this time, instead of her normal dark brown. Her tan skin stands out in her white shorts and navy blue shirt. When she pulls back, she gives me a once over. She then pulls a classic Belle move and gives a flirty wink to Mason.

"Hey, big guy. You can join my team, so just pick a table." She points to the table in front and behind her, each with a guy about the size of Mason sitting at it.

Before joining Belle, I turn back to him, "Remember our deal. You will eat."

He gives me a cocky half smile.

"A deal a deal." He says.

I nod and sit down with Belle.

"Girl, we have so much to catch up on. Did you really go on tour with the guys?"

"Yeah, Landon convinced me to sing two songs at each stop."

"Oh, I'm so jealous I wasn't there. We really should do a duet. I think it would be killer."

"I'll have my people call your people." I joke, as we place our drink orders.

This place makes the best sweet tea, and the food is all true southern cooking. The first few times we were here, we did the buffet to try it all. Now, we order from the menu, because we know what we like. After I order, I turn my head to Mason and watch him order, before nodding in approval.

"So, what's with Mr. Sexy Hulk?" Belle asks.

"See! I'm glad I'm not the only one who thinks he looks like The Hulk. I wonder if I can get him to let me paint him green for Halloween?" We both break out into giggles.

"You could dress as Black Widow and hang over him all night." Belle jokes.

"His wife wouldn't be too happy, and my brother would freak!" I laugh.

"Speaking of, how is your brother?"

"Ahhh, he's been busy. He's working out of town. Some sponsorship he's working with, and a charity that he's on their board. But we are... okay, I guess. I'm not his biggest fan at the moment."

"Why, what happened?"

"Oh, you know he's told me who I can and can't date. No one's good enough. The usual." I wave my hand at her and sigh.

"Isn't this why you moved to Portland?"

"Yeah, but here's a story for you." I go on to tell her about Branden, and how it was casual, and he proposed after three months, and then randomly showed up on my doorstep a few days ago. I leave out the part that my brother is looking into him, and that's why I have security today.

"What!" She screeches just a little too loud, making heads turn.

"I couldn't get my boyfriend to propose after two years, and here it only took you three months. Damn girl." She shakes her head.

"It would be nice if that was my goal, but him being good in bed was all he had going for him."

"Damn."

"Yeah," I agree.

"So, I heard a rumor, and I need to confirm it, because if it's true it will break my heart."

"Oh, what's that?" I ask.

"There's a rumor that some girl tamed Dallas. He's done with his playboy ways, and also cut off contact with all his hookups. I need to know if it's true, and who this lucky bitch is."

I take a deep breath. Shit. I can't tell Belle, before my brother knows, but I also hate the idea of lying to her. I know I can trust her, but Dallas and I hadn't agreed to tell anyone yet, so I need to keep this under wraps for now. But I need to give her something.

"Well, I know he's done with the sleeping around. Has been for months, and he's just tired of the lifestyle. Landon doesn't seem to believe he's changed, but I've seen it. I'm proud of him." I tell her.

"And the girl?"

"I don't know of one. He's pretty much a homebody. He doesn't go out anymore or anything, so I don't think there's a girl. If there is, I haven't met her."

"Damn."

"Did you ever sleep with him?" I ask her.

Belle had a bit of a wild side, when she first started making a name for herself. She was always partying and was known to sleep with other singers. She calmed down and started dating her ex and was happy, until he dumped her for no reason a few months ago.

"No, and not for a lack of trying. He said he would never sleep with one of your friends. I told him you gave me the go ahead, and he still said no. Then, he avoided me like the plague the rest of the tour. Think I should come over and try to get a date?"

I'm relieved they never slept together, but the thought of her flirting with him doesn't sit right either. What's one more white lie, right?

"I don't think that's a good idea. He doesn't want to date right now and complains about everyone asking him out. How did you hear about this rumor?" I ask.

"Oh, it's all over the biz, since your tour. I guess, the girls he hooked up with had some pillow talk, and the word spread."

I shiver, "Gross."

Belle shrugs, as our food gets there.

We take our time eating and talk about her last tour, a few bad dates she's been on, and the gossip at the label. We get to dessert, before people start coming up to her asking for autographs and photos. She agrees, because like Landon and Dallas, she knows she's nothing without her fans.

I help take photos, kind of happy to fly under the radar. I can tell Mason doesn't like this at all. He's right by my side and making sure everyone keeps a distance, until their turn. Then, one of the guys recognizes me.

"Score! Austin Anderson, too! My buddy is going to be so mad he ditched lunch! Can I get a picture with both of you?" He asks.

I agree, and after that, Belle has Mason take a few photos of just the two of us.

"Since we have been outed, might as well make our own posts," Belle says.

Mason leans down to my ear, "We should get moving. They'll be posting those online, and we don't want people to track you here."

By people he means Branden. Great.

"Belle, I have to get going, but how long are you in town for?" I ask.

"Oh, I leave tomorrow."

"Damn, call me, when you get back, and we can hang out at our pool, working on our tans."

"Sounds perfect." She hugs me and not just a quick hug. This is a huge I'm going to miss you like crazy hug.

Mason walks me out to the SUV and helps me in once again. Then, we are on the road home, and all I can think about is Belle's comment about wanting to ask Dallas out. I don't doubt she's the only one.

CHAPTER 22

Dallas

I haven't been able to concentrate on a damn thing, since Austin walked out that door. I know she's in good hands with Mason, but he has to be sick of me texting him every thirty minutes asking for an update.

I had to know she was okay, and with her brother looking into Branden, he'd never forgive me if something happened to her, while she was out. He has no problem locking her up and throwing away the key, but I can't do that to her.

I'm pacing the house, when I hear the notification that the gate is being opened. Running to the monitors, I see the black SUV they took and breathe a sigh of relief. I don't want her to know I've been a mess, since she walked out of the door, so I head to the living room and sit down. I unmute the cooking channel I had on and wait for her to come to me.

It doesn't take long, until she's in the doorway, and I'm up across the room, pulling her into my arms.

"I hated you being away." I pout, as I pull her back to the couch with me and put her on my lap. "I've gotten so used to you being around. It's going to be torture, when Landon gets home."

I lean in and kiss her, just a short one to ground me, before pulling back.

"Did you have fun?" I ask her.

"Oh yes, it was great to see Belle again. Can you believe we got all the way to dessert, before someone asked her for an autograph? I think it was giving her a complex." She laughs. "She did tell me about an interesting rumor that has been circulating."

I instantly tense up. People are great at spreading rumors to benefit themselves. The three of us have dealt with our fair share, and we never let it drive us apart. But that was before Austin was mine, and that changes a lot.

"What's that?" I ask.

"There's a rumor going around that some girl has tamed you. She wanted to see if I knew who. She's heartbroken and totally made it no secret she wants to make a pass at you now that you seem to be relationship material."

"Fuck, I bet she won't be the only one. No one linking us together?"

"Nope, doesn't seem to be. I didn't want to lie to her, but I figure we didn't want her to know either."

"Baby girl, I want everyone to know. You say the word, and I'll blast it on every social media network out there. But it's probably best Landon is the first to know. I don't think that's something he should find out from someone else."

"I agree. He texted me on the way home. He'll only be home for a week, before heading out again. I was thinking we don't tell him this time, keep our bubble a little longer, and tell him, when he gets back from his next trip?"

I don't like hiding from him and having to pretend she isn't my everything for an entire week. It's going to kill me.

"We have to be super careful. No climbing into my bed. No sneaking around."

"So, we get him out of the house, or we leave the house to sneak around. We could rent an Airbnb outside of town; meet up there. It's not ideal, but just a week, and then he's off again for two more weeks. We build us up, and then we tell him. He's going to be mad no matter what. I'd rather he be mad here where we can fix things than mad thousands of miles away."

I rest my head on her shoulder. I know her and Landon will fix things, but I don't voice that in my heart. I have a feeling this is something he and I won't be able to fix. My biggest fear is I don't know if there will be any coming back from this for us, but I won't worry her about any of it. Landon is my best friend, but I know I couldn't live without her. There's no question.

This is what Austin wants, and there's nothing I wouldn't give her, so of course, I'm going to agree. I will do whatever she asks and will have her back.

"That's fine, baby. Let me book a place for us, okay? And we can trust Mason, he's been assigned to me from the start. We tell him the truth, that we plan to tell Landon, and he'll be your security guy. Landon will insist any time you leave the house anyway."

"We will make this work D, I know we can."

I lean in and kiss her, because I don't have a choice. Words fail me right now, and I need her to know how much I care about her.

We're interrupted by my phone going off.

"It's Landon," I tell her, before answering it, and then putting it on speakerphone.

She gets an evil smile on her face and turns to straddle me. This girl is going to be the death of me.

"Hey," I say to Landon.

"What were you thinking?" He says without even a greeting. At the same time, Austin grinds down on my cock.

I plead with my eyes to go easy on me, but I doubt she will.

"What do you mean?" I ask.

"You let her go out with Belle. To a restaurant downtown. Anything could have happened to her. It was all over social media where she was."

"Mason went with her. We can't keep her locked up like a princess in a tower, as much as you may want, too." I tell him.

That earns me a smile from Austin, as she starts a slow, steady rhythm of grinding on me. I throw my head back on the couch, looking up at the ceiling.

"I still haven't gotten any information on this Branden guy. She doesn't need to be going out, security or not." Landon bites out at the same time Austin does a swivel with her hips, and I almost groan out loud. I set the phone on the back of the couch next to my ear. Two can play at this game.

"You will not keep me locked up, Landon. Mason was with me, and I was fine. I'll take him with me, when I go out, but that's it. You can't control me, and I won't let you, and you won't try, if you want me to stick around."

Oh, she did not just threaten to leave. I whip her shirt and bra up, exposing her delicious tits to me and lean in to give one a hard nip. There will be no leaving; no walking away from me, I remind her by sucking on her tits, as she grinds on my cock.

"Damn, Austin. I just want to protect you."

"No, you want to control me. Telling me who I can and can't date, what to do, where I can go, and when. You know who does that? Cult leaders." She snaps, and then covers her mouth, as she moans.

I smile with her nipple in my mouth. We're going to get caught, but hell if I care, and I certainly am not going to stop.

"You understand the length some of our more obsessive fans will go to. Dallas and I have seen it and lived it."

I pull back from her just a bit.

"Landon, I've told her the stories, and she knows. You have to remember she grew up with this, but she didn't sign up for it like we did. We may not have known in detail what we were giving up, but that's on us. You can't punish her for our choices." I say, and then move to her other breast.

"Whose side are you on?" He snaps.

"I want Austin safe, too. I just think your vision is a bit

clouded, because you're in parents' mode, not brother mode. I promised to keep her safe. Do you trust me?" I ask, and then hold my breath.

We have been through a lot lately, so I really am not sure how he will answer. He doesn't trust me to date Austin, so will he trust me to protect her?

He sighs. "Of course, I trust you. I just hate not being there, and hate we're having such a hard time tracking down this Branden guy. It's like he went poof into thin air."

"I love you, Landon, but you've got to relax just a little. I'll keep Mason with me, but I don't have a lot of plans to leave the house. This was the first time, since the day Dallas and I went to the record label, okay? Trust us?" Austin says.

I bite her nipple, and she doesn't mask her surprise this time.

"Shit." She groans.

"Austin? What's wrong?" Landon says.

Her eyes go wide. We've been caught, but thankfully, she thinks on her feet.

"Just got an email from a client. I need to go and fix something, but we'll see you in a few days." She says.

I grind up into her harder and faster, watching her tits bounce at the movement.

"Okay, talk to you later." He says.

"Bye." We both say, as she hangs up the phone, and I double check to make sure the call has been disconnected. Then, I give us what we both want and flip her over on to the couch and grind into her, like I'm fucking her. Hard and fast, but our clothes are still between us.

"See what you started? We were almost caught, because you couldn't keep your pussy off me for ten minutes. How wet are you? The thrill of getting caught soak your panties, baby girl?"

"You should find out." She says.

"Oh, no. Your punishment is no skin to skin. You will come

like this." I wrap my arms around her wrists and pin them above her head.

"Just like this," I say and grind into her harder.

I try to memorize this. Her stretched out beneath me, her breasts pushed against my chest, and withering for me to give her relief. I only get one more stroke, before her body locks up, and she cums screaming my name.

The sound alone is all I need to follow her groaning out her name. I couldn't stop myself from collapsing on her if I tried, and thankfully, she doesn't seem to mind, as she wraps her arms around me.

"We need to go shower." She says and sounds about as breathless as I feel.

"In a minute, I don't want to move," I say into her neck.

When we finally do make it to the shower, it's a repeat from the other day. We spend the day cuddling on the couch, watching movies, and just being.

I try to soak it in now, while I can, because it all ends, when Landon gets home.

CHAPTER 23

Austin

Landon gets home today, and he's already called to tell us not to worry about dinner. He was stopping at the store to get what he needs to make us this casserole dish he tried last week.

He raved about this meal for a whole ten minutes, before I threatened to hang up on him. Our easy banter seems to be back, since the other day on the phone, but I know we need to talk.

I've been working all day, so I can take tomorrow off and spend it with Landon. Dallas has been soaking up the last of our free time with his hands on me anyway he can. Right now, that means I'm sitting on his lap, trying to work with his arms wrapped around me, and his chin on my shoulder watching me.

"I booked the Airbnb. I'll text you the address and the code, because there's no way I'm going to be able to be around you and keep my hands off you for a week." He says.

I sigh and save what I was working on and close my computer. In one quick movement, I turn on his lap, so I'm straddling him. I wrap my arms around his neck, and we stare into each other's eyes.

"It will be worth it, though. When we talk to him, we'll have a month under our belts, and he'll have to take that seriously. He has to, right?" I'm asking myself, as much as I am him.

"You nervous about telling him?" He asks.

"Yeah, what if he doesn't approve and won't accept it?"

This is the worry I've been trying to push out of my head for days. If I'm honest, it's the biggest reason I don't want to tell Landon this week.

"It will change nothing for me. I'm not walking away from you, I can't. He doesn't approve then that's on him, baby girl. We have done nothing wrong, and I'll keep proving to you how perfect we are together." He says and kisses the tip of my nose.

"It won't change anything with me either. Though, I don't like the idea of my brother mad at me. Never been a fan of it. I can't walk away from you either." Then, I lean in and kiss him.

He wraps his arms tightly around me, holding me to him, and starts kissing down my neck. I grind in to him and feel his hard cock right where I need it. His hands grip my ass, pulling me closer, as the alarm beeps telling us the gate has been opened.

"Damn," I say and rest my forehead against his.

"Exactly. Tomorrow, lunch at the cabin." He says, and I nod, as I climb off him.

He gets up and moves to sit at the kitchen island, while I unplug my computer and get ready to put it away.

As soon as Landon walks in the door, he beelines right to me, sweeping me up in a hug.

"I've been on edge the whole time I was gone. I was worried about you." He whispers in my ear.

"I'm fine thanks to Dallas," I say.

He sets me down and gives me a once over.

I roll my eyes. "No marks, bruises, or even a hair out of place, I promise."

Over Landon's shoulder, Dallas smirks. There are a few love bites on my inner thighs. Dallas couldn't help himself, but my brother doesn't need to know about those.

Once satisfied I'm okay, Landon turns to Dallas and pulls him in for a hug, too.

"Thank you for watching over her." He says barely above a whisper.

Dallas's face clogs with emotion, and his eyes get misty, before he gets it back in check.

"Always. She means a lot to me, too." He says, and I freeze, worried he's revealing too much.

My brother pulls from the hug and studies him, but says nothing, before turning away.

"Okay, dinner! Wait until you try this. It's chicken pot pie in casserole form, but with a twist, and it's amazing." Landon says, as he turns and starts pulling items out of the bag he brought in.

I glance over at Dallas, shrug my shoulders, and he gives me a wink. I go grab the cutting board for my brother.

"Need help?" I ask.

"Nope." He grabs me by my waist and sets me on the counter just like normal.

"So, this trip was about the sponsor deal?" I ask and steal a few of the baby carrots from the bag.

"Yeah, it was boring as hell. I hate to say, but I leave again in a week this time to go work with the charity." He looks at me. "I can stay if you need me."

I rest my hand on his shoulder. "Landon, I don't want this to interrupt our lives. Dallas is here, and if I go out, I have Mason. I promise, I'll be fine. Tell me about this charity."

His face lights up, and I love seeing him like this.

"Oh, Austin, you'd love it. The organization works with companies to provide scholarships to kids in the arts. They provide small scholarships for summer camp all the way up to college. I've been focusing on the music side of it and helping set up some after school music programs across the country."

He goes on to talk about the details of the program, while he continues preparing dinner. Every so often, I look up and find Dallas, staring at me with a heated look on his face. It's barely been an hour, and this has been torture. How am I going to last a week?

Like he can read my mind, Dallas stands up and comes over to where I'm sitting.

"I'll set the table." He says, as he starts getting placemats and drinks. When my brother goes to the fridge, he comes over towards me to get silverware.

I glance over, and my brother's head is in the fridge, so I lean in and give Dallas a quick kiss, before moving my legs out of the way. He smirks at me and grabs a little higher on my thigh than he should to move them from in front of the drawer. Wanting to drive him as crazy as he drives me, I spread my legs wide, so one is on either side of the drawer.

Dallas visibly swallows, as he looks up at me, then quickly gets the silverware and heads to the table. I notice the outline of his cock in his pants and smile, knowing he's trying to hide it from my brother. This is a dangerous game we're playing. I know it but can't seem to stop.

Over dinner, Landon tells us more about the charity and the work he will be doing, when he visits next week.

"Landon, dinner was delicious. Why don't you go unpack and get a shower, and Dallas and I will do the dishes, and then we can watch some TV." I suggest after dinner.

"Sounds perfect." He grabs his bag and heads upstairs. Dallas and I stare at each other, but neither of us moves, until we hear his bedroom door close, and then Dallas has me pinned to the wall, before I can blink.

His mouth is on me and his hands try to cover every inch of my body.

"Dallas." I gasp. "We have to do the dishes, or he will know."

"Tomorrow can't come soon enough." He mumbles into my neck, before pulling away.

We work on cleaning up the kitchen and doing dishes mixed

with quick kisses. Lots of touching and lots of laughs. We finish just as Landon comes back into the kitchen.

"Ready?" He asks, tilting his head towards the living room.

We follow him, and I sit down in one corner of the couch, and Landon sits beside me, forcing Dallas to the other corner.

I couldn't tell you what's on TV, because I'm watching Dallas out of the corner of my eyes the whole time.

When he picks up his phone, I finally pull my eyes away. Maybe, this isn't as hard on him as it is on me. Those thoughts fly out the window, when my phone goes off, and I see a text from Dallas.

I turn my phone on silent so not to draw Landon's attention, and then open my messages.

Dallas: This is torture. I want you in my arms.

Me: I don't even know what we're watching, because I've been watching you.

Dallas: Same here. You look so sexy and relaxed over there. Nights like these were always hard on me, even before, because I couldn't take my eyes off of you.

Me: Ah, you're so sweet. I always loved nights like these, too.

"I like seeing you this happy. I want to meet whoever is putting that smile on your face." Landon says, and I look up to see him watching me.

Just beyond him, Dallas has a huge smile on his face, too.

"You will, but not yet. It's too soon." I tell him, as honestly as I can.

He seems to accept that and nods, turning back to the TV.

Dallas: I'm not sweet. I can't stop thinking about what we did on this couch. Your head was right there where you're sitting, and how wet you were with what I was doing to you.

Me: Dallas... Play fair.

Dallas: You gave me some incredible firsts that night, baby girl. But there's another first I can't wait for.

Me: Yeah? What's that?

Dallas: Being able to introduce you as my girlfriend, and you introducing me to Landon, as your boyfriend.

Me: You ready for that?

Dallas: More than ready.

Me: The night he gets back from this next trip, we'll tell him everything.

I glance up, and Landon is watching me again. I know he can't read my phone, because I'm sitting somewhat sideways on the couch, but a blush still creeps up my cheeks anyway. Landon just smiles and shakes his head.

"Well, I'm going to bed. I'm beat." Landon says and stands up.

"I won't be far behind you," I say.

"Night," Landon says and heads upstairs.

Dallas doesn't move just stares at me from across the couch with a lazy smile on his face.

"Go to sleep, baby girl. See you at lunch." He says but makes no move to head upstairs himself.

I just smile and go up to my room. As I get ready for bed, I read the texts again. No one would believe how sweet and caring this man is. They all see the playboy and part of me is excited to have this side of him to myself. I don't want to share it, which is why I want to put off telling Landon for just a bit longer.

I flip through social media and realize I've been up here for an hour, and all I can think about is cuddling with Dallas. So, turning my lights off, I go and peek my head out of the door. The house is silent, and the lights are off under my brother's door. Traveling always wears him out, so my guess is he's dead asleep already.

I close my door and head across the hall to Dallas's room and quietly sneak in, closing the door behind me. When I turn to face the bed, there's enough light to see him, sitting up staring at me.

"Get over here." He says, his voice gruff.

"Did I wake you?" I ask.

"I couldn't sleep, and I was about ten minutes from coming to your room." He pulls me in, as I get under the blankets. My back is plastered to his front, as he holds me tight.

"I don't think I can sleep without you anymore." He whispers in my ear. "I've gotten too used to it. Sleep, baby girl. I'll set an early alarm, so you can get back to your room, before Landon wakes up."

I turn in his arms, facing him so both our fronts are molded together.

"I don't think I can sleep without you either," I tell him and bring a hand up to cup his cheek.

I kiss him nice and slow, not looking to take it any further, just needing to reconnect with him. When he pulls back, he tucks my head under his chin, and it's the most comfortable I've ever been.

CHAPTER 24

Dallas

Sneaking around for a few stolen moments with my girl each day sucks. I want her in my bed to hold her every night. I want to wake up with her. We are both exhausted from having to be up early, so Landon doesn't find us together, but any time with her is worth it.

Landon left for his trip today. We survived a week barely. We were meeting every day at the cabin I rented. I cited meetings, and she used excuses from business meetings to get togethers with friends. This still only got us an hour or two of time together.

Mason was very understanding, when we told him about our situation and promised not a word, until we were ready. I owe him so much for helping take care of Austin. I made sure the increase in his pay showed him how much I appreciated him.

Our afternoons in the cabin were amazing. Just holding her in my arms and reconnecting was what I needed, but I craved making her cum too. She tried a few times to take things further, but then accepted when I told her I wanted to go slow with her. Who knew I'd crave the most basic activities with her more than I would want sex?

I want to have dinner with her, hold her while we watch TV, and sleep next to her every night. I want to talk about our day and kiss her, until she's breathless.

I know I need to tell her the real reason I haven't slept with her, because it's becoming harder and harder to stop myself from sinking into her, when she spreads her legs. I crave her, but I won't sleep with her, until she knows all of me. I also want Landon to know about us. I don't want him to think this is about sex, so I want to look him in the eye and tell him I haven't slept with her.

Austin and I have known each other for so long, but there's still a side I have kept from her, from everyone. I think Landon has an idea, but we don't talk about it. I want Austin to know me, before we take that step.

Tomorrow, is a hard day for me. I need to explain it to her and open up to her about my feelings. Explain she isn't one of the many and also what she means to me. I want to tell her everything. I think she's ready, and I need to do this, open myself up to her. I want to admit how long I've liked her; how long it's been only her.

I've been going over and over in my head today what I want to tell her, and how I want to tell her. I try not to think of it sending her running, but it's a possibility.

I'm in meetings all day today. Ones I couldn't get out of, no matter how hard I tried. I've been texting with Austin all day. Neither of us can wait for me to get home. Landon was still there, when I left this morning, but he's gone now.

Austin: I never realized how big this house really is. It never felt so big with you guys here.

Me: Yeah, I don't like being there alone much either. What are you doing?

Austin sends me a picture. Making sure no one is around to see, I open it, and I'm instantly hard. She's in the bathtub, in my room, and covered in bubbles. You can't see her face or anything inappropriate just her long legs on the side of the tub, but it's enough to drive me crazy.

Me: Baby, you can't do this to me. I still have this dinner meeting, before I can get back to you.
Austin: I'll be waiting, don't worry.

I figure maybe I can change the subject.

Me: Did you eat dinner?
Austin: Yes, I ate the last of the leftover fried chicken.

Damn, those were the best leftovers in the fridge. Landon made them last night, and his fried chicken rivals many restaurants here in town.

Me: Thief. I had called dibs on those leftovers.
Austin: Mmm, maybe you will have to punish me.

Fuck. I excuse myself and head to the restroom to get myself under control. I can't sit in this meeting with her tempting me. She's playing dirty, and she knows it.

Me: You can't do this to me, baby. I can't sit in this meeting hard as nails for you.
Austin: Okay, I will stop, but I promise to take care of you, when you get home. Don't make me wait.

Something about this moment makes my heart race. It hits me this girl will be at home waiting on me. I have someone to go home, too. Not just someone, but Austin. The truth I had been trying to deny for years slaps me in the face. I love this girl with everything that I am.

I want to tell her, but she needs to know all of me first. Because if I'm lucky enough to have her say those words back to me, I want to know she loves all of me, the good and the bad. I have to know she loves all of me.

Me: I promise to hurry home to you as fast as I can. I miss you.

Those words are the best I can give this girl right now.

Austin: Miss you, too. I'm going to read some after this and wait for you.

Me: Wait in my bed. I love knowing you're in my space.

Austin: I love being in your space. I'll be here.

Me: No more dirty photos.

Austin: No promises.

I groan. This girl is perfect. As I get back to my meeting, they're finishing up, then I meet with a few guys, and we head down to dinner.

These meetings are the first steps of Landon and me starting our label. We have so many details to work out, and I told Landon I'd get this all settled, while he was gone, and then we can dive into setting it up, when he got home.

We have to be careful, because we're still under contract with our label and manager for now, but there's plenty we can do to get set up and start working with some other artists.

Landon has been scouring the internet for videos and found two people he wants to meet with, who he thinks would be great to sign. We want to help people get their foot in the door, more than we want to sign huge names. Someone took a chance on us, and we want to offer others that same opportunity.

There's so much about starting a label we didn't know, and that's what we're covering today. The amount of paperwork I'm bringing home fills a box. No, I'm not joking they handed it to me in a filing box.

Over dinner, all I can think about is Austin. In my bath tub, in my bed. I try to focus on the men talking, but I just want to get home to my girl.

When the meeting is finally over, I'm the first one out the door and heading home. The house is quiet, and if I didn't know she said she'd be up reading, I'd worry she went out for the night, because it feels like no one is home.

I run up the stairs and see a light on in my room and smile. I make my way to my door, and the sight in front of me takes my breath away. Austin is lying in my bed asleep. Her reader is beside her, like it fell out of her hand. It's after nine p.m., and since we have been up really early getting back to our rooms each morning so Landon doesn't catch us, we have both been tired.

I slowly remove my clothes down to my boxer briefs and go to the bed. I pick up her reader and check out the book she's reading. Holy shit, this stuff is dirty. I close out of the book and go to her library and email myself a few names of the books she recently read. I will find time to read them. I want to know what she likes; especially, if it's as dirty as the book she had open.

I set the reader on the nightstand and just take her in. Her dark brown hair scattered across the pillow, and her perfect tits barely contained by the tank top she has on. Her cotton shorts have ridden up, and the curve of her ass is visible. The long, tan legs stretched out, and her feet under the covers.

I chuckle, because her feet are always cold, and it could be the hottest day with no air conditioning, and she still needs her feet covered to sleep. Just one of the many quirks I love about his girl.

I turn off the light and climb into bed. As soon as I reach for her and start pulling her into me, she moans.

"I'm sorry I fell asleep." She says, her voice sexy and sleep laced. She places her head on my shoulder and wraps her body around mine.

"It's okay. We have all day tomorrow to ourselves. Besides,

coming home to you in my bed was a dream come true. I want that every night." I kiss the top of her head.

"I love your room. It feels more comfortable than being alone in my room."

"You should just move your stuff in here," I say without thinking.

"Let's not give Landon too big of a heart attack, but maybe soon." She kisses my chest, and this feels like the most normal thing in the world. Coming home after a long day and talking.

"I want more of this," I tell her.

"More what?"

"Coming home to you. Cooking dinner, or in our bed. I want more just talking, while I hold you. All the normal day-to-day things couples do. I want more of it."

"Me too, Dallas. Soon, I promise."

"I know."

She drifts back off to sleep pretty easily, while I lay there soaking her in. I know I won't get much sleep tonight, because tomorrow, I'm going to have one of the most difficult conversations of my life.

This is sink or swim. Either she will embrace me, or it will send her packing. Opening yourself up raw to someone and asking them to love all of you, is the scariest thing a person can do. To give yourself to someone on a silver platter.

Austin isn't just someone, though. She's the *one*. The girl I want to spend the rest of my life with. The one I will fight for, until my last breath. The one I can't live without and don't even want to think about trying, too.

I start running over in my head again what I'll tell her. I want to make sure I lay it all out on the line and hold nothing back.

CHAPTER 25

Austin

I can't believe I fell asleep, before Dallas got home last night. We have been waiting for a week for my brother to leave, and I was so excited for that time to ourselves. I remember him crawling into bed with me, and I guess, I drifted back off again shortly after that.

I smile and reach for him but find a cold bed. When I open my eyes, I see Dallas sitting by the window just staring outside. His chair is turned slightly towards the bed, like he might have been watching me at some point.

He's in sweatpants, and his hair is messy, like he's been running his hands through it. His tattoos are on full display, and the ink next to his tan skin is always a huge turn on for me.

The look on his face isn't the happy to have me to himself look I was expecting. He appears sad and almost depressed. A sinking feeling hits me, as I sit up in bed. My movement catches his attention, and he turns his head to look at me. His eyes run over me for just a moment.

"Come here, baby girl." He holds a hand out to me, and my legs carry me to him almost against my will. Pulling me into his lap, he hugs me tight, like he needs the comfort. Then, he rests his head on my chest, and I rake my fingers through his hair, trying to offer him whatever comfort he needs.

"I know I have to be open with you. I want you to know all of me." He says without lifting his head. "Today, is the anniversary of the day my mom died."

I knew it was about this time frame, but couldn't remember the exact date, and I never asked him, because it made him so sad to talk about it. He would share things here and there about his mom, but it always brought a look of sorrow to his face. One I didn't like seeing there, so I never asked many questions about her.

"I'm so sorry, Dallas," I say and lean down to kiss the top of his head.

His mom was a single mom and raised him. She worked hard, and oftentimes, he spent the night at our place, while she picked up extra shifts at the bar. Every now and then, she would have Landon and me over, and then she would bake cookies with me. She's the one who taught me to make the chocolate chip pecan cookies Dallas loves.

He was sixteen, when she passed, and his aunt moved to town, so he could finish school with us. She pushed him to pursue his singing career. I remember that much. I remember his mom's funeral, and how he was shut down. He spent a lot of time with Landon that summer, and that was also the summer he started putting space between us.

"This day always hits me hard. Landon says I haven't dealt with it. I think it's just too hard to remember. Every year, I would spend it..." He trails off, and his entire body trembles.

I frame his face with my hands and force him to look up at me. His icy blue eyes find mine, and for a moment, I'm frozen in time. There's so much pain and vulnerability in them. I would do anything right now to take that pain from him and make him feel better.

"There's nothing you can tell me that's going to stop me from wanting to be with you. No matter what you say next, I'm staying right here." I tell him.

His hold on me tightens, but he drops his head and buries it in my neck.

"Normally, I spend the day having nothing but mindless sex with whatever girl was available." He pauses, and I don't say anything. I'm not sure where he's going with this.

"But you are different. I won't do that to you. You knew my mom; you knew me back then. I won't use you to forget."

I just hug him to me and run my hand through his hair, as we sit in comforting silence.

"Is this why you won't let us go any further, when I tried?" I ask, thinking about the times he stopped me in the cabin this last week. I wanted him so badly, and we'd get to that point, and he'd pull away and focus on me. Though, I enjoyed myself, I knew there was something bothering him.

"Yes. If I'm honest, I'm scared to sleep with you, because you mean so much more. I don't ever want you to feel like you aren't the most important person in the world to me."

"Dallas, you show me every day how much I mean to you. From little things like the way you look at me, to fighting my brother, to making sure I'm allowed to go out and not be trapped here. The biggest way is how much you make me cum versus how much you let me make you cum. That says a lot about a guy." I smirk.

He gives a dry chuckle, and then pulls me in even closer to him.

"I remember the first day I saw you. You were eight, your hair was in those pigtail braids, and you had on your dance recital outfit. While Landon and I played in the yard, you'd spend the afternoon, practicing on the back porch. I felt this urge to protect you even then. I always thought it was because you were Landon's little sister, and Landon was like a brother to me." He says.

"I remember that day, too. Landon almost hit me with a ball, and he said it was an accident, but I knew he did it on purpose, because he smirked at me. I wanted to punch him in his face. I also almost got hit, because I couldn't take my eyes off of you." I kiss the top of his head.

"A few years later, you went away to that summer camp you begged your parents to send you, too. That whole summer I felt like a part of me was missing." He says.

"I was twelve that year. I loved the camp, but I hated the other girls there. They were so mean to me. Fun fact. Several have tried to reach out to me over the years now that the band has made it big. I told them to fuck off."

"That's my girl. I remember the day you got home from the camp." He lifts his head and finally looks at me. "You were wearing shorts and a t-shirt tied at the waist. You were so tan; your hair was longer but had highlights in it."

"From using lemon juice and sitting in the sun, all the girls were doing it. My hair was sticky for days."

"You stepped out of the car, and I knew right then and there I was yours. You stole my heart that day. I couldn't take my eyes off you. Landon noticed, and that was the day he told me you were off limits. Bro code rule number one. You can't date your best friend's sister. I was crushed and went home and cried that night. I told my mom why and she said things change, when you get older, and if I really felt the way I did, the best thing I could do was to be your friend, your best friend. So that's what I did."

He leans in and gives me a soft kiss.

"When she died, it messed everything up. I shut down. I'm grateful my aunt took me in, but she was very cynical after having three husbands cheat on her and one run off with all her money. I think it rubbed off on me, because I didn't think someone as perfect as you would ever go for a guy like me."

"I remember that summer you started putting distance between us, and I hated it. Then, you got the record contract and were gone with Landon. I'd never felt more alone. In my senior year, you seemed to be my friend again, but it was never the same."

"Then prom happened. I wanted you so bad that night. I never thought I'd be there with you, but in that moment, I didn't feel good enough, because I had sunk so low with the groupies. When we went on tour, I just sank lower. I think..." He stops and bites his lip. "I think I did it to push you away, even if I didn't realize it was what I was doing."

"I had the biggest crush on you growing up. When I left for school, I tried dating, but I was always comparing the guys to you, so by my senior year of college I decided to just do casual relationships. I was always single, when I came here to visit on the off chance you showed any interest. But of course, the time you decided you wanted me was the one time it was the last thing on my mind." I tell him.

"It was me who insisted you stop wearing bikini's around the house. You would lie out in the sun, and all I could think about was moving the triangles to the side and sucking on your nipples, until I made you cum. I'd get so hard I couldn't hide it, and I'd hate how the other guys would look at you." He admits.

"I didn't mind switching to a one-piece. I didn't like how they looked at me either. You were the only one I wanted to look at me in the bikini anyway."

He kisses the side of my neck but says nothing.

"I'm going to treat you so good today, so all you'll have will be good memories on this day. Not just bad ones." I say.

His whole body shutters, "What did you have in mind, baby girl?"

"Let's start with the pecan French toast you love. Then I'm going to kick your ass at pool. I'll bake you some chocolate chip pecan cookies, and even let you lick the bowl. Then, we can watch the new spy movie, and I plan to make you feel extra good during it."

His cock starts getting hard under my ass, and I know I described the perfect day.

"Maybe, we should start with a shower?" He says.

"Maybe, we can have a little fun, before our shower?" I suggest.

He makes me cum twice, before we get in the shower and get ready for the day. Just like I described we spend the day making good memories, and I take every chance I can to make him laugh from smearing cookie dough batter on his chest and licking it off, to showing him I know all his tickle spots.

His laugh is real and vulnerable. It's like the last of his walls have dropped for me, and this Dallas is too easy to fall in love with. As much as I try to guard my heart, I think it has always belonged to him.

CHAPTER 26

Dallas

Today, has been a good day. The anniversary of my mom's death is always a dark day for me. I try to forget it, but Austin did as she promised and made it a great day. Today, I have fun memories to look back on.

I opened up and showed her my darkest side that I was ashamed of, and she didn't push me away. Hell, she pulled me closer. She accepted all of me, and she opened up.

I'm still in a bit of shock we had crushes on each other at the same time. If we had only known, what would have happened? Would we have been together all this time?

Part of me wants to think so, but another part of me knows we were so young. We had a lot to figure out along the way and getting together back then could have destroyed us. I finally decide we are right where we need to be.

After dinner, we settle in to watch some TV, but TV is the last thing I want to be doing right now.

"You ready to head upstairs, baby girl?" I ask her.

She smiles up at me, "Yeah."

"Go on up, and I'll lock up down here." I walk her to the stairs and watch her ass, as she makes her way upstairs.

I make the rounds, making sure everything is locked up, and the alarm is set for the house and the gate. Then, I turn off the lights and switch on the library light, which is on a timer.

Making my way upstairs, I see the light on in her room, so that's where I head. She's sitting in bed with her back against the headboard, checking her phone. When she sees me, she puts it down, as I climb into bed, facing her with my back to her footboard and just take her in.

"I was at school, when I found out my mom died in a car crash on her way home from work." I start. "They pulled me from class and told me. When they asked who to call, I said Landon. I learned later he called his mom, too. I stayed with you guys a few days, until my aunt could pack up and move down. Do you remember that?"

She nods. "It broke my heart how sad you were, and I had no idea how to fix it. I was scared to say the wrong thing, and Landon told me to just leave you be, so I did. I baked like crazy, hoping it would help, if even a little."

"I remember. I ate everything, because it was you who made them. That night I couldn't sleep. It was about one a.m., when it started raining."

I pause, hoping she remembers that night.

"It was the first night we shared a bed." She whispers.

I nod. "I didn't want to be alone. I was hurting, and I didn't care what Landon or anyone said, I needed you. I meant to just come and watch you sleep for a few minutes and slip back to my room. No one would have known, but then loud thunder crashed, and you woke up, and your eyes landed on me."

"You said you didn't want to be alone, and I said neither did I. You laid down in bed over the covers, and we held each other all night." She smiles.

"I didn't sleep even a moment that night, and I snuck back to my bed, before anyone woke up."

She chuckles. "I never put it together that our little routine started off that night. I always thought it was after my parents died."

"I lived for those nights, even when you slept on the other side of the bed and wouldn't touch me. Just getting to see you sleep and watch over you for the night was such an honor."

"You were always up and gone, when I woke up, no matter how early it was." She says.

"Because every morning, all I wanted to do was wake you up by making you cum. I imagined it hundreds of different ways, and I had to leave at the first light of dawn, so I wasn't tempted."

"I would have let you." She whispers, and I groan.

Needing to get the rest of my story out, I try to put those thoughts out of my mind.

"After the funeral, I started channeling my feelings into song-writing. Some of those songs have been number one hits. Being around you, helped more than you know. You were and still are light, smiles, and sunshine. On my darkest days, I just wanted to be in your light, and you would lift me up without even knowing it."

"I wanted to help you, Dallas, but I just didn't know how. I would have done anything you asked. If you just wanted me to sit with you, I would have and still would. That hasn't changed. Whatever you need, just ask."

"This right here is what I need right now. I want you to know me. Opening up to you like this, I've never done it. Not even with Landon, but I need you to know me, all of me."

She looks at me hesitantly, like she wants to say something, but isn't sure where to start.

"What is it?" I ask her.

"Well, I don't know if you want to hear this." She pauses.

"I want to hear anything you want to tell me," I say and hope I won't regret that statement.

"Your mom, well, I think she knew we would end up here someday."

That statement knocks me a bit out of balance. I want to ask her how she knows that, but I can't seem to find the words. Like she can read my thoughts, she continues.

"One day, we were baking, and you and Landon were outside in the yard. It was the day she was watching the neighbor's dog, so you two were running around with her."

"I remember," I say.

"Well, she caught me watching you through the kitchen window and smiled. She said you kept things inside, but for the right woman, you would open up one day. She made me promise that if I wasn't that girl that I would vet anyone who tried to get close to you." She chuckles. "Your mom laughed, when jealousy surged through me at the thought of you with another girl. She said she didn't think I had anything to worry about. That was the day I realized I needed to get my feelings for you in check. So, I learned to hide them better."

We are both quiet for a bit. The silence is comfortable and welcome, as we both process what was said.

"When Landon and I got on the road, girls were just easy." I admit. "I could shut my brain off for a while with someone, who didn't know my past, and only knew rock star Dallas. But I'm telling you now, I never knew we'd be here to today. If I knew I'd be given the chance to be with you today, I wouldn't have touched a single one of them. I would have waited for you." I admit to her.

She strokes her foot up my leg.

"Hey, none of that. We were different people, and we both have pasts. We had to go on that journey to figure out who we are, so we would be good for each other. The girl I was back then wasn't good for you. I know that with my whole heart now. It wasn't our time. Our time is now, and the girls don't matter to me, so long as you don't touch them again." Her voice gets stern, and she glares at me.

"Fuck, you're sexy as hell. When I made the choice to stop the one-night stands and flings, that was it for me. I still didn't think

I had a chance with you. Even before you showed back up, when a girl would touch me, it made my skin crawl. Then, you came back, and we fell asleep on the couch. Waking up with you laying with me, I felt... peace."

She nods. "I felt safe. For the first time in months, I felt safe."

"I will always be your safe place, Austin. No matter what happens, I will always be your safe haven."

She smirks. "You know you weren't the only one with fantasies, when we were in bed together."

She licks her lips, and my cock is already starting to get hard.

"What where your fantasies, baby girl?" I ask her.

"Why don't you lay down like you're sleeping in bed with me, and I'll show you."

I move to lay down next to her, as she turns off the lights. I pull the blanket up and lie on my back and close my eyes, like I'm asleep. There's no movement or sounds at first, then the bed shifts, and she pulls the covers back. My heart races, and I want nothing more than to open my eyes and watch her, but I want to give her this fantasy, too.

Her hand rests on my knee and slowly makes its way up to the waistband on my sweatpants, before pulling them down, and my cock springs free. I'm already hard and ready for whatever she has in mind.

The bed shifts again, and it almost feels like she's straddling my leg. I'm trying to make sense of it, when her warm, wet mouth takes my cock. She doesn't start slow with some licks. No, she sucks half of me down in one stroke.

"Fuck!" I groan, unable to pretend to be asleep now. I look down and see her perfect lips around my cock, sliding up and down, taking a little bit more of me each time.

I reach down and move her hair out of the way, so I have a better view. It's then I notice her bathroom light is on, and it's enough light I can see the blush on her cheeks, as she slides off my cock and looks up at me.

"Good morning." She whispers. Ahhh, still playing.

"Don't stop, baby girl," I growl, and she smiles, before taking me into her mouth again. "Grind that sweet pussy on my leg. Take what you need. I want to watch you cum." I tell her.

She obeys and lowers herself on to my leg and starts grinding on me. When she moans around my cock, it's the sexiest thing in the world.

"If you had woken me up like this? You would have sealed your fate. You would have been mine. I never would have let you go. Now? Nope, there's no way I'll let you go. You can run, but I'll always find you. You. Are. Mine." I growl and cum down her throat, screaming her name.

She lets out a long moan, and I can feel her pussy flutter through her barely there shorts, as she cums and soaks the leg of my pants.

Sliding my cock from her mouth, she gives the tip a kiss, before I pull her up to me. She lays her head on my shoulder, and I kiss her head.

"Feel free to wake me up like that any time."

I strip down to my boxers and crawl under the covers with her. I don't remember falling asleep, but I never thought I'd wake up the way we did either.

CHAPTER 27

Austin

"What the fuck is this?" Is not the phrase, you want to be woken up by. It takes me a minute to get my bearings. I'm in my bed with Dallas wrapped around me. I feel warm and safe, but when I turn towards my door and see Landon, standing there fuming, the warm feeling fades fast.

Shit, this is not how I wanted him to find out. What is he even doing home?

"Dallas." I nudge him siting up, but he's already waking.

No time like the present to bite the bullet and get it out in the open, right? Though, I had this worked out in my head much different than this clusterfuck. Several different ones in fact. If I know my brother, straight to the point will be best.

"Landon, Dallas and I are dating; we have been for a few weeks." I tell him.

His eyes shoot to Dallas, like this is his fault. Feeling the need to protect Dallas, I continue, "Now, head downstairs, let us wake up and get dressed, and we will come down to talk about this like adults." I use my stern voice.

Pure anger like I've never seen is all over Landon's face, but after a moment, he turns and slams the door. I can hear his pounding footsteps going downstairs, before I flop back down on the bed. He's been gone barely forty-eight hours, and we were supposed to have two weeks.

Dallas pulls me in close. "Hey, we're in this together, okay? I choose you. It will hurt like hell to lose him, but I can't live without you. I made that choice a while ago."

My heart races. I look over at him and see the vulnerability in his eyes. He's worried I don't feel the same.

"Dallas, it's the same for me. These last few weeks proved that even more." I tell him and lean in to kiss him soft and sweet. This moment, even with my brother mad as hell downstairs, is everything I've ever wanted, to be someone's first choice. Isn't this what every girl wants?

"This is not how I planned for you to wake up this morning." He smirks at me, and I laugh. After talking about all the fantasies of waking each other up last night, it definitely wasn't on the list for how I expected to wake up.

"Let's get dressed and go try to talk to him. Though, I doubt there will be any talking to him." I sigh and cover my face with my hands and dig the heels of my hands in my eyes, trying to fight off the building headache.

"One more thing." He says and waits for me to look over at him. "Now that the cat's out of the bag, I want you to consider moving to my room. Or I can move in here, but I want our stuff together."

"Dallas..." I start, but he holds up a hand.

"Just think about it, okay?"

I nod. If he's sure this is what he wants, then I have no doubts about it. But I want to ease Landon into this, no matter how big of an asshole he's about to be. I don't want to overwhelm him all at once.

As we get dressed, Dallas can't seem to keep his hands off me, despite his angry best friend downstairs. It's like after all the talking yesterday he's happier, lighter, and more like the boy I remember. If I thought for one moment, we had the time I'd let his hands wander and give us both the wake up we had planned.

We make our way downstairs hand-in-hand to find Landon, sitting at the kitchen island with coffee in front of him and his back to us.

"How long?" He asks, before we are even in his line of vision.

"Officially, since the last day of the tour," Dallas says.

"We had decided to tell you, when you got back from this trip. All we wanted was a few more weeks in our bubble."

"Who else knows?" Landon asks.

"Mason, and that's it," I tell him.

Landon looks right at Dallas, his voice even but angry. "You should have talked to me first!"

For some reason, this sets me off. We tried on the tour, but any time we looked at each other, as more than friends, he would go off on us. Did he really think we'd chance upsetting him, before we even knew what this was?

"Why, so you can tell him yet again he isn't good enough? Do you realize we have both been fighting this, since before his mom died? Do you understand how miserable you made us, because we didn't think we could have the other? Then, to tell Dallas he isn't good enough, because of choices he made, because you kept us apart?" I yell.

I know it isn't fair, but I'm so mad I want to hurt him. I want him to feel an ounce of what I've felt over him keeping us apart.

Dallas wraps his arm around me from behind. "Baby girl, don't. Don't say something you can't take back. We talked about this, and it's in the past. We are where we are meant to be. I have you now, you have me, and that's all that matters." Dallas's voice is steady, soft, and calm.

I take a deep breath and look back at Landon, who is watching us his face still full of rage.

"Why would we chance upsetting you, when we didn't even know what this was? I was the one who didn't want to tell you, because I knew you'd act like this, and Dallas and I are in a good place. I didn't want you to ruin it, like I knew you would. He's your best friend, the one you trust most in the world. If he isn't good enough for me, then who is?" I ask surprised at how steady I was able to keep my voice.

"No one!" Landon shouts.

I stumble back against Dallas's chest, almost like Landon slapped me. Dallas's grip on my hips tightens, a silent warning to think, before I speak.

He can't mean that, can he? I always thought no matter what, Landon had my best interests at heart, even when he made things difficult. But this? I don't want to believe he really thinks this.

"So, I'm supposed to die alone and miserable to make you happy? Fuck you, Landon." I break from Dallas's hold, grab my purse, and the first set of car keys I can and run out to the garage, ignoring Landon and Dallas, yelling behind me.

Seeing I grabbed the keys for Dallas's SUV, I hit the unlock button and leave, before one of them can stop me. Tears are rolling down my face, and I have to pull over, once I'm out of the neighborhood to get myself in order, so I can drive.

I take a few deep breaths and realize these aren't tears, because I'm hurt, they are tears of anger. The one quality of myself I have always hated was when I get really mad, I cry. And I can't remember the last time I was this mad at someone, much less my brother of all people. We've always been a team, him and me. There's no way he believes that, but he still said it.

Once my emotions are under control, I start driving. I get on the highway not even paying attention to which way I'm going, but I end up downtown. I randomly take a few major exits and put Nashville in my rearview mirror. I crank up the music and try not to think. I want to let all the anger and emotion go and clear my head.

Of everything I expected to come out of Landon's mouth, I never thought it would be that no one was good enough; that he could be that selfish.

Then again, I never thought I'd see the day he was so harsh to his best friend either, and that he'd put him down that way. It makes me wonder what else he has been feeding to Dallas over the years.

For a fleeting moment, I have a thought, is all this worth it? I can easily pack up and point my car west and be somewhere new in a day or two, and everything can go back to normal.

But it can't, can it? After having this time with Dallas, my heart will never be the same, and we will never be the same. The thought of walking away from him rips my heart out, and I know I'm in this for the long haul no matter what happens with Landon.

There's a sign for a scenic overlook ahead, so I take the exit and park. The view is amazing. I'm on top of a small mountain, overlooking a small town with more mountains in the background.

I sit on the low stone wall and let the wind hit my face. Here all my problems feel so small.

A car pulls in a few spaces down, and a couple, slightly older than me, gets out. They have huge smiles all over their faces, as they take in the view. You can tell how much in love they are just by the way they look at each other.

He stands behind her and wraps his arms around her, as she leans back into him. My eyes water, because I want that so badly. I thought I had it, and if I'm honest, I still do if Dallas meant what he said, and I know he did.

In that moment, I know I will fight for Dallas and me, because I meant what I said this morning, too. He's worth it, and I choose him. I choose us.

I sigh. If I'm honest, I didn't run, because I was unsure of my feelings for Dallas. I ran, because I was unsure if I can live with Landon right now. I don't want to be around him; I want our bubble back.

I want to be wrapped in Dallas's arms. I want to fall asleep that way and wake up that way.

I get back in my car and reach a spot where the highway splits. I can go south towards the beach or keep heading towards the mountains. With how small my problems felt on that overlook, the choice is easy. I continue towards the mountains.

The highway narrows, and I'm not sure what I'm looking for, but I see an exit labeled scenic drive, so I get off, figuring at the very least, I can have some pretty views, while I figure things out. I only make it a few miles, before the answer to everything sits right in front of me.

Talk about a sign.

CHAPTER 28

Dallas

Now, it's my turn to be mad. The hurt is Austin's eyes and making her run out of here like that, fuck. No one does that to her. I don't care who you are; I won't even let Landon treat her like that. What the hell has gotten into him?

I turn to Landon, who is still staring at the door Austin just slammed.

For a moment, I think about running after her, but I know she needs to think and clear her head, and I will give her that while I deal with Landon. Even though, all I want to do is tell him to fuck off and go after my girl.

When he finally turns his gaze back to me, I speak the one truth that trumps everything else. It's also the last thing I'm sure he's expecting me to say.

"I love her and have since high school," I admit for the first time out loud. It feels wrong that Landon is the first one to hear it, but it needs to be said. I'm putting all my cards on the table.

He just stares at me. There's no emotion on his face, so I say what I had planned.

"Yeah, I slept around, but I was always honest with them, and I didn't want commitment. I didn't want it if it wasn't with Austin. I had it in my head she would never want me. I want you to know I haven't slept with her. She's different, and she's more

190

important."

"You haven't slept with her?" He looks shocked.

"I haven't. This time with her has only made me fall in love with her even more, and I realized I can't live without her."

I pause and let that sink in.

Landon studies my face, while his is still blank of emotion.

"I hate to lose you. You're my best friend, but I can't live without her. So, don't make me choose, because there's no contest, it will always be her."

He sighs and runs his hands over his face.

"I remembered what yesterday was, and I canceled my trip and got back as fast as I could," he says. He's talking about the anniversary of my mom's death.

"I had Austin. We talked, and I told her everything, even how I used to spend the day. You always said I hadn't dealt with it, and I think you were right. There was a part of it I couldn't talk to even you about, because during that time, I needed her. When I was with her, it was the only time I felt happy, and the dark cloud over me lifted. She and I talked a lot yesterday. We talked about the good times, the bad ones, and everything we didn't get a chance to say to each other back then."

I pause and smile, remembering our time sitting on her bed, talking about anything and everything.

"I needed that more than I realized. I needed her. Yesterday, I laughed, I smiled, I and remembered the good times with my mom, not that horrible time, after she was gone."

"What couldn't you talk to me about?" He asks, looking hurt.

"Well, did you know, when it storms Austin crawls into bed with me at night? She has for years." He looks shocked, but not angry. "Do you know why?" I ask him.

"Why?" He asks quietly.

"That night my mom died I couldn't sleep. It started storming really bad, and she woke up. I needed someone. She was there for me and held me all night. We didn't make the connection, until yesterday, but it started then. Storms make me think of my mom, and when Austin is there, she chases those thoughts away. She's never liked storms, since your parents died, so I've been there for her, too."

"She's been climbing into bed with you for years, and you expect me to believe you never touched her? Damnit, you were her prom date. I know what happens on prom night!"

I just laugh. I don't know what else to do.

"Until today, have I ever given you a reason not to trust me? Did I want to put my hands on Austin? Yes, I wanted her so bad it hurt. I would hold her, and she would cuddle up to me, but that was it. And again, I didn't touch her at prom either. After the dance, we went and lay in the field on a blanket and talked. She was upset about her ex and needed someone to talk, too. I just wanted to soak up time with her. If you don't believe me, ask her yourself." I say.

"She was so much younger back then, and it didn't seem right you liking her." He says.

"She's barely two years younger than me. Your dad was five years older than your mom, and they dated in college." I remind him. "You know you have to let her lead her own life and not try to control her, right? The harder you try to hold on to her, the more you'll lose her. You'll put yourself in a no win situation. Even if I stepped away from her, which I won't, don't you think she will blame you? You know what heartache is like. Do you really want to be the one responsible for causing your sister that kind of pain?" I ask him.

He cringes but says nothing, as my phone rings. I breathe a sigh of relief that it's Austin. I look at Landon, before stepping out of the room and answering it.

"Baby girl, are you okay?" I ask.

"Yes, I'm more than okay. I'm sorry I walked out and left you to deal with him alone. Are you okay?" She asks, and I just laugh.

"I can handle him, so don't you worry about me."

She's quiet for a moment, and I don't want to push her.

"I want our bubble back." She says.

"Me too," I admit.

"Good, I'm going to text you an address. Pack a bag for each of us for five days. Actual clothes, Dallas and bathroom items, and I'll meet you there."

I smirk. She knows me well. My first thought was to pack as few clothes as possible. Who needs clothes in our bubble? I plan to keep her clothes off her as much as possible.

"Meet me where?"

"At the address I'm going to text you. I kind of took your car, so bring mine, or have Mason bring you, if you want."

"I'll be there. You're safe, right?"

She laughs a carefree laugh that wraps around my heart.

"I'm better than I've been in a long time. See you soon."

I don't bother going back in to the kitchen to talk to Landon. I just head upstairs and find one of her bags in her closet and start grabbing clothes. Shorts, jeans, some of my favorite tops, and everything else she will need. I get her phone cord, tablet, and laptop too just in case.

Once her stuff is packed, I go to my room and do the same. I pull up the address she has texted me, and I see it's about an hour away.

I head downstairs with both bags over my shoulders to find Landon still in the same place. He looks over, but I don't offer any information.

"You're leaving?" He sighs.

"Austin called. She asked me to pack a bag for a few days. She said she wants our bubble back, and so do I. You both need to cool down and think this out, you especially. We'll be back, and if you don't want to lose her, you need to talk not yell."

I grab her car keys and look him over one more time. He looks deep in thought, so I just shake my head and head out to the garage.

"I want you both to be happy, I do." He says and stops me in my tracks. "It's hard having been lied to for so long."

"We tried to tell you our intentions, but you made it impossible to talk to you. Maybe, you need to ask yourself why?" I tell him, before I close the door behind me.

Landon has always been my biggest cheerleader, but it seems like the last few years he's changed, and I can't put my finger on it. From not believing that I was changing, to putting down Austin and me, when we tried to talk to him. He just seems off. I need to talk to Austin about it, because she knows him just as well.

I plug the address into the navigation and take a deep breath. The car smells like her, and it's comforting but also makes me hard at the same time. I head towards the highway, ignoring my cock that is trying to find her, find our home. Because above all else, that is what Austin is for me. *She's my home.*

On the drive, I send up a silent prayer that we are okay, and this doesn't break us. She sounded happy on the phone, and like things are going good, and I just hope it stays that way.

I decide it's time to give her all of me, and the last piece I have been holding back. If she still wants me, I plan to make love to her and show her how much she means to me. I want to feel her around me, when she comes and hold her in my arms, when we're one. I want that connection, a connection I never wanted with anyone else.

The further I head out of Nashville, the better I start to feel. This isn't how I wanted Landon to find out, but I'm glad he knows. Hopefully, he will get his thoughts together over the next few days, and we can come back and talk like adults, like family.

I have this overwhelming need to make sure things are okay

for Austin's sake. I will do whatever it takes to make that happen, except let her go.

No more hiding, and no more sneaking around. I won't hold back anymore.

CHAPTER 29

Austin

This cabin is perfect. Right at the base of a mountain; it's close to hiking trails, a lake, and the cute, small, little town. This is the perfect place for Dallas and me to get back into our bubble and figure out our next steps together.

Because we're moving forward together; I made that choice at the overlook. I'm going to fight to be that happy couple. That starts here.

The billboard for Mountain View Cabin rentals was just the sign I needed. I stopped in and asked for the one with the best view, and I have to admit this cabin is amazing. I'm not sure how someone else hasn't rented it.

I also stopped at the grocery store in town and got us food, and a few other things to last us over the next few days. Everyone here is so friendly, and it's just the kind of place I would move to, if I was looking to relocate.

I check on our late lunch or early dinner, depending on how you look at it, and see that Dallas should be here any minute. I light a few candles and set the table, as he knocks on the door.

Butterflies take flight in my stomach. I know I shouldn't have left like I did, and while he sounded fine on the phone, he has every right to be mad at me, and I wouldn't blame him if he is.

I open the door to see my handsome man, but that light and

carefree look he had this morning is gone. I make myself a promise to get it back, before we head home.

I stand aside and let him in, as he sets our bags down and takes a look around.

"What's this?" He asks, as his eyes run over the large open concept cabin. The front door opens right into the living room with a massive fireplace. The dining room is to the side with the kitchen just beyond that. It all leads to the massive picture windows with the breathtaking mountain views you can see from just about any place in the cabin.

"I rented this cabin for us for the next five days. You and me. We figure out what our next steps are, and then we go back and talk to Landon, together. We can go public to everyone or not at all. I'm done hiding us."

He answers without hesitation, "We go public. I want all of you, and I want to tell everyone you're mine."

"My brother?" I ask. I almost don't want to know what happened after I left.

"We talked, and I made it clear I'll pick you and asked him not to make me choose. He hasn't, and I don't think he will."

A sudden thrill goes through me that he really did mean what he said this morning. A part of me still can't believe we're doing this. He's after all the unattainable guy I had a crush on in high school. The one thousands of girls have pinned to their walls, and yet, he wants me.

"Then, you have to give me all of you. No more holding back for either of us." I tell him.

"I'm scared." He whispers, as he reaches for me.

"I am too, but we're in this together." I wrap my arms around his waist, soaking in his warmth. This is what I needed to just reconnect.

We stand there locked in each other's arms for a few minutes, before I pull back and place a hand over his chest. Even with his shirt on, I can feel his heat, as if we are skin to skin. The sparks between us are undeniable, but it still takes my breath away, leaving me unable to speak.

"I have something for you." He says, his voice gruff. He pulls a piece of paper from his pocket and hands it to me.

"I got it done the week I asked you to wait for me on tour. I just didn't know when to give it to you, but now seems like the right time."

It takes me a minute to understand what I'm looking at. It's a clean bill of health from his doctor. He's STD free.

When I look up at him, there's a light blush on his face, and he looks a little shy. I can't remember the last time I've seen him blush. He can be vulnerable and open around me, yes, this blush isn't something I've seen, since he was that shy teenage boy, who I had the biggest crush on all those years ago.

I lean in and kiss him, because words fail me. Without words, I try to show him what this means to me, and he seems to understand. I pull back and rest my forehead to his.

"I don't have one for you," I say.

He shakes his head, "You don't need one. You have nothing to prove."

"You have nothing to prove either, Dallas. But this is perfect." I tell him and kiss him again. Just a short, sweet kiss, before pulling away to check on the food.

"What can I do to help?" He asks.

"Why don't you get us some drinks, but otherwise, we're ready."

I set the food on the table, and he pulls me into his lap and slides my plate over in front of us next to his.

"Let me feed you, baby girl." He whispers next to my ear. The heat from his breath sending tingles to my core.

He feeds me each bite of food, and then himself in-between feeding me. One hand remains on my waist the whole time, holding me close to him, like he's afraid I'm going to try to get up and run. Not a chance.

He's constantly nuzzling my neck or placing kisses all over my face, while I eat. It's an easy going time, while I tell him about my drive up here, and the couple I saw at the overlook. I want him to know I'm in this.

"Dinner was amazing, baby girl. I want many more days like this. Dinner and just conversation. This was perfect."

"It was perfect, and I agree. I want many more nights like this, too." I rest my head on his shoulder and enjoy the moment.

"There's a hot tub on the back porch. Want to go for a soak?" I ask.

"I didn't bring swimsuits." He admits.

I shrug, "Do we need them?"

He just stares at me, heat in his eyes, "No we don't." He admits.

I stand up and leave the food on the table and make my way to the back door. I stop and look over my shoulder. Dallas is standing with his eyes on me, but he hasn't moved.

I turn back to the door, and before I open it, I whip my shirt off and let it fall to the floor. I leave the door open and shed my shorts next followed by my bra. I'm standing in front of the hot tub, turning on the jets in just my black lace panties, when I feel his body heat come up behind me. He pins me with his hips to the side of the hot tub. His shirt and pants are gone, and he's in just his boxers.

"You are so damn beautiful." He whispers, as he slowly pulls my panties off, his hands trailing down my legs. "Get in." He whispers into my ear.

I do as he says, and then turn my eyes back to him, watching him strip his boxers off and follow me into the hot tub. He sits across from me, and I slide my feet up his legs, until they're in his lap. His arms are stretched out along the side of the hot tub, but his eyes stay on me the whole time.

So, I settle in and sink down, until the water covers my shoulders. The hot water is easing my tense muscles from the fight with my brother today, but that's the last thing I want to talk about. We both stare each other down, waiting for the other to make the first move. It's almost a battle of wills, before he breaks a second, before I do. He leans in and pulls me into his lap.

I'm straddling him and feel his cock against my core. With my eyes on his, I grind, and we both groan. His hands roam over my hips up to just below my breasts and to my back.

"You're so beautiful, baby girl." He whispers, before his lips land on mine. He takes control of the kiss, as he moves my hips over his cock, the tip hitting my clit with each slow pass.

I throw my head back and moan. "More, Dallas."

"Cum for me. Then, I'm taking you inside and making love to you." He says, as he lowers his head to suck one nipple into his mouth.

I shove my chest into his face, needing more, and he sucks harder. He picks up the slow place just enough that it makes me shatter, like the tension cord was just cut. My orgasm over takes me, as I scream his name. Thankfully, there are no neighbors to hear.

Before my body has even relaxed, Dallas is wrapping my arms around his neck and standing up from the hot water with his hands under my ass.

"Wrap your legs around my waist." I do as he says, and he carries me inside.

"Which way?" He asks, since I never got to give him a tour.

"Bedroom behind the kitchen," I mumble into his neck. He chuckles and heads to our bathroom and bypasses the bedroom.

Before I can even ask what he's doing, there's a towel being wrapped around me. He sits me on the counter and takes his time drying me off, before drying himself off. His eyes roam over me, and I let my eyes look over him as well.

His muscles seem even more defined, standing in front of me in the bathroom light, and the tattoos on his chest catch my eye. I trace my fingers over the Texas one again, and he places his hand over mine.

"Austin, Texas." He says.

"For me?" I ask, and he just nods.

"You've held my heart longer than you know. I got this one done in Austin, Texas. Every time someone said Austin, or I saw Austin, I would miss you."

Without thinking, I lean forward and place a kiss on the tattoo right over his heart.

"You've held my heart for longer than you know, too." I pull his hand to the tattoo of their band. "Everyone assumes this tattoo is pride for my brother, but it's not. It was pride for you. Even if you and Landon hadn't demanded I stop wearing bikinis, I would have, because I wasn't ready for either of you to see it yet. Landon still hasn't." I smirk.

He runs his fingers over the guitar tattoo, before his eyes meet mine again. This time his arms go around my waist, and I barely have enough time to hang on, before he swoops me up and carries me back into the bedroom. He lays me on the bed, like I'm the most precious thing in the world, before standing back to look at me.

I can feel every place his eyes land, because they send little heat waves.

"Don't move." He says and disappears out the bedroom door and is back, before I can even think of sitting up. He tosses a box of condoms on the nightstand, before he falls to his knees beside the bed. When he pulls me to the edge, I spread my legs. His warm breath ghosts over my pussy, and I can feel how wet I am.

He leans in slowly and gives me one slow, firm lick from slit to clit, before latching on to my clit and doing that thing with his tongue he knows drives me wild. He's learned my body and knows just the right amount of pressure to put on my clit and just the spot to hit. When he slides two fingers into me, as he stretches me, it pushes me over the edge. My hand pulls at his hair, keeping him close, as I scream out his name.

As my body calms, I catch sight of him, rolling on a condom, and I don't think the action has ever been so hot before. He wraps his arm around my waist and moves up to the center of the bed, like I weigh nothing. Then, he settles himself over me, as he takes both my hands in his.

I wrap my legs around his waist, and I see the fear in his eyes, the uncertainty mixed with lust.

"This is us, Dallas. We're just beginning. No walls between us. Lean on me, I've got you." I whisper and pull his hips towards mine with my legs.

The head of his cock nestles at my entrance, and his eyes lock on me.

"Eyes on me. I've never needed someone's eyes on me as badly as I do right now." He says.

I nod, keeping my eyes on him, as he slowly slides into me. Slow, short thrusts have me groaning and fighting not to throw my head back and close my eyes. With each thrust, he grips my hands a little tighter. I've never felt so full or been stretched so perfectly.

When he's filled me to the hilt, he lets go of my hands and braces himself on his forearms, leaning down to kiss me. His pace is slow and languid, like he's not in a hurry for this to be over, and I'm not either.

Each thrust pulls me closer to the edge and tightens all my nerves to the point they are balancing on the thinnest line, and he's the only thing stopping me from going crashing over.

"You feel so damn good." He moans. "Never felt like this before, baby girl."

"Faster, Dallas," Is all I can get out, before his mouth is over mine again, and he picks up the pace.

Shifting my legs higher up his waist, he moves faster and finds the perfect spot. I gasp, trying to meet his hips to get him closer, deeper.

He kisses a trail down my neck and nips at the skin, where my neck meets my shoulder.

"Oh, Dallas." I moan.

"Yes, baby?" He whispers against my ear.

I catch him off guard and manage to flip him on to his back with me on top and still keep him inside me. A huge smile crosses his face, as he runs his hands over my body, and I begin riding him.

"I love this position." He says, as he pulls me down, so he can take my nipple into his mouth.

Somehow, even from the bottom, he remains in complete control of the pace. He has me so close, but I'm not able to climax like this.

"Please, Dallas," I beg.

He takes mercy on me and picks up the pace, pulling me down for a kiss. My nipples running over his coarse chest hair, and the angle allow him to hit my clit each time he thrusts into me.

"Come for me. I want to feel you pull the come from my cock for the first time." He says, as his thumb strums my clit and sends me into an orgasm.

"Fuck, you're squeezing my cock so hard." Dallas moans, as I blackout at all the sensations, running over me.

I come to just as Dallas thrusts into me again and moans my name. Dallas, losing control, while inside me, sends off another mini climax, as he rolls to the side.

"Fuck that was amazing," I say barely able to open my eyes.

"Yes, it was. Get some rest, baby girl. We will be doing that a few more times tonight." He says, as he pulls the blankets over me and heads to the bathroom.

When he climbs in bed and wraps himself around me, then I'm

in my safe place. There's no way I could give this up.

CHAPTER 30

Dallas

I wake up with Austin next to me and smile. This is the most content I have ever been. How did I think I'd fall back into my old habits with her? Old me with other women would have pushed her away, as soon as sex was over, but with her, I couldn't get her close enough.

Old me wouldn't have wanted them to look me in the eye, but with Austin, I didn't want her eyes to ever leave mine.

I lean up on my elbow and watch her sleep. The sheet is around her waist, leaving her beautiful breasts on display. They're round and perfect with red marks from my loving on them all night.

One time wasn't enough. She had barely gotten to sleep, when I was waking her up and needing her again. I would have felt guilty, if it wasn't for her doing the same to me a few hours later.

Pulling the sheet back over her, because I don't want her to get cold. I simply watch her sleep, thanking whoever is listening that she's mine.

When she rolls over and opens her eyes, the world instantly seems warmer, brighter, and perfect.

"Good morning, baby girl," I say, as I lean down to kiss her forehead.

"Mmm, any morning I wake up next to you is a good morning.

But I love it, when I wake up to that huge smile on your face."

I hadn't even realized I was smiling. I tuck some hair behind her ear and cup her cheek.

"I love you, Austin. The soul crushing, once in a lifetime love, that I'll write songs about, until the day I die."

Her eyes mist over, and I rub my thumb gently over the corner, catching her tears.

"I love you too, Dallas. I think I've loved you from the time you saved me from the giant spider in my bedroom." She smiles.

I remember that. She was about twelve, and Landon and I were hanging out at the house, and she came home to get her math book she forgot, before going to a friend's house to study. Landon went outside for something, and I heard her scream. My heart stopped.

I raced to her room, finding her frozen with an enormous spider on her math book. I killed it and checked her whole room to make sure he didn't have any friends.

I chuckle. "I remember that day. You let me hug you for the first time, and I think that was the day you stole my heart, too."

I pull her into me and kiss her. This girl loves me! I will do everything I can to make her happy. Always.

We are interrupted by her phone ringing. I get out of bed and find it for her on the kitchen counter.

"It's Landon," I say.

"Ugh! Just turn my phone off." She calls back.

I send him to voice mail and turn her phone off, and then my phone rings. I write a quick text telling him we're fine and will talk to him in a few days. Then, I turn off my phone as well, before heading back into the bedroom.

Austin just slipped one of my shirts on and smiles at me.

"Let's get breakfast, I'm starving." She takes my hand and pulls me into the kitchen.

I push her back up against the kitchen counter, because I need to hear her say it again.

"I love you," I whisper against her lips.

"I love you, too." She whispers back, and then her lips land on mine. I suck her bottom lip into my mouth and run my tongue along it, before pulling back.

"I want to take you again, but I'm going to feed you first. Because I'm going to prove that I'll always take care of you." I tell her.

Her hand comes to rest on my chest, right on my Texas tattoo over my heart.

"You have proven time and time again you'll take care of me and not just since we have been together, but before then. I think I knew it, when you dropped everything to make sure I went to prom and had an amazing night. You proved it again and again every time I'd visit, or I'd need someone to talk, too. I want to take care of you too, Dallas."

"You do, baby girl. Just being here and talking to me is all I'll ever need. Now, it's simple things like your touch." I place my hand over hers. "It steadies me, grounds me. On my worst days, just being in the same room as you, always helps."

With a soft kiss, we pull apart and make breakfast.

"What do you want to do today?" I ask.

"Besides you?" She asks with a smirk.

"I can easily spend all day in bed making you cum over and over again, but I think we should spend some time outside, too," I say, as I look out of the window at the mountain view.

"Well, the lady at the office said there's a path out the back door that leads to a river, and then if we go to right around the bend, there's a waterfall. Maybe, we can check that out?"

"Sounds good."

After breakfast, it takes us twice as long to get dressed, because we can't keep our hands off each other.

We head out in search of the waterfall, and the hike is pretty easy.

"Was I why you didn't date in school?" She shocks me by asking.

I chuckle and shake my head. "Pretty much. I had it in my head if I dated the wrong girl, I'd ruin my chances with you."

"Well, if it had been Chelsea Milton, I don't think I'd have talked to you again." She cringes.

"Oh, Lord no. She may have been pretty, but I couldn't stand to be around her. She was a horrible person and still is, by the way. She came to a show about three years ago, and she's even trashier now, if you can believe it."

Austin gives me the side eye, and I know what's running through her mind.

"No, I didn't sleep with her. I told her off and actually had security keep her away from me. I was never into trashy girls."

As we round the corner, the waterfall is right in front of us.

"Wow!" She gasps. The waterfall isn't very tall, so the surrounding water is relatively calm and perfect for swimming.

By the water's edge, there's a fallen tree ideal for sitting on and being able to get your feet in the water. Austin must have the same idea, because she's taking her shoes off and heading that way.

We spend the rest of the afternoon enjoying our secret oasis and the sun, before going back to the cabin.

✳ ✳ ✳

Each day at the cabin is spent almost the same way. Breakfast together before leaving to explore. On day two, we went into the small town nearby, and it was charming. Either they had no clue who I was, or they were being respectful, because we weren't approached once.

The town is small and built around a square park. We had fun taking in the shops, eating lunch, and catching a movie. One day, we came into town for brunch. We made another trip out to the waterfall, before we left, too.

Every night, we'd come back to the cabin and have dinner. I'd feed her, while she sat on my lap, and then we head to bed, where I'd make love to her, until we both passed out. If only we could stay in our bubble.

Today, we head home. We had finished packing up the cars and doing the final sweep of the cabin to make sure we didn't leave anything.

"Do we need to stop at the office on the way out?" I ask her.

"Nope, she said to leave the key on the counter and call, if we aren't gone by eleven." She says.

It's just after ten, so we are good.

"We'll take it slow, and I'll follow behind you," I say.

I hate the idea of having to drive back in separate cars, but it will be a good chance to call Landon, give him a heads up we are coming home, and take any anger he has for turning our phones off, before he lashes out at Austin.

As soon as we hit the road, I turn my phone back on and let it load. The most recent text from Landon catches my eye.

Landon: Austin's ex was outside the house. When I confronted him, he said he was waiting to talk to Austin. Cops can't do anything, because he was on the street.

Fuck. I hit the button to call Landon, as his voice fills the car over blue tooth.

"Took you long enough to call me back." He sounds irritated, but I can't blame him.

"We both turned off our phones. I just turned mine back on and saw your text. We're on our way home now." I tell him. "What happened with Branden?"

"I saw him standing outside the gate on the camera, so I went to confront him. He keeps saying he wants to talk to Austin. I said she wasn't here, and that she left a few days ago, after we had a fight. He hasn't been back, and I'm hoping he thinks she won't be back."

"Okay, well when we get closer, I'm going to call you and make sure he isn't there, because the last thing we need is for him to see her get home."

"Yeah, I thought he could be watching from a side street or the neighborhood gate. No way of telling. I almost debated having you guys stay away longer, but I think it's safest to get her home." Landon admits.

"You know we have to tell her. I don't want to scare her, but she has to know. She needs to be on alert."

"I agree," Landon says.

"Listen, I know we need to talk, and you're probably still mad at me. That's fine. But can we agree to put this aside for right now for Austin's sake and work on making sure she's okay?" I ask him.

He's quiet a moment, before he sighs.

"Yeah, I only want her safe, and I'll do anything to make sure it happens." He says.

"Okay, she said you were looking into this guy. What have you found?" I ask.

"Nothing. That's the problem. He doesn't exist."

"So, he was lying to her, which means he has something to hide. What's our next step?" I ask.

"The private investigator is trying some facial recognition software with pictures I sent him. I had to break into Austin's cloud storage to get them. She gave me the password years ago, but I've never used it. I don't know if she'll be too happy, but I couldn't reach you guys."

"I'll smooth it over. I would have done the same thing."

"The PI says the best thing is a fingerprint. If he's running, he'll probably be in the system, but I'm not sure how to manage that."

"Not without using Austin as bait, and I don't like that idea," I growl.

"Me either. I don't think we're to that point yet. Also, have you heard from Dave? It's like after your meeting he's dropped off the planet."

"No, I wasn't in a rush to call him again. Have you tried Mitch?"

"Yeah, Mitch doesn't even know where he is. Oh, well. We need to meet about this label, so we can get away from all of them anyway."

"You still want to do this with me?" I ask.

"Of course, I do. I'm not happy about you and Austin, but you two are my family. I'm not turning my back on either of you."

I take a moment to compose myself. Those words mean more to me than he will ever know.

"I had an idea, and this is more for Austin than anything," I say.

"Lay it on me." He sighs, and I can tell he's lounging on the couch, his favorite place to talk on the phone. He always sighs like that, when he lies down.

"Austin and the receptionist at the label hit it off really well. I'd like to bring the receptionist over with us, so Austin has a friend and no reason to go back to the label."

"Deanna, right? She's always been nice, when I'm there. I'm good with that, but let's not talk to her, until we're out of our contract. No need to ruffle feathers just yet."

"I agree."

We spend the next bit talking label stuff.

"Hey, I need to let you go. Austin is pulling into a gas station. I'll talk to her about Branden. We're about twenty minutes out." I tell him.

"Okay, stay safe."

This conversation with Austin could go one of two ways. Here's to hoping she trusts her brother and me to keep her safe.

CHAPTER 31

Austin

As soon as Dallas steps out of the car, I can tell something is wrong. He looks like he doesn't want to tell me something, so I'm instantly on edge. I get the gas pumping to my car, before crossing my arms and turning to look at him.

"Okay, out with it," I say.

He sighs and steps up to me hold each of my arms.

"I just talked to Landon. He caught Branden outside the house. When he confronted him, he said he wanted to talk to you. Landon let him believe you took off after you fought with him. As in moved out, took off."

He bites his lip, as he holds my gaze. I don't even have to ask him what else he has to tell me, because he launches right into it.

"Also, Landon's private investigator has been digging into Branden hard, and basically, he doesn't exist. Which means, he's probably using a fake name to hide from something. So, Landon logged into your cloud account to get a few photos of him to run some photo analysis on."

Dallas's grip tightens on my arms, as he says this. I'm kind of pissed Landon was in my account without permission, but we did have our phones off, and I did give him the password a while back. Anyway, I don't keep anything on there I don't want him to see.

I sigh and shake my head.

"Okay, what now?" I ask.

Dallas just stares at me, like he's waiting for the other shoe to drop.

"What?" I finally ask.

"I expected you to get upset or freak out. I don't know."

"What good is it going to do? You and Landon already talked, and I'm guessing you have a plan?"

"Yes, we both agree having you at the house is best. We can protect you better there. As normal, you take Mason with you, if you leave the house, and he'll be there, if we have to leave you alone. Which will happen, because we have some meetings lined up."

"Okay," I say.

"Okay?"

"Well, I don't want to be alone anyway. This is all giving me the creeps. That day he showed up, he seemed off. I can't put my finger on it."

"Alright, then we're heading straight home. I'm going to call Landon and you on a three-way call, as we get closer, and he'll watch the cameras to make sure Branden isn't nearby. If he's there or if you see him, you keep driving past the house and circle the street back out the gate. Then, head back this way to the cabin, and I'll be right behind you. Okay?"

"Fine. Wouldn't it just be easier, if I hit him with my car?" I try to joke.

A forced smile finds its way to Dallas's face, before he pulls me into a hug.

"I love you, crazy girl." He whispers in my ear.

"I love you too, my protector."

Thank God for automatic shut off pumps, because I'm pretty

sure my gas tank was filled a while ago. I finish up, and once Dallas is ready, we get back on the road. The closer we get to home, the more my nerves kick into gear.

Will he be there? What does he want? Is all this because he wants me back? After three months? What is wrong with this guy? Why won't he leave me alone?

In no time flat, I have myself worked up, so I do the one thing that will calm me down. I call Dallas.

"Hey, baby. You okay?" His voice fills the car, and instantly, I feel better.

"Just talk to me. What's going on with the label you're starting?"

He talks, until it's time to call Landon, and then the two of them control the situation. I might admit it to Dallas, but never to Landon that I feel so much better, when they take control, that way and I can just clear my mind, and do as they tell me, too.

Again, a tidbit my over controlling brother doesn't need to know. Another fact that might work out great in the bedroom with my sexy-as-hell boyfriend. Such confusing thoughts. I smile at that thought, as I pull into the garage and shut off the car.

The call disconnects, and Dallas is at my door, before I even get a chance to open it. He pulls me into his arms, and everything is okay again.

When I walk inside, Landon is standing there, looking unsure and watching us. Though Dallas has his arm around my waist, he doesn't seem mad, he's just watching. I drop my bag, walking to him and wrapping my arms around Landon, and he holds me just as tight.

"Thank you," I tell him.

"Always. For you, always." His classic line he's been telling me, since we were kids. I know right then things will be okay with us. I just need to make sure they're okay with Dallas and him, too.

"Let's go sit down and talk," Landon says, as he lets me go, and I follow him into the living room with Dallas right behind me.

I sit on the couch with Dallas beside me, and Landon sits across from me on the love seat just watching us again.

"I'm not sure what Dallas told you," Landon starts. "But my guy was able to track Branden down to his last job and all his info is fake. He says he only sees things like this, when they're running from the law. He thinks if we can get fingerprints, then we can track him, but we don't have a way to do that."

"Unless I do it," I say, connecting the dots.

"Which is not an option," Dallas growls. "He's getting desperate, and we don't know what he wants. This isn't normal behavior, and if he's running, we don't know what his plans for you were. Again, I repeat, it's not an option."

"I agree," Landon says. "But in the meantime, you're not to be alone, ever. I want you to limit going out. I won't keep you trapped here, but I don't want you going out more than needed either."

"When you leave, you take Mason with you, even if you are with me or Landon," Dallas says taking my hand, as I nod.

"When we can't be here, Mason will be with you at the house. We are tightening security and having people here around the clock. I did file a police report, but they said there was nothing they could do, because he was on the street not on our property." Landon says.

"If he tries to get in contact with you in any way, you tell us immediately. Phone, text, email, social media, skywriting, or however stupid it might be, tell us no matter what." Dallas says.

"I will." I agree.

"Did you notice anything off, when you were together?" Landon asks.

I think about the short time I'd known Branden.

"Well, his place was bare, but I chalked it up to him being a bachelor, it's not uncommon. We never hung out with his friends, and he only met mine on accident. He never talked about his family, but it never raised a red flag. We didn't date and went to dinner three maybe four times and saw one movie. We didn't talk on the phone or really text, unless it was about getting together. The rest was just. Well." I can't bring myself to say it was just sex, but they get it, and thankfully, they don't push it.

"Okay, well, let's hope the photos will bring us something. Sorry about that by the way. You guys had your phones off, I tried to call first." Landon looks like he means it.

"You have my password, so I'm not worried about it." I wave my hand at him.

Neither of us says anything for a moment.

"Do you think he's dangerous?" I ask in a low voice. Though, I don't want to admit all this worries me, and all the extra security scares me a bit. I feel like it's overdone, like there's something they aren't telling me, but I'm happy to live in my ignorance for now.

I shiver at the thought of what they could be keeping from me, but Dallas is right there, pulling me into his arms, despite my brother being in the room.

"We don't know if he's dangerous, more than likely he's harmless, but you're the most precious thing in the world to both of us, and we'll always protect you. That means we'll we go overboard more times than not, but it will always be with your best interests at heart." Dallas says, rubbing my arms.

"I know," I say, resting my head on his shoulder, as they start planning out their schedules for the next week, and who will be with me when.

The rest of the evening passes almost like normal. Landon makes us dinner, and we sit at the table and talk about the cabin, and the small town we visited, and our hikes to the waterfall.

We watch some TV, and I was able to snuggle up to Dallas's

side on the couch. I caught my brother shaking his head a few times, but he never commented on it.

I guess, I started drifting off to sleep, because the next thing I feel is Dallas's chuckling and picking me up to carry me upstairs.

"Come on, baby girl. Let's get you to bed." He says.

"Night," I say to Landon, but don't get a response.

Dallas is a perfect gentleman. He takes me upstairs, helps me get ready for bed, tucks me in, and turns to leave.

"Get in bed," I tell him.

He smiles, "I think it's best we don't push our luck with your brother, don't you?"

"No, we should push all our luck, because I want you in bed with me." I pout.

He chuckles and leans in to bite my lip that I stuck out at him.

"Good night, baby girl."

I watch him walk out the door and close it behind him. I try to sleep, but all I can do is toss and turn, and every time I close my eyes, I see Branden. After over an hour, I give up and sneak across the hallway to Dallas's room.

Even with his lights off, I know my way to his bed, like the back of my hand. The moment my knee hits his mattress, he turns to face me. Then, he pulls me to him and makes sure I'm under the covers.

"You lasted longer than I thought you would." He says.

"I tried, but I'm just too used to sleeping in your arms now."

"Me too, baby girl. Me too." He kisses the top of my head, and I finally feel safe enough to sleep.

CHAPTER 32

Dallas

It's been a few weeks, since Austin and I got home from the mountain cabin, and there has been nothing from Branden. Landon and I have talked about this a few times, and we agree we don't want to let our guard down. We worry the moment we do that's when something will happen. Austin indulges us, but she's made it clear she thinks we are either hiding something from her, or even going a little too overboard.

I think we're both on edge that there's no information on him, and that he disappeared into thin air, the same way he appeared into Austin's life.

We have seen so many of our musician friends' deal with crazy fans and stalkers, and it's always been a worry for us with Austin. She tends to stay out of the limelight enough that they have left her alone.

I think she was getting a little stir crazy being home so much, so this last weekend we invited Ivy and Dom over for a BBQ and pool party. Austin was attached to Ivy's side. I think she needed that girl time, so I made a mental note to see if she wanted to do a book club thing with Deanna later this week.

If she needs girl time, I will give it to her, and the safest way is at our house. Landon agreed it's easy to control security there.

I had a talk with him about that. I wanted to pay for half the security bill for Austin and half of the bill for the private investigator. He fought me on it like I knew he would. I said I wanted to help take care of her, and I know he's her brother, but she's my girl, my whole life. I have no plans of going anywhere, and if I have it my way, someday it will be my responsibility to take care of her. That seemed to shut him up, and he finally agreed.

We still haven't talked about our relationship or worked on our friendship. It's all been about Austin, and that's what it needs to be for now. It's helping us keep the peace and things are good. So, for now, we focus on Austin.

Today, I'm taking my turn to meet with the private investigator, who has some news for us. For the most part, we have done well at keeping one of us home with her at all times. Only twice did we both have to be out, and Mason stepped right in.

Austin did say the other night how she feels like she's in a fishbowl. Always someone right there, even when she takes a shower. She knows it's for her own good, but says she missed just being alone.

I step into the private investigator's office. The waiting room isn't bad, a little older, but the magazines seem to be new, and his receptionist is cleaning, when I walk in.

The first time I walked in, her eyes went big, when she saw me. I knew she recognized me, but she did her best to keep her composure and didn't bother me, so on the way out, I offered her a photo and an autograph as long as she didn't post about running into me at work. She was so excited.

"Mr. McIntyre, Kurt's expecting you. I'll just let him know you're here." She says with a huge smile. I don't have to wait long, thankfully.

"Dallas, come on back." Kurt, the private investigator, says, as he peeks his head out the door.

I follow him back to his office, and I swear it's just like all those old movies. The walls are all brown wood paneling, and it's dark. Everything is brown, the floor, the walls, the furniture, all but a dark green curtain over the window that blocks the only source of natural light. A wall of bookcases takes up one wall, and a row of file cabinets takes up half of another. I'm thankful the only thing missing from those old movies is the smoke smell.

Despite all that, Kurt's office is perfectly organized. It's clean and everything seems to be in place. No massive stacks of paper, and all that's on his desk, is a folder I assume has all the information on my case.

I also like that Kurt is a straight shooter. No small talk, he just cuts straight to the point.

"So, your buddy Branden wasn't easy to track down. As you know, Branden is not his real name. It took some digging and greasing some of the right people, but I finally got his real name. Jimmy Buckerton."

"Buckerton, as in our manager, Dave?" I ask, because that's the only time I've heard that last name in my life.

"Exactly. It's his son." Kurt says and pauses, letting me digest it. Dave being shocked she was here, and Branden showing up a few days later, and then Dave going MIA.

"What do you have on Jimmy?" I ask finally.

"Nothing good, I'm afraid. He was pretty heavy into drugs, the nasty shit, too. That led to some petty crimes, mostly theft, I'm guessing to pay for more drugs, before he moved on to a bigger job that got him caught. He did two years in jail, where he went through a forced rehab program, and a month after, he got out just vanished. That lines up with when Branden Lewis shows up, and he beelines right for Austin from what I can tell."

"Any idea why?" I ask, my throat tightening, as I start shifting around in my chair. Staying still doesn't seem possible right now.

He purposely sought Austin out is what it looks like, which doesn't sit well with me. That means he was up to something, and with that quick proposal to Austin, who knows what that would be.

"That I'm not sure about. If he's tied to your manager, I'd start looking at your books. It's always a safe bet to follow the money. They might be working together. Has anything changed there?" Kurt asks.

"Well, our contract is coming to an end, and we have been talking about starting our own label, instead of renewing the contract. Especially, after how Dave acted towards Austin, when he saw her after the tour."

"I'm guessing you're one of his biggest clients, so how much money would he be out?" Kurt asks. I know he doesn't expect an answer, he's just making a point.

"A lot," I whisper. I have a rough idea of what the band makes and his cut on it. He'd be out a whole fuck of a lot of money. We assumed the label would move him on to their next big fish, since that's how we met up with him. He's good at what he does, so he won't have trouble getting more clients, especially with our band on his resume.

"Sounds like motive to me. I don't have proof, but I've seen it more times than not. Like I said, I'd have someone look at your books. I'm guessing this isn't his only way to attack you guys. I will keep an eye out for him and see what else I can find. Want me to dig into your manager, too?" Kurt says.

"Yes," I say without hesitation.

"Okay, tell me what you know about him."

I give him what I know about Dave, and everyone who works with him. Kurt takes notes and asks a few questions here and there.

"This gives me plenty to go on. I'll get started on this, and call you, when I have something." Kurt says, as he stands.

"Okay, thanks," I say and mindlessly walk to my car. My first thought is to call Landon and talk it out, since he stayed home with Austin today. Knowing she's okay will steady me, and then I can focus.

"Hey, what's wrong? I'm getting ready to head into a meeting," Landon says, and I hear people talking in the background.

"What meeting? You're supposed to be home with Austin. I had the meeting with the private investigator today."

"I'm meeting with the lawyer for the label contract, your meeting was tomorrow." He says, as I get a sinking feeling.

"No, it was today. Did you call Mason, before you left?" I ask.

"No, I assumed you were home with Austin, since she was still in bed, when I left. Shit." He says, as he realizes Austin is now home alone. "I'm packing up now, but I'm an hour out."

"I'm on my way now. Depending on traffic, I might make it back just before you, but Landon, what the private investigator found? It's not good."

"How not good?"

"Branden's real name is Jimmy Buckerton. He's Dave's son." I say and let it soak in.

"Son of a bitch!" He yells, and I hear his car door slam, as he starts up the car, and I get switched to the blue tooth.

"Give me all of it." He says.

I tell him about the drugs, the jail time, and what Kurt said about checking our books.

"I think we should take his advice and have someone else not connected to the label look over our books," I tell him.

"I agree. I'll take care of it, as soon as we know Austin is safe."

"Also, I have him looking into Dave, and everyone who works with him. My gut says whatever Branden is involved in that Dave is connected to it as well. I think it's why he was so shocked to see Austin that day at the label, and it wasn't a coincidence Branden showed up at the house a few days later."

"Want to bet that Dave is how Branden got the address? Remember Austin was trying to figure out how he found her?" Landon says.

"Shit, I bet you're right." I agree.

"Call me as soon as you get home and let me know she's okay." He says, before we hang up.

I send up a silent prayer that she is and press down on the gas pedal, speeding ticket be damned.

CHAPTER 33

Austin

Finally! I'm alone for the first time in weeks. Weeks! No one is watching my every move, timing my bathroom breaks, giving me weird looks, and making notes of every little thing I eat. I love those guys, but they can be too much! I didn't think I'd mind it, until they were always right there.

I hit my limit, when I went to take a bath to get a break from my brother, and he knocked on the door and threatened to barge in, because I had been in there too long. Seriously, I had only rewarmed the bathwater once!

I know they're trying by inviting Ivy and Dom over, so I can have some much needed girl time. I didn't leave Ivy's side, and she had a good laugh at how protective they were being. Glad she thought it was funny, but what I need even more is to soak in the bathtub without someone waiting for me in the next room, which is exactly what I'm doing right now.

The hot water soothes most of my nerves, and the wine takes care of the rest. I don't care that it's not even lunchtime yet. This wine is hard earned. I'm reading one of the books Deanna recommended and not paying much attention to the time, until the water gets cold. After the third time of rewarming the water, I bite the bullet and get out of the bath.

I dress in sweats and one of Dallas's shirts and keep my hair in the messy bun I had it in from the bath. I head downstairs and crank up the stereo in the living room and have a dance party for one, complete with all the crazy, stupid dance moves you wouldn't dare do in front of anyone. It's a good workout though, and after half an hour, I'm sweating and muscles I didn't know I had hurt.

I debate on letting my little girl out and running upstairs to jump on the bed and hide things in the guy's rooms to drive them crazy. But settle for grabbing a water from the mini fridge, and then sitting down to watch the shows I'm way behind on, because the guys refused to watch them.

There's nothing like the guilty pleasure of reality TV shows. I don't care how many times the guys try to tell me it's scripted and not real, it's still fun as hell to watch. After a few episodes, I'm starving, and I think I hear the guys coming in from the garage, so I head to the kitchen to get lunch going for us.

Only it's not the guys I find in the kitchen, it's Branden. He's standing in the kitchen, but this isn't the Branden I remember. This one looks like he hasn't slept in days, his clothes are wrinkled, he's dirty, he smells, and his eyes are red-rimmed and glassy.

My best guess is he's on drugs. I've seen people on tour look like this after a night out of heavy partying with drugs and alcohol. I know they can be unpredictable, so I have no idea what my next move is.

"Took long enough to get you alone." He sneers.

I suddenly realize no matter how annoying Dallas and Landon have been the last few weeks, they were right. Now, I have to wonder, *why am I alone?* Why didn't they call Mason? Why aren't the extra guards around the house? How did Branden get on to the property, much less inside?

With all the questions in my head, all I manage to get out is, "What the fuck?" This pretty much sums them all up nicely.

"That's what I said. I did and said all the right things. Dated your way, did romance, made sure the sex was great, and when I proposed, you said no."

"We weren't dating, it was just sex, and it was only for three months." I try to reason with him. What person in their right mind would agree to marry a guy you barely talked to once a week for three months?

He just shakes his head, "Then, you ran back here. It couldn't have been more perfect. Dear old dad saw you, and then we knew exactly where you were. He got me their address and their schedules. Yet, when I showed up here again, you turn me down and slam a door in my face."

"Dad? Who's your dad?" I ask, trying to put the pieces together.

"Dave," he smiles, like he just solved the biggest mystery on the planet.

Dave, the guy's manager? The one who has the most to lose over the guys starting their own label, because they won't be bringing him with them.

"Shit." The dots all start connecting. Dave's reaction to seeing me that day, and how quickly Branden showed up after. I knew he was lying about the mail.

"You know they plan to stop touring?" He continues, as he takes a step towards me. "They want to open their own label, and put Dad out of business. The label is insisting he retire, once the guys break off on their own. But when he retires, he gets barely five percent of what he's making now. You see the problem?"

Oh, I'm seeing the problem, but I don't think it's the one he sees. Daddy's pay gets cut, and there's less money to fund what looks like his little drug problem. What I don't get is what I have to do with all this.

If he has been saving for retirement, he should be loaded. I have an idea of what the guys make, it's closer to the billions number, and he gets a slice of that, so he's making millions.

Yeah, I know the cut in income will be hard to swallow but a change in lifestyle, and he's set for life.

The guys have been saving for retirement. Hell, they have saved for their retirement, mine, all our kids, and even the grandkids would be set. They don't blow money. The biggest thing they bought was this house and live together to save money.

I'm guessing Dave didn't do all that. He's up there in age, so he had to have known he'd be forced to retire soon anyway.

I don't realize how close he's gotten, because my brain goes down a path it shouldn't have been. The next thing I know he grabs my wrist in a hold so tight I cry out in pain.

"So, here's how it's going to be. You break up with your little boy toy here and marry me, or we will destroy the band and them. We have enough dirt on them to send them to federal prison for a long time." He laughs.

"You have nothing on them! They have done nothing!" I yell and start to fight to get out of his hold. Big mistake, because he tightens his grip, making the tears I was holding back start to fall.

"Doesn't matter what they did or didn't do, there's enough evidence to put them away. It's great to know the right people."

In other words, they manufactured enough evidence. My mind starts racing. They have always put me first and protected me. Now, it's my turn to protect them. I can do this.

I guess, I was quiet for too long, because he jerks my wrist and slams me against his body. The pain shooting up my arm has me worried it might be broken, and when he twists my wrist, it hurts so badly, I start crying. I try to turn away from him, because his breath is putrid and is making me sick.

"You have one week. Break up with him and make it believable. Maybe, tell him he has a small dick, something good that will hurt. Pack your shit and move out."

He places a key into my other hand, along with a card that has an address on it.

"Your new apartment, sweetheart." He leans in and kisses my cheek, before turning and leaving.

The moment the door closes, I collapse on to the floor crying. How could I be so stupid? He pursued me, and I fell for it. Now, look where I am. I don't dare try to call the guys, my luck he has my phone tapped. I don't know what to do, but I know crying on the floor isn't it. If the guys see me like this, they will know something is wrong, so I need to get moving. Besides, crying on the floor won't get anything done.

I move my wrist, and it doesn't seem broken, but it hurts like hell. I can focus on this. One task at a time. I head up to my room and find the wrist brace I use, when I'm on the computer for long periods of time. The guys won't question it if it's this one. I switch out of Dallas's shirt and put on one of my sweatshirts. The need to cover the most skin overwhelms me.

I grab a suitcase and start packing, deciding what to take with me, so he thinks I really packed, but making sure what I take is stuff I don't care if I never see again, because that might happen. I will set his place and him on fire, before I marry him, and I won't let the guys go to jail. They do too much good with the music, the band, and the charities.

I will figure this out. But for now, I need to buy us all some time and let him think I'm doing as I'm told. Then, I need to figure out how to end it with Dallas that will do the least amount of damage, but still be enough that he will believe me.

As I'm packing, I hear a door downstairs slam and I freeze. Is he back? He said to go to the apartment, and he can't expect me to have packed that fast! What could he want? Can I get out my window and run safely, before he finds me?

I turn to lock my door, but my whole world crashes, when I hear it.

"Austin!" And then, the pounding footsteps.

CHAPTER 34

Dallas

The second I get home, I hit the ground running. I run in, slamming the door behind me. "Austin!" I yell but hear nothing in return. I run through the living room, and then up to the stairs, my panic rising.

"Austin! Answer me!" I yell again and then listen, before heading upstairs.

Just as I get to the top of the stairs, I hear her door close, so I beeline for her room. I jiggle the door to find it locked. What the hell is going on?

"Open up, Austin, or I will break this door down, so help me God!" I yell.

There's some shuffling from the other side, and finally, she opens the door. She looks a mess, but she's safe as I pull her into my arms and just hold her. She's secure and is here in my arms. Everything else I can deal with. When my heart finally calms down, I notice the state of her room.

Her closet is open, lights on, and it's a mess. There are bags on her bed. With clothes strewn around them. She's packing.

I pull back from her and hold her at arm's length to get a good look at her. She's been crying, and she's in the oversized clothes she wears to comfort her, when something is wrong. Even though, she looks beautiful to me, I know something is wrong.

"What's going on?" I ask her.

She shakes her head and pulls away, walking to her bed and turning her back to me.

"I can't do this anymore." She says, but she refuses to look at me.

Who knew those five little words could break my heart? But I refuse to accept it. Something else is going on here. I'll get to the bottom of it and won't let her push me away.

"What the fuck happened?" I ask, trying to keep my emotions under control and failing. I walk towards the bed and notice she's crying and my heart shatters.

Something isn't adding up. Something is very, very wrong.

I pull out my phone and text Landon.

Me: Did you talk to Austin?

Landon: No. Tell me she's OK!

Me: Physically, yes. But she's really upset and won't talk to me.

Landon: Well, she'll be fine. Give her some time.

Me: No, she's so upset she's packing, saying she can't do this anymore.

Landon: Do what?

Me: She won't say. Maybe us? Maybe living here?

Landon: I'm twenty minutes out. Keep her there, until I get home.

Me: Will do.

I sigh and run my hand through my hair.

"Baby girl, talk to me. Tell me what happened." I say in a soft tone, hoping she will open up to me.

She cries harder and covers her face with her hands, and that's when I notice the wrist brace she wears, when she works on the computer. I gently take her hands in mine, and she winces in pain. Her wrist was fine, when I left this morning.

I start to remove the wrist brace, and she tries to pull her hand away, but I hold her hand above her wrist a little tighter. When the brace comes off, and I see the bruises, my throat closes up. They're dark purple and nasty looking.

Someone did this to her. Someone put their hands on my girl and hurt her, and I wasn't here to stop it, because we mixed up the dates.

"Baby girl," I say, but get choked up, before I can say anything else.

I keep eye contact with her, as I remove her sweatshirt, so she's in just the tank top she wore under it, and I see some scratches and light bruises up her arm.

"Who did this?" I ask, keeping my voice gentle, but my insides are raging. Whoever did this to her is going to suffer.

When she doesn't answer, I say the first thing that comes to mind and hope it's not true.

"Was it Branden?" I ask, in a whisper praying I'm wrong. But he's in the forefront of my mind after talking to the private investigator earlier.

She nods, then bursts out crying again. "Oh, God." She says, as I pull her into me and hold her.

I swear when I get my hands on that little asshole. I want to kill him, but the only thing stopping me from doing so is this girl in my arms. Killing him will take me away from her, and I can't have that.

I grab my phone and call Landon and get him on speakerphone.

"Hey, what's wrong?" He says.

"Austin has a nasty bruise on her arm and some scratches on her arm. She admitted Branden hurt her." I tell him.

"Motherfucker. I'm going to kill him myself!" Landon lashes out.

"Austin, baby, tell us what happened. Please." I keep my voice soft and coaxing. I can tell the last thing she needs is me upset, too. "We can't help if you don't tell us."

She takes a moment to get herself under control, before she speaks.

"I was just relaxing, when you guys left. I took a bath, watched some TV, and then, I heard the kitchen door. Thinking it was one of you, I went to start lunch, but it was Branden. He wasn't himself." She pauses.

"I think it was drugs. He was dirty, wrinkled clothes, red eyes, and acting off. Like some of the guys on tour who would party all night, before you guys put the drug ban in place. He's Dave's son, did you know that?" She asks.

She tosses that in there, like it's no big deal.

"We just found out today from the private investigator," I tell her.

"Well, he was going on and on about how, when Dave doesn't manage you guys, because the label is forcing him to retire all the money he'll lose, when all this happens. Then, he grabbed me."

I tense up. The thought of his hands on her kills me. I have to remind myself she's here, she's safe, and she's in my arms.

"Then, he demanded I break up with Dallas. He knew we were together. How I don't know. I swear Landon, you're the only one who knows. He said I was to marry him, or he'd send you two to jail for a long time with some evidence he has. From the sound of it, it's fake, but I don't know. He gave me one week. He handed me a key for an apartment." She says, and then buries her head in my chest.

"Where is this key?" I ask her.

"Over there on my nightstand, along with the card with the address."

She doesn't move, but I turn my head and see a sliver house

key, sitting on top of a white card with an address scribbled on it just like she said.

"Of course, this is all for the money," Landon says and sighs. "Okay, we're pressing charges. Austin please don't fight me on this. We'll get our lawyers on it. We have the best ones there are, and there's nothing in our pasts that can send us to jail. But he will be going. I need you to trust us."

"Okay." She whispers.

"I'm upping security. Today, was our mistake. We both thought the other was with you. The three of us will have body-guards around the clock, and security around the house. That's the way we can deal with this. I know you hate not having alone time, Austin, but this isn't forever just until he's behind bars, okay?"

"After today, I'm okay to never be alone again." She sniffles, and I hold her tighter, but smile a little. I know she doesn't mean that in the long run, but right now, I will give her that and make sure she's with me as much as possible.

"We'll talk more, when I get home," Landon says.

"Drive safe," I say, before hanging up.

Austin and I just stand there with our arms around each other. Neither of us moving or talking. Soaking in what we might have lost today. Her mind is racing as much as mine is, so I let her think as I hold her. I will stay here like this, as long as she needs me.

Finally, I sigh, and then do the one thing that will calm me. I pick up her bags and carry them to my room and start unpacking them. I made room in the closet and dresser the other day, but I will get Landon to help me move her dresser in here, too. There's plenty of room for her stuff, and after this, there won't be a single night where she's not in my arms, so it's time to make it official.

She can keep stuff in her room. Turn it into a reading nook or whatever she wants, but she won't be sleeping there anymore.

I turn, and she's standing in the doorway, watching me with a look of love on her face. In this moment, all the day's horror from her ex is forgotten. It's me showing her that I'm taking a stand, and that she isn't pushing me away.

"You are mine, baby girl. Always. I will fix this." Taking her hands in mine, I give her a soft, comforting kiss. "I love you so much."

"I love you too, Dallas. I never was going to marry him. I was just trying to buy us some time, until I came up with a plan."

"That's for us to do; the private investigator gave us a few leads that will help us. We'll talk, when Landon gets here." I pull her into my arms.

When the door closes downstairs, she stiffens up again. This time I'm here for her and nothing is going to happen.

CHAPTER 35

Austin

Hearing the door close downstairs, makes my heart race, even though I'm in Dallas's arms.

"Guys, it's me!" Landon calls up the stairs, and I relax.

"I got you, baby. I promise you'll be safe always. Let's go talk to him."

I nod, and he ducks into my room to grab my sweatshirt, because he knows I will want to put it back on, once Landon sees my arm.

He takes my good hand, and we walk downstairs hand-in-hand. We find Landon in the living room, and he jumps up as soon as we enter. His eyes zero in on my wrist.

"Christ. I want to take you in and have it looked at." He says, as he pulls out his phone.

"Let me get some pictures." He says and starts snapping photos of my wrist and arm from all angles.

The whole thing makes me uncomfortable, but Dallas holds my eyes the whole time, letting me know without words that he's here for me.

This is why I don't notice Landon moving to touch my wrist, and I flinch away in pain, which sets both guys on edge.

"It's not broken," I tell him and show them I can move it, but it's swollen already.

"Let me get some ice," Dallas says and heads off to the kitchen.

This time it's Landon's turn to pull me into a hug. He might be trying to comfort me, but I think this hug is more about comforting himself.

When Dallas walks back into the room, he settles with me on the love seat, placing my wrist on his lap and putting the ice on it. Landon sits across from us, watching Dallas but not saying anything.

"I called Mason, when I got off the phone with you. He's meeting with the security team and bringing in a few more guys. They already have some on the grounds, but the rest will be here soon. Once the bodyguards get here, I want to take you to the emergency room and get that looked at."

I just nod, because I know he won't budge on this. I stubbed my toe once, while he was babysitting me, and he rushed me to the emergency room. Mom and Dad laughed at him for weeks over it. The only way he will feel better is when the doctor tells him I'm fine.

"We need to have the security system on the house replaced. Somehow, he knew how to hack it, because I know I set it before I left." Landon continues.

"So, did I." Dallas adds, and they both look at me.

"I didn't touch it. Didn't go outside. I was in the tub, and then here in the living room."

"I don't think Dave ever had access to the house or to the system, but I wouldn't put it past either of them at this point," Dallas says.

"Agreed," Landon says.

"Also..." Dallas hesitates, before he continues, "I'm moving Austin into my room. We talked about it a few weeks ago, and we were going to wait, but after this, well. I know I'll sleep better, and I think she will too, knowing she isn't alone."

My eyes bounce between Landon and Dallas. I'm waiting for my brother to explode and not allow it. I'm waiting for any emotion really, but there isn't any.

"Okay." He nods.

"Okay?" I have to ask and make sure I heard him right.

"I'm trying here, Austin. My main concern is you, and even at night, you shouldn't be alone, especially at night. So, this is the best option." Landon says.

I'm in shock. I expected some yelling or more of what happened, when he found out we were together, but maybe, that will come later, after the buzz of the day wears off.

Landon's phone goes off, and he checks it, and then stands up.

"Mason is here. I'm going to go let him in, and we can go over the new security protocols. Then, we'll get Austin to the hospital," Landon says.

As he walks out of the room, Dallas wraps his arm around me and pulls me closer.

"That went over better than I thought it would." He says.

"You and me both." I agree.

Dallas kisses the top of my head, as Mason and Landon enter the room followed by six other guys and one woman.

They waste no time and get down to business. I guess, we will each have two people assigned to us during the day, when we're out, and then at night, there will be security in both the grounds and house. As in people inside the house at night. Lovely.

Landon and Dallas both insist Mason, who I'm learning is the head of their security team, stay on my detail, and the woman will also be with me to accompany me to places a male cannot, bathrooms, and dressing rooms were a few places he mentioned.

I didn't interject and tell him I had no intentions of really leaving the house, much less going shopping and trying on clothes.

They go over details of where security will be and protocols, if someone gets on the property and a bunch of other things.

Once again for Mason and the security guys, I have to go over in detail what happened with Branden for Mason. He has some questions, while Landon runs upstairs to get the key and the card from my nightstand.

"It's a Nashville address," Mason says, as he plugs the address into his phone.

"It's not in a great part of town and looks to be an apartment complex. I'll dig more into it. My guess is with enough money the landlord will give us anything we want. I've worked with those types of guys before."

They talk about what the private investigator found, and Mason agrees they need to look into their books. He asks for a copy of the file and any info they find on Dave. I guess Landon texted all this new info to the PI as well.

"Okay, let's get her to the ER, and I'll call a detective buddy of mine, so he can come down and get a statement. I'm sorry, Austin, but you'll probably be repeating the story several more times, before the day is over." Mason says.

"Super," I say sarcastically.

"Wait. Branden knew when I was alone, which means he's been watching not only me, but this place. He's going to know something is up the moment we step outside. Hell, he might have known the moment you guys showed up." I say.

"Good. Best case he comes at us, and we can get him behind bars tonight. My guess is he's going to stay to the shadows and try to get you alone again, which we won't let happen. Let's get you checked out, talk to the police, and we'll work on the next steps."

I nod, and then there's a flurry of activity. Both Dallas and Landon insist on coming with me to the Emergency Room. That means there will also be six bodyguards following us. Oh, what fun we will have.

Mason drives us with another guy, and the rest of them follow in another SUV. Dallas sits beside me and keeps the ice on my wrist. Every so often, he turns his head and plants kisses at my temple. While It's a simple gesture, it comforts me.

Once we get to the hospital, we're whisked right to a private room. They don't even blink at the bodyguards. I guess one of them called ahead, and this being Nashville with loads of musicians, it's pretty normal.

After I talk with the nurses, the doctor comes in and agrees with me that it's probably not broken, but he still wants to get an X-ray done to be sure.

Mason and Dallas go with me to get the X-ray and stand behind a wall the entire time with their eyes on me.

When we get back, the detective Mason mentioned is waiting on me, and I have to tell the whole story over again. This time starting from when I met Branden, his proposal, me leaving, running into Dave at the label, and all of it. It's exhausting.

As we wait for the doctor to come back in, I guess I drift off. I wake up, and I'm sleeping on Dallas's chest, who is on the hospital bed. Landon is in a chair next to us, and the six bodyguards are on the couch and standing around the room.

When the doctor walks in, he just shakes his head at everyone, before focusing on me.

"No broken bones; no fracture. Just a sprain with lots of swelling. I'm going to have a nurse come in and wrap it, but keep ice on it, and take some ibuprofen for the swelling." Dallas and Landon are both hanging on the doctor's every word, but I just want to go back to sleep.

A different nurse comes in to wrap my arm. She's older, about the age my mom would be, if she was still alive.

"Where's the other nurse?" Dallas asks.

The nurse chuckles.

"She fangirled a little too hard and got reassigned." She says.

"On the way out, we'll sign autographs, but just want to make sure she gets taken care of first," Dallas says.

"The rest of the staff will appreciate it."

"Also, remind them of the HIPPA laws, and they apply to us being here. We will follow up on anyone who leaks anything regarding Austin's visit." Landon says.

"Oh, rest assured, they have already been given that lecture twice, since you've been here. Once from the head ER doctor, and a second time from the head of the hospital that happened to still be here. That's why I got sent in. The only people I'd fangirl over are dead."

"Thank you," I mumble. She starts on my wrist that's resting on Dallas's chest. He refuses to move, and I don't have the energy to sit up, so she just uses Dallas, like a counter to wrap me up.

"Out of curiosity, who would you fangirl over?" Dallas asks her, before she leaves.

"Elvis and Johnny Cash." She smiles and turns to leave.

"Elvis got all the girls." My brother jokes.

"Wake me, when we get home," I mumble, closing my eyes again.

"Go to sleep, baby girl. I got you." Dallas says.

I don't remember getting home, just that Dallas wakes me up to feed me and get me some medicine, before taking me up to bed, so I can go back to sleep.

CHAPTER 36

Dallas

It's been four days, since Branden attacked Austin. There hasn't been a peep from Branden or Dave. That's fine by me. It gave us plenty of time to make our plans. Austin has spent a lot of time relaxing and reading, since she can't do much else with her wrist. This has allowed us plenty of research and planning.

Today, is the first time I will be away from her, since that day. Landon is also with me, so it's the first time she will be home alone. She has her bodyguards and a hand full of other security with her, but she still didn't want me to leave. I didn't want to leave her either, but this meeting has to happen today.

We were able to finally get a meeting with Dave on the threat of contract violation. That got his attention and got us a meeting.

We walk into the label, and Deanna greets us with a huge smile.

"Hey! I wanted to ask if Austin was okay. She's been going through books like crazy the past few days, but she says she's fine and changes the subject." She asks.

I step up to her desk. "She's okay just hurt her wrist, so she can't get much work done. If you have time this weekend, we'd love to have you stop by." I lower my voice. "We'd like to talk to you but, not here." I look towards the office, so she understands.

She nods. "I'll stop by this weekend to check on Austin."

I grab a card and scribble our address on the back, before Dave enters the reception area. It takes everything in me to not lunge and beat him to a bloody pulp. Landon has told me several times that won't help matters, but I told him give me a sign and I'd make it happen.

We follow him back to his office, and he closes the door behind us. As soon as we're seated, he speaks first.

"I'd like you to drop the charges against my son."

"He attacked Austin. In our home." Landon says.

We agreed he'd do most of the talking, because he's the more levelheaded one and doesn't anger as quickly as I do.

"He needs help, and I can't get him that help with a warrant out for his arrest," Dave argues.

"Oh, he needs help all right, but he sang a very different song, when he attacked Austin," Landon says with a smirk.

"He needs help, he isn't stable," Dave says, and this is where I've had enough.

"Let's cut the bullshit. We aren't dropping the charges. He attacked Austin as a way to get back at us for dropping you. It all adds up, because when you saw her here at the office, your son mysteriously shows up at the house. A house we never gave him the address, too. He sought her out, why? To marry her, and, then use her as blackmail for us?"

Dave's face goes tomato red, and I know his cool composure is gone. Good. This is what I wanted, the angrier he gets the more he will let slip.

"What did you expect? You're trying to end me. As soon as you drop me, the label wants me to retire. They won't put me on another band. Do you know how much of a pay cut that is for me?"

"Oh yes, we do, because we had someone go over our books." Landon full on smiles this time.

Dave's face pales, but he tries to regain his composure.

"What?"

"Yeah, once we found out Branden, well Jimmy, was your son we took a closer look at you. You're paying three employees who don't exist from our record earnings. The money is going to accounts, and then gets filtered and lands in your offshore account. How convenient. Offshore accounts that have hundreds of millions of dollars by the way. You're not hurting for money; you're just mad the gravy train has dried up. So, you set all this up, didn't you?" Landon says.

"You guys would be nothing without me. I lost my wife, and my son turned to drugs, because you took up all my time making you into stars. You weren't easy to deal with in the beginning, and the pay was horrible."

"What I don't get is your legit pay is still several million a year. Are you really that greedy?" I ask.

He grunts. "I do all the work. All you two do is sing. Why should you get all the money? And no, I didn't set all this up, Jimmy did, but it made sense, so I went along with it. Got him addresses and info."

"Great, well we're done. You are released of your job as of today." Landon says.

"Like hell, I am. You still have another year on your contract!" Dave yells.

This time it's me who smirks. "Hard to do your job from a jail cell."

We walk out of his office and right to the studio big-wigs, who have been waiting in a conference room for us. We close the door and sit down.

"So, what's this about that we all had to rearrange our schedules?" Milton asks. He is the owner of the label, and while his tone is nice, I know he was none too happy, when we called. He knows this is serious, because we have only ever called one other meeting with him, and it was when we did the drug ban on our tours.

Landon pulls out the tape recorder and sets it on the table, as everyone eyes it.

"We just had a meeting with Dave that we wanted to inform you about, before we go to the police and the media gets wind of it," I say, and everyone sits up straight. They never like even the slightest hint of a scandal.

Landon starts, "As you know, we have been upfront and honest with you about wanting to go off on our own and turn around and help the next generation."

All the heads around the table nod.

"Apparently, Dave didn't like that. His son sought out Austin in Portland and started trying to date her. When he proposed after three months of seeing each other, she left and came home. That was right before the last tour." I tell them.

Landon goes on to tell them about the run-in with Dave and Austin after the tour, his son showing up at our house multiple times, him attacking Austin, and down to the meeting we just had. Then, he plays the recording of the meeting.

Pens are flying across paper, as everything starts to come to light, along with many angry and worried faces.

Once the recording is finished, Landon leans forward in his chair.

"We want out of our contract with you and Dave as of today. This evidence and everything we've learned we'll be taking to the police, and we're pressing full charges against Dave and his son. Any money recouped will go to charity. You let us out of our contract, and we'll spin this story about how helpful you were, once it came out and we'll sing your praises. You don't? We will assume you were involved, and you'll be the next investigated." Landon says and sits back.

We both wait, and finally, Milton looks back at us.

"Will you gentleman give us a moment to talk? You can wait in my office. Also, I had our security detain Dave. He was trying to make a run for it." He says.

That explains what he was doing on his phone, as we talked.

We head to his office and collapse into his leather chairs.

"Think this office is bugged?" I ask.

"Wouldn't surprise me, if they are listening to us now. Text Austin and check on her, please." Landon says.

I pull out my phone and shoot her a text.

Me: Hey, baby girl. How's your book?

Austin: Good. Just finished it and started a new one.

Me: You doing okay?

Austin: Yes, I'm good. Hurry home.

Me: I'm trying. I did invite Deanna to stop by this weekend. Give you time to talk books and have girl time.

Austin: Thank you. I love you.

Me: Love you, too.

"She's fine just reading. I told her about inviting Deanna over, and she's excited." I tell Landon.

"Good. I like she found someone who shares her interest in books," Landon says.

"Me too." I agree.

"Boys, we're ready for you." One of the ladies who were in the conference room earlier peeks her head in. I think she's a secretary, but I can't remember her name.

We follow her back into the conference room and take our seats. Since they didn't talk long, I hope it's good news.

"Gentleman." Milton starts. "I will let you in on a little secret. We had always planned to let you out of your contract early. Yes, we hate to lose you as clients, but I love what you're doing to help the next generation. But we have a few stipulations, and if you agree, I can send you home with a contract to have your lawyers look over."

"What are they?" I ask.

"The biggest one is we ask that you don't poach any of our clients. If they choose to leave us and go to you it's one thing, but what we don't want is you pursuing them."

I look over at Landon, and he looks at me and nods.

"We agree to that. We want new talent we can help grow, and not old ones who need their handheld," I say.

That earns a few laughs around the room.

"That describes some of our clients perfectly." Milton says.

"But we ask the same of you in return." I say.

"Agreed. Next, we'd like you to consider working with us." Milton says.

"What do you mean?" Landon asks.

"Well, you're a huge name and have many fans that will follow the people you sign strictly, because you signed them. Whereas we have a huge marketing team and contacts. We'd like to be a sister company. You'd be your own company, and do your own things, but we'd like to work with you on marketing. Honestly, we don't want to lose your band completely. We work together. We promote your artists, and you help promote ours."

I look at him and shrug and mouth the word 'drugs'. He gets what I mean instantly.

"We'd be up to talking about it with one condition. Any artists we promote have to be drug free. We made that rule for our band and roadies and will make it for our artists. Anyone we promote must follow the same rules." Landon says.

Milton smirks.

"Done, and I'll let you in on something that isn't widely known yet. After all, the support you guys got about banning drugs from the tour; we started working it into all our contracts as well. As of the beginning of the year, all of our artists have a no drug clause in their contracts. As does everyone who works on their tours, and those here in the office as well." Milton says.

I'm a bit shocked if I'm honest. I've seen some managers with other labels feed their client's drugs to get them on stage in order to manipulate them. Labels have turned a blind eye for years.

Milton takes advantage of our silence.

"Here are the contracts we drew up. They're fairly simple. No poaching for either of us, no drugs, different promotions, and ways to work together, and the legalities of parting ways. Take a look at it and read over it. Either way, we'll let you out of your contract, as of today." Milton says.

We stand up, and everyone shakes hands. Milton hangs back, and when it's just the three of us in the room, he turns to us.

"You two remind me of me and my partner, when we first started. We were never a band though." Milton says.

His partner died of cancer a few years back, and he had taken over the main operations of the label.

"With that being said, I'd like to be a mentor to you guys. Be a sounding board, answer questions, and help get you off the ground." He says.

"Why?" I ask.

"Honestly, because it's what Charlie would have done." He says, speaking of his partner. "He always loved your band, as a fan, and as your label, he was proud of you taking the stand on drugs. I think that will help revolutionize the music industry and help clean it up. I want to be a part of that."

"We'd like that," Landon says.

We say goodbye and head out to the car. Our next stop is the police station, and then on the way home, we both do nothing but read the contracts in our hands.

CHAPTER 37

Austin

This is the first time I've been alone, since Branden attacked me. Okay, let's face it, I'm not alone, alone. Mason is here, along with the woman who doesn't talk to me. There are also two other guys in the house who don't talk to me. There are at least six outside that I have seen. The only one who talks to me is Mason. He said he's my point of contact. So damn formal.

Today, is my first day alone without one of the guys here. I feel safest with Dallas, but Landon runs a super close second. Without one of them here, I'm a bit jumpy. Every time I see movement from the corner of my eye, I spin around. Every time, it's been Mason. I try to shake it off, but for some reason, I just can't.

So, I've started pacing the living room. Mason has his back to the wall with his arms crossed watching me, and another guy is standing by the back room. This room is large, I could probably run laps around it for a decent exercise, but the pacing is enough right now.

"Austin, why don't you try to watch some TV?" Mason says.

I shake my head.

"Okay, why don't we do some baking? Dallas is always talking about much he loves your cookies." He says.

"I'd probably burn them all," I say.

"Well, you're making the guys nervous." He says.

This makes me stop in my tracks, and I look at the guy by the back door and see another one in the doorway that leads to the small hallway to the kitchen.

"Sorry." I sigh and try to slow down my pacing, until a door closes, and I full on panic. I run right to Mason, who puts me between the wall and him.

"It's okay. It was just one of my guys coming in from doing a garage sweep," Mason says.

I don't move right away, and finally, he sighs.

"If you're going to pace, let's at least go do it in the upstairs hallway and give these guys a break, yeah?"

"Okay." I nod. He follows me upstairs, and I start to pace not just the side of the hallway where my old room is along with Landon's and mine and Dallas's room. But also, down the guest side and make the 'L' turn to the game room and the loft. Mason follows me the whole way.

They still haven't found Branden or Jimmy, whatever his name is. The cops have a warrant out for his arrest, because on top of attacking me, he missed several probation check-ins and being back on drugs is a violation of his parole.

I know the cops are searching for him, and I know Dallas and Landon are working with Mason, too. One night, I heard them talking to Mason, who had hired on a bunch of extra men to start their own search for Branden.

I asked Dallas about it that night, and he told me the guys are all ex-military and happy to help find someone, who attacked a woman. Dallas said this is also a trial run for security for their label and their tours. Mason is going to be working with their clients too, not just as their personal security.

That made me feel a bit better. Mason is good at what he does, and I know they trust him, because they ask him to watch over me. Dallas also told me once everything is over with Branden, I will be assigned a new guard, because Mason will take on a desk job, managing the security team.

That makes me sad, because I really like and trust Mason, but I know this is a huge promotion for him, so I'm happy for him, too. It will allow him to be home more with his wife.

After several passes of the long hallway, Mason finally speaks.

"Dallas and Landon's car is at the gate." He says.

I sigh and start to feel better. "Thank you."

Making my way downstairs, I enter the kitchen, as soon as they do. And I don't stop, until I'm in Dallas's arms, and finally feel safe and calm again. Things are okay. I won't let go of him, and he just chuckles and carries me into the living room, collapsing on the couch with me in his arms. Landon follows us and kicks his feet up on the coffee table.

"It's over, baby girl," Dallas says, as he rubs my back.

"What do you mean?" I ask him.

"We had a meeting at the label today as you know, but we kept some stuff from you, because we didn't want to worry you," Dallas says.

"It didn't work. She was a nervous wreck, jumpy and pacing, and freaked at the sound of a door closing," Mason interjects, sitting at the edge of the love seat.

"Thanks," I mumble and snuggle into Dallas even more.

The guys chuckle, before getting back to business.

"So first, we finally were able to get a meeting with Dave. As expected, he just kept asking us to drop the charges. He was all sweet at first, saying Branden couldn't get the help he needed in jail and all that, which we know isn't his motivation. Then, we revealed how we knew he was stealing money and things got ugly. He admitted to it, and of course, I was recording it all, though he didn't know that." Landon says.

"So, after that, we met with the label execs and laid out what Dave has been doing, the stolen money, and all about his son. We gave them two options. Let us out of our contracts now, and we'll spin this in a positive light for them, or if they don't, we will assume they were working with Dave." Dallas says.

"How did they take that?" Mason asks.

"Better than we thought. They said they had planned to let us out of our contract early anyway, and they want to work with us on our label, help with tour promotions, and still use our name. We have contracts to look over. Then, after the meeting, Milton shocked us both and offered to be our mentor. So, all in all, it was good." Dallas says.

"After that, we went to the police station with the recording. Milton had his security hold Dave, so he was easy to arrest, and he turned Jimmy in to try to save his own ass. A few minutes ago, we got a call saying they picked Branden up, too." Landon says.

"So, it's over? They're in jail?" I ask, hesitantly.

"Yes, and will be for a very long time," Dallas says.

I sag in relief, and even though I'm happy, I start crying. Crying in relief, it's all over and letting out all the emotions from the last few days. So many emotions.

"Come on, baby girl. Let me take you upstairs. I just want to hold you." Dallas says, and he picks me up in his arms.

All I can do is nod, as I let him take control. He carries me upstairs like it's nothing and lays me in our bed. The bed we have been sharing every night, since he moved my stuff in. This room already feels like home. When I wouldn't change anything, Dallas did. He added stuff from my room and mixed it in with his stuff.

I grab his hand and pull him into bed with me.

"Lay with me," I say to him. "I hated you being gone today. I feel so safe in your arms."

With this, he wraps his arms around me and pulls me to lie on his chest.

"I will always protect you. Though, I hated being away from you today too, but it had to be done, to put an end to this. I wasn't expecting him to turn on his son the way he did. I thought we'd still be hunting him down, but I'm so happy he's behind bars, too. They can't hurt you anymore, and it got us out of our contract, so I'd say it's a win."

"You guys excited to start your label? Are you ready to start early? I know you weren't planning to for another year. This won't set you back, will it?"

"Calm down, baby girl. We'll be just fine. It will still take some time, because we want to do this right, but we'll be okay. This also means there won't be a final tour, so I'll be home. No more going on the road for a while." Dallas says.

"Will you ever tour again?" I ask him. I can't imagine *Highway 55* never touring again.

"We will. Landon and I have been tossing around the idea of being part of the first tour, as we bring the people we sign on. We'd draw a crowd, and it'll be a good way to get them out there. Maybe, have each person do a song with us that would be on their albums. We know our name will sell and to get them off the ground we aren't afraid to use our names. But because of that, we will be extra selective of those first few artists."

"Oh, you won't join some music competition show and just take the winners?" I joke.

"No, we won't be part of those horrible reality shows you watch. Those guys get a huge fan base, even if they don't win. We want undiscovered talent. We've been watching videos online and pouring over the demos people send us. There are at least seven possibilities, and I'm sure there will be more. We'll bring them in and audition them to see who can cut it."

I love seeing Dallas like this. He's in his element, and that calms me in a way I didn't know I needed tonight. He must sense me getting tired, because he starts running his hand through my hair.

"Get some rest, baby girl. I'm right here, and we aren't leaving again tonight."

That soft touch of his hand in my hair makes the whole world right. Our next battle is working things out with Landon, but right here, right now, everything is perfect.

CHAPTER 38

Dallas

I lay there with Austin, as she falls asleep. It's been a long day, but the texts we got from Mason said she was stressing herself out, while we were gone. She was on edge, and when we got the call that Branden or Jimmy was picked up and in custody, Landon and I both breathed a sigh of relief.

Once I'm sure she's asleep, I gently move off the bed, making sure she doesn't wake up. When I see she's sleeping soundly, I make my way downstairs. I need to talk to Landon, and I want to do it without her hearing. I want to make things good with us, before she wakes up.

I find him in the kitchen with a beer in one hand and his phone in the other.

"Now that all this is over, we need to talk, and I want to do this, while Austin is asleep. I'd like to have this settled, when she gets up, so it's one less thing she has to worry about. She's been through enough." I say.

"I agree. May I talk first?" Landon asks.

"Okay." I agree and sit down.

"I've been watching you two for the last few weeks. I've seen how you are with her, and how she is with you. Something I should have noticed years ago. Maybe, I knew that and chose to ignore it, I don't know. When all this happened, you took care of her almost without thinking. Your first thought was her, always her." He pauses and shakes his head.

"You did what I would have done to protect her, but she takes care of you, too. She calms you, and I've seen this change in you I can't put into words. She makes you a better person, and you do the same to her. Yeah, I was upset before, but I think I let that cloud my vision, when it comes to not just you, but her, too."

This shocks me. He's right. I don't think twice, when it comes to her. I've known her so long I know what she needs, and I just do it. I don't think I make her a better person, but I know she makes me a better man. She makes me want to be better for her.

I open my mouth to say something, but he holds up his hand, so I nod and let him speak.

"I have spent a few nights thinking, and I always kept coming back to one thing. I trust you with my life. Why wouldn't I trust you with Austin? The thing is, I do trust you with her. That doesn't mean I like the idea, but I don't think I could trust any-one else with her the way I trust you. I don't think anyone else would take care of her like you."

"Or love her like I do," I state, as I look him in the eye.

We stare at each other for a minute, before he nods.

"You really trust me with her?" I ask, having to make sure.

"Yes, and I'm sorry about how I reacted. I knew you guys liked each other back in school. I just thought it was silly teenage crushes, and that you would outgrow them. I never imagined it was big enough to lead to this. Then, I was dealing with my own stuff, when Opal turned me down, and I wasn't in a good place. I let it all cloud my judgment."

"All is forgiven as long as you make it right with Austin," I tell him. "Everything you told me might make this go over easier," I tell him, as I run my hands over my thighs and sit on the edge of my chair.

"I'd like to ask her to marry me, and I want your blessing to do so," I say. I have no idea how this is going to go.

A week ago, I would have expected a no, but at least, I would have tried. I plan to ask her to marry me no matter what, but I'd like to have Landon on our side. I know she will want him to walk her down the aisle, and I want him to be my best man. Things won't be the same, if he isn't behind us.

Landon sits back and crosses his arms. There's no emotion on his face, so I let him work through whatever he has to, before giving me an answer.

"You don't think you're moving a bit fast?" He asks in a flat voice.

"Some might think so, but we've known each other as long as you and I have. It's always been her, Landon. It will always be her. If she turns me down, it doesn't mean I'm going to stop asking, because she's it for me."

Landon turns his head and looks out the window. Then without a word, he gets up and walks out of the room. I'm in shock, I at least expected him to say something.

Looking to the security guy in the corner of the room, his eyes are wide, like he isn't sure what to do either. Then, I decide I'm going to give him a piece of my mind, and at least, let him know I plan to ask her anyway.

I head upstairs and to his room, where I assume he went. His door is open, and his back is to me, as he faces his dresser. Before I can even say a word, he starts speaking.

"My parents would always tell us the story of how they met and fell in love. My dad made a grand gesture and bought mom her dream house. He proposed there surrounded by candles and rose petals. He gave her this ring." He says and turns to face me with a ring in his hand. "When planning the funeral, I debated whether to bury my parents with their rings or to save them."

"I remember," I say, choked up. "You never said what you decided."

"I decided to save them. Mom's set for Austin, and Dad's ring for me. If you're going to ask her, it should be with this ring. Austin always loved it growing up. There's no one else I'd trust her with, and no one else I'd rather she spends her life with. I already consider you family, so I guess it's time we make it legal." He holds up a ring box with his mom's wedding set.

He has tears in his eyes, but somehow, he manages to keep his voice level. Losing the battle, tears fall down my face. I take the ring from his hand and stare at it. I remember it from when we were kids. His mom never took it off, and it caught my eye a few times. It's a unique ring, and I know Austin loves it.

The vintage setting almost looks like a rose, which was her mom's favorite flower and is also Austin's. I think she likes it, because it reminds her of her mom. I'll plant her a whole rose garden if she wants.

"I have a plan, but I need your help." I tell him, once I get my emotions back under control.

He nods, "Let's head back downstairs."

We spend some time going over my plan, and I fill him in on what I've been doing the past few weeks with every spare moment I've had. We make notes and do some online research. This needs to be a grand gesture to show her I'm all in. Landon is excited to help, and it feels great to be back on the same page again.

Once our plans are in place, there's just one more thing to take care of.

"We're keeping security on the three of us, right?" I ask.

"Yes." He says.

"You know this means I'm paying for Austin's, right?"

He smirks. "I know. It's going to be hard letting her go and letting someone else take care of her, so just go easy on me, okay? Let me get used to it, before you have any ideas of turning me into an uncle." He gives a fake shiver, and I laugh.

God, it feels good to laugh.

We finish up, and I go to the kitchen, making Austin and me

a sandwich and grab some chips and water and head upstairs. I know she's tired, but I want to make sure she eats, too.

She starts to stir as soon as I enter our room and turns to look at me.

"You need to eat, baby. Then, I thought we could watch a movie in here and just cuddle." I suggest.

She nods, as she sits up in bed. I hand her a plate, and she digs in.

"I didn't realize how hungry I was. Thank you, Dallas." She says, after her first bite.

I lean over and kiss the side of her head and dig into my sandwich, too.

We eat in silence for a bit, before I speak again.

"Your brother wants to take you out for lunch tomorrow. We talked, and I think he wants to speak with you. I want you two to work things out." I tell her.

She nods. "Okay."

"Save your dinner plans for me, though. I plan to take you out, show you off, and tell the world you're mine with a fried chicken dinner at the diner and a movie."

She laughs. "That sounds perfect."

It does sound perfect. This life with her is perfect.

CHAPTER 39

Austin

Today, Landon asked me where I wanted to go to lunch; he said anywhere I wanted the only condition was that I was to wear a dress and look nice for him. He has something up his sleeve, but I will go along with it. I picked my favorite deli, something light, since Dallas has something planned tonight.

I dress in one of my favorite maxi dresses. With sleeves to my elbows, a tight fitted top and flowy from the waist down, it's all one color, a grayish baby blue.

It's comfortable, just enough to stay cool in the Nashville heat, and dressy enough for whatever my brother has planned. I pair it with my favorite sandals and step out of the bathroom to find Dallas sitting on the bed.

"Think this will satisfy my brother?" I ask him.

Slowly, he eyes me from head to foot and back again with a hungry look in his eyes.

"Stop looking at me like that, or I won't make it to lunch with my brother." I tease him.

"Keep that dress on. I want to peel it off you later tonight." He growls.

"Mental note to buy it in every color, check." I laugh, though I'm not joking.

"Have a good lunch, baby." He says, as he gets off the bed and wraps his arms around me.

With a chaste kiss, he steps back and slaps my ass. "Go, before I drag you to bed." He says.

Landon is waiting for me at the bottom of the stairs, and he's dressed in dark jeans and a button up shirt.

"You look very nice. It's a girl, isn't it? Am I meeting her today?" I ask. I never see him get dressed up, unless it's for a girl or a holiday.

"Yes, there's a girl." He smiles, as he opens the door for me. He's already pulled his car around to the front.

"Ha, I knew it!" I say, as he opens the car door for me.

"And her name is Austin, and she's a pain in my ass." He says just before he closes the car door. My jaw drops open.

As he gets in the car, I turn to face him.

"I dressed up for you, don't overthink it, okay. It's just the first time either of us will be out in public, since the whole Branden thing, and it's just starting to hit the news, so I thought we should be dressed in case." He says.

I turn to the back seat to face Mason and the other bodyguard. "He really expects me to believe that?" I joke with them, and they smile.

Mason will be with me for a few more days, until he finds someone to replace him. I think it's more, until Landon and Dallas approve of whoever is to take his place.

The first part of the drive is quiet, before I ask, "Have you read what is being reported about Branden?" I ask.

"I've looked, and we had our PR manager release a statement to get ahead of it and control the story. She's good at what she does and is also coming with us to the new label." He smirks.

That would be my subtle hint to change the topic. So, I do and ask him about the label, and that's all he talks about for the rest of the drive. He talks about who they have gotten to come with them, employee wise. "Deanna will be over this weekend.

She's coming to see you, but we want to ask her to join us at the label. Our contract says no poaching clients but nothing about employees. We don't want to steal anyone, but many have been working with us for so long that they want to follow us over. Deanna coming is just as much for us as it is for you."

"I like her, and it's nice to have a normal friend, even if she gets a little star struck over you and Dallas every now and then. And I feel like I need to put this out there. She's off limits for now. Until we establish our friendship, give us a little time." I tell him.

"She's sweet, but I have my eye on someone else," he says.

"Oh, do tell."

"Oh, look at that, here we are." He says.

We enter and get a table in the back. Every head turns, and I know it's because of the bodyguard. Everyone knows they mean we have to be someone, and they don't want to miss out on who.

"This is why I never wanted a bodyguard. I get why you want me to, but all this attention is not something I like." I tell him, once we're seated.

"I know, but thank you for humoring us."

We place our order, before I turn to him.

"So, why are we here?" I ask.

"First, the not fun stuff. On advice from the private investigator, we had someone look over all the books. He stole upwards of fifty-million dollars from us by paying several people that didn't exist and using some other write offs. His accounts have been frozen, and it will be a bit of a battle, but our lawyer is certain we will get most, if not all that money back."

"Well, that's good news then."

"Yes, but here's the rest. Some of that money is yours, too. Dallas and I want to donate the money to charity, we haven't missed it, but we wanted to talk to you first."

"Of course, I agree to that. I barely touch the money you have deposited into that account for me. I haven't missed what he stole. But fifty-million is life changing to some charities. Any idea where you want to donate them?"

He pulls a list from his pocket and hands it to me.

"We thought ten charities to get five million each." He says.

I recognize several musical charities on here, but the last three I've never heard of.

"What are the last three on here?" I ask him.

"Oakside is a rehabilitation facility for veterans wounded in action. It's a place for them to heal and transition back to the civilian world. Mason was a patient and met his wife there, or they started the relationship there I'm not sure. He also has a friend whose brother was there. The other two are also military related. One helps with prosthetics, and one helps with reconstructive surgery."

"These are all good choices. I agree to all of them."

"Perfect. Now, for what this lunch is really about." He says, as the food gets here.

Once the waitress leaves, he turns to me.

"I was an asshole for the way I acted, when I found out about you and Dallas." He says in a serious tone.

I feel like all the air has been let out of me. I know we have to talk about this, but I guess, I didn't think it would be today.

"I was blindsided, though after thinking about it, I guess I always had an idea of how you two felt about each other back then, but I told myself it was a crush, and it would pass. You'd both grow up and move on. Then, seeing everything on tour, I was fighting it myself, which wasn't fair to either of you."

"Landon."

"No, Austin. This had nothing to do with you or him, this was me. I was being selfish, because I didn't want to lose what we have. I didn't want to lose my two best friends to each other, and I didn't want to be the third wheel. It didn't help that I had just asked out the girl I want, and she turned me down, because of me being a musician and the tour. I was just in a weird place, and that wasn't your fault. If I had the pick of any man in the world for you, I'd pick Dallas."

"Really? You wouldn't pick some prince who would be king one day?" I joke.

"Not a chance. Prince charming isn't good enough for you, but Dallas is. He's always been there for both of us; he's protected you and me more times than I can count."

"He has, but we've been there for him, too. Don't forget that. You'll always be his best friend no matter what happens with us, and that won't change."

"I know it won't, he promised me that, too."

We talk a bit about Dallas and some of our favorite childhood memories of the three of us, until we're finished with dinner.

On the way out, we get stopped by a table of three girls, who recognize Landon.

"Oh my, gosh, it's Landon Anderson!" They squeal, and I just smile. "Can we get your autograph?" The tall blonde one asks.

"Yeah." Then, he turns to me, "You got a pen, A?" He asks.

That's when their eyes flash to me. I figure it will go one of two ways. Either they will recognize me, or they will turn back to Landon and ignore me.

Boy, was I wrong. The shorter brunette turns to Landon.

"Is this your girlfriend?" She asks.

Landon's eyes go wide, as he looks at me, and I start laughing so hard my eyes tear up, and I stop to search in my purse for a pen.

"How the hell is that funny?" He asks, and I shake my head, still laughing.

I look up at the girls who are looking at me like I'm a bit crazy.

"I'm sorry. After the conversation we just had over lunch, and then you asking that question." I laugh. "Yeah, no, I'm his sister."

They relax after that and laugh a little, too. Finally, I pull out a pen and a small notebook I carry with me for situations just like this. Landon signs a few autographs, and I take some pictures of him with the girls.

A few people stop us on our way out, until Mason leans in.

"Boss, we're going to be late." He says.

This is the phrase used to get us out of what will turn into a never ending line of autographs and photos.

There are lots of sighs and a few people snapping photos, as we walk out of the door, before we're back in the car.

Landon looks over at me, and I start laughing again, and he just shakes his head and starts the car.

"One of these days, I'm going to say yes and let them post it, and then the people who know better can tear them apart just for entertainment. Because your real fans will at least recognize me, even if they don't care about me." I tell him. That's why I laughed so hard. I pictured doing that but couldn't stop laughing long enough to pull it off.

I pull down the visor and check my eye makeup, which isn't as bad as I thought.

"Okay, where to next?" I ask.

"One more stop, it's a surprise."

We drive back towards the house but keep driving further outside of town. We pull up to a dirt driveway with an old iron fence that is propped open. There's a for sale sign near the street, but you can't see the house from here.

"Let's go take a look?" He says.

I nod. I love historic homes and getting to peek in them, while they're for sale is one of the benefits of having a famous brother. This used to be one of our favorite pastimes, when I lived with him. He has the bank account to pay for any of them, so we'd set up appointments to go look, and then he'd tip the real estate agent, because we started to feel bad about not buying them.

Yet, it didn't stop us.

It's been a while, since we did this, so I'm excited to check it out. It's not too far from our place and downtown. Who knows? Maybe, I will fall in love with it and buy it for myself with that money I never touch. I've always thought of buying an old southern home, and then fixing it up. *Someday.*

As the house comes into view, I gasp. It's beautiful and like one of those old southern homes used in the movies. White with green shutters and two-story columns, along the front porch. It looks like it's been kept up pretty well, and there are some really old trees in the yard. It's breathtaking.

Parking, I can't take my eyes off the house.

"I thought you'd like it. Let's go check out the inside." He says, and then his phone rings.

"Shoot, I need to answer this. Go on in the front door. It should be open, and I'll be right in."

I don't even argue and just make my way up the path to the front door. It's beautiful. The front porch has plenty of room for several seating areas, and I can see the three of us out here just talking. Maybe Ivy, Dom, and Deanna joining us.

The front door is open like he said, but the inside is the last thing I was expecting. The lights are dim, and there's a trail of rose petals from the entryway, leading into the house.

What the heck is going on? Curiosity wins over, and I slowly follow the rose petals to the back of the house, where there's a wide-open room with views over the back of the property.

The room is surrounded by hundreds of tea light candles all glowing, and in the middle of the room, is Dallas.

CHAPTER 40

Dallas

I have never been so nervous in my life. Today, is the day that can change my whole life, one way or another. Things will never be the same. Knowing I have Landon's support, means everything.

As soon as Landon and Austin left the house, it was time to get my plan into action. Landon helped me load up the car last night, and Mason wanted to help too, so he sent some of his guys ahead to help get started.

Mason has been texting me updates on where they are this whole time, and now that they are almost here, I take one last walk through the house. I make sure the front door is unlocked and get ready to call Landon for his cover story.

I stand back in the shadows and watch Austin take in the house, as she steps out of the car. I knew she'd love this house the moment I saw it. It's everything she's always wanted.

Shooting off the dummy call to Landon, I watch, as she takes a step towards the front walkway. Then, I head back to my spot in what I think will make an amazing family room. Everything is in order, and my security team is standing out of the way in the kitchen. They didn't want to miss this either.

The front door creaks open, and a moment later, it clicks shut. I wait anxiously for her to appear in the doorway to the room, all she has to do is follow the flower petals. When she does, she freezes.

Her eyes take it all in, the hundreds of lighted candles, the rose petals, and me in the center of the room. The surprise is written all over her face, as she tries to figure out what is going on. Though, I don't think she has any idea just yet. She looks so beautiful lit by the candlelight. The house's dark curtains give a feel of sunset, even in the middle of the day.

"What is all this?" Austin whispers.

I hold my hand out to her, "Come here, and I'll tell you." I just need to touch her to ground myself again.

She comes willingly to me and takes my hand with no hesitation. Though, there's a slight shake in her hand from nerves most likely.

"Do you like the house?" I ask her.

"Oh, Dallas, I love this place. It's so beautiful." She runs her eyes over the details of the room. The original woodwork, hardwood floors, and original moldings.

"The house sits on fifty acres. The property is fenced in and has good security, won't be hard to add to it, and tighten it up. It was remodeled about twenty years ago, and they kept as many of the original details as possible, but it needs updating again, and I know you'll love doing it." I tell her.

"Dallas, what do you mean?" She asks, her eyes making their way back to mine.

"I bought this house for us," I admit.

"What?" She says, as it all sinks in. Though, she's shocked, this isn't all I have up my sleeve for her.

My heart racing, I hold both her hands in mine and take a deep breath.

I drop down to one knee and look up at her. Her eyes go even wider, as she looks down at me, but otherwise, there's no hint on her face on which way this will go.

"After all this time, you're still the one I see a future with. The one I want a family with. I want kids, dogs, grandkids, all of it with you, in this house. I already talked to your brother, in fact, he helped me plan this today. Now, I'm asking you. Will you marry me and be my wife? Live this life in this house with me?"

Her eyes have watered over, and she opens her mouth to say something, but closes it and clears her throat.

"Yes, of course, I will." She says, as the tears start to fall down her face.

I open the ring box, and she gasps, when she sees her mom's ring and falls to her knees in front of me.

"Where did you get this?" She asks.

"From me," Landon says behind her. "I knew how much you loved the ring, so I made sure to save it for you."

"I don't remember you doing that." She whispers, as she runs her finger over the ring.

"I almost didn't. At first, I was going to bury them with their rings, but then, I had a flash to a moment just like this, and I knew this was the best way they could be here with us. I saved Dad's ring for me someday, too."

Picking up the ring with shaky hands, I place it on her finger, and it's a perfect fit. Austin is now full on crying, and I don't care. Then, I lean in and kiss her.

My fiancé. My life just agreed to marry me. I hold her close and bury my head in her neck.

"Let's fix your makeup, so we can take some pictures!" Ivy says.

"Ivy!"

"Dallas asked us here to get photos. Your face was perfect, and you're going to love these!" Ivy gushes.

"I got it on video, too," Landon says.

Austin turns back to me. "You thought of everything!"

"I tried. Now, go get ready for some pictures. Then, I'll give you a proper house tour." I tell her.

She shakes her head. "I can't believe you bought this place!"

"Anything for you, baby girl. Always."

Ivy whisks her off to do her hair and makeup, and Landon walks over and gives me a hug.

"You really will be family now, even though, you have been for years. Congrats. That house won't be the same without you two."

"Well, I've been thinking about that," I tell him and turn to walk over towards the back window. He follows me, but I know he doesn't see it.

"How do you feel about the guest house? It's got three bedrooms, you'll have your own privacy, and we can remodel it any way you want. But you can still be here often or as little as you want, and we can carpool to work."

He just looks at me, almost in shock.

"It's just an idea. I know Austin will want you close. This way we can eat dinner as a family almost every night, but you still get your space." I tell him.

He nods. "I'll talk to Austin, and if she's on board, then I think it would work. I don't want to be too far from you guys either. You're family."

We spend an hour taking photos, and I give them all a house tour. The best part is it has a library for Austin. Not quite as big as The Biltmore one, but still one that's bigger than we have back at the house.

We talk to Austin about Landon moving into the guest house, and she practically begs him to, so he couldn't say no. Though, we agree to stay at the big house, while renovations happen.

As the day winds down, Ivy and Dom bring in the dinner they snuck away to pick up for me and I kick everyone out, even the security guards, who go hang outside.

"Now, for our first meal in our new home," I say, as I spread the food out on the kitchen counter.

"The first meal with my fiancé." She says, and my heart skips a beat.

As we eat, we make plans for the house. What she wants to do, things to change, and things to add. She even gets on her phone and looks up the history of the property. I think she's just as excited about the history that comes with it, as she is about the house.

After we finish dinner, I take her phone from her and set it on the counter behind me.

"Hey, I was reading about the crops they used to grow here!" She pouts.

I nip at her lower lip that she was sticking out just before I grab her hips and set her on the kitchen island.

"And I want to make love to my fiancé in our new home right here in the kitchen," I tell her, as I start kissing her neck.

She moans but still looks around for the security guys.

"They're all outside. I kicked them out. They won't be coming inside." I reassure her.

I slowly push her dress up to her waist, before pulling her to the edge of the counter and dropping to my knees. I can see from here that her panties are already soaked.

"It's so sexy how you're always wet and ready for me, baby girl." I moan, as I pull her panties to the side.

I waste no time, running my fingers through her folds. She gasps, as I slide two fingers into her. She's so wet they just glide right in.

"I love you," I tell her right before I suck on her clit.

"Oh, God. I love you too, Dallas." She says, as she falls back on the counter and wraps her legs over my shoulders.

I love the sounds she makes, as I drive her closer and closer to climax. When I hook my fingers on her G-spot on the next thrust and suck hard on her clit, she cums hard, arching her back with my name and a curse on her lips.

As her body relaxes, I stand up and undo my pants, pulling a condom from my pocket.

"Mmm, you don't have to use that if you don't want, too." She says, and I freeze.

"It's just... I've been on the pill for years, and you had that test. I just thought..."

I lean over and kiss her to stop her rambling.

"I would love nothing more than to take you bare, baby girl. Never done that before." I whisper.

"Me either." She says.

I nod and toss the condom on the floor, along with my pants and boxers, before I step back between her legs.

"Come here and sit up. I want you to watch the first time we're together with you, as my future wife." I tell her, as I help her sit up.

With a quick kiss, I watch, as I slowly enter my fiancé for the first time. The sensations of taking her bare almost overwhelm me.

"God, baby. You're so warm and tight."

After a few short stokes, I'm seated fully inside her and looking up I lock eyes with her.

"I love you," I whisper.

"I love you, too." She whispers back, and I start thrusting.

She wraps her arms around my neck, and I hold on to her waist, but we never break eye contact the whole time. Something about the moment feels deeper than any time before, bigger than saying I love you; bigger than her agreeing to marry me. It feels like in this moment our souls are fusing together and won't ever be letting go.

As I start to stroke her clit, she starts moaning again.

"Give me one more, baby girl. I want you to cum on my cock for the first time in our house. Cum for me, baby." I whisper in her ear.

The grip of her legs around my waist tightens a second, before her entire body locks up, and her pussy clamps down on my cock. I only manage one more thrust, before I'm spilling into her, and she's collapsing against me.

I've never climaxed so hard in my life, and I'm holding on to her, like she's my lifeline. How I'm still standing, I will never know.

After a moment, I help her get cleaned up, and we both get dressed, before we head outside to the car. She pauses at the driveway and turns back to the house, lost in thought.

"What is it?" I ask her.

"I just remembered, when we were kids, they were building that new house down the street, and we were riding our bikes by it. I said I never wanted to live in a new house and wanted an old southern plantation."

"And I said I'd make sure you had it one day." I finish for her.

"You have made all my dreams come true, Dallas. Now, it's time for me to do the same for you. You'll see. I'm going to be the best wife."

I just laugh, because I know she will be. Austin as my girlfriend was better than anything I could have dreamed up. I didn't dare dream of Austin as my wife, but I know she will hit it out of the park, too.

EPILOGUE 1

Austin

6 months later

"Austin, I have seen enough tulle, chiffon, and beading to last the rest of my life. The fact that I know what those things are proves it. You have Ivy, Deanna, and Belle, so I'm going to hang out with the men." Landon whines, but he kisses my cheek, before heading out.

"Men, they're always weird at weddings." Ivy laughs.

"Not your man, he's perfect." Deanna jokes.

"I took too long to get ready on our wedding day, and he barged his way in and dragged me down the aisle, mumbling about having too much time to change my mind." Ivy laughs.

"Well, I still can't believe you lied to my face about the whole Dallas thing." Belle pouts.

"I've apologized a million times. We hadn't told Landon, so I didn't know what to say, and I thought he wouldn't want people to know, before he did. But I'll never live this down, will I?" I ask her.

"You will, once you plan my over the top mega fabulous wedding!" Belle squeals.

"You're engaged?!" Ivy squeals right back.

Belle flops down on the couch. "No, I'm not even seeing anyone. But someday, and until then, I get to hold this over her head."

I roll my eyes and turn back to the mirror. I look like a bride. Well, I should it's my wedding day after all. But with the hair and the makeup and the dress, I really do look like a bride.

There's a knock on the door, and when Deanna answers it, Landon is on the other side.

"I was instructed by the groom to give this to you and not leave, until I watch you read it," Landon says with a small smile on his face, as he hands me a sealed envelope.

Taking it, I step away to the window to open it. Inside is a letter, and I recognize Dallas's handwriting instantly.

Austin,

I remember your dad sitting me down to give me a speech on how to treat the woman in my life. He said it was always the little things she never expects that mean more than flowers and candy on Valentine's Day.

I asked him how he showed your mom he loved her. He told me how he proposed and about his wedding day. He sent your mom a letter much like this, telling her everything she meant to him.

He said the wedding was delayed, because it made her cry so hard, they had to redo her makeup.

So, I won't be doing that, because I'm already going crazy waiting to marry you, so instead, I want to tell you that I think your brother is more nervous than both of us put together.

It's part of the reason I'm having him deliver this letter, because he's driving me crazy. But this is also how I know I'm making the right choice. I'm calm and excited about marrying you. I'm not nervous or scared. I just can't wait to call you mine and whisk you away on our honeymoon for two weeks out of the reach of the media. Just you and me and very little clothes.

 I love you with all that I am.

 You very soon to be husband,

 Dallas

The letter is perfect. I don't cry, and I laugh, which earns smiles from the girls, but a confused face from Landon.

"He didn't want to mess up my makeup, so he made me laugh instead," I say and shake my head.

I turn to the window and peek through the curtains to the media circus outside.

When news broke of our engagement, it split their fan base. Half of them were so excited for Dallas and me, while the other half were upset Dallas was off the market. A small portion of them were just mean and nasty, so much so, the band and I shut down our social media accounts for a month.

Landon was our rock during that time. He worked with their PR manager and got us an interview that went viral. We told our story about growing up together and being apart, not knowing the other one liked us. We left out the part of Landon keeping us separated, and by the time the interview was published, we had a massive following for our happily ever after.

We turned our social media accounts back on, and the few nasty comments we got, well, the fans took care of for us, so we have been able to only focus on the good.

The downside, the media is now crowded outside, waiting to see us and get any photos. We allowed the reporter we gave the interview to, to come in and is the only one allowed in the ceremony for photos, but no video. She helped us win our fans back over, so we wanted to help boost her career. Plus, it never hurts to have a reporter on your side.

She did such a good job with our story; we have been approached to have it turned into a movie. After lots of talks, we decided to do it and donate all the money to charity.

So, the movie guys are here today to witness the wedding, and then we sit down with him, after we get back to give the writer our story and work on turning it into a movie. He even agreed to put part of the movie's profits towards charities, when he heard that's what Landon, Dallas, and I were planning to do.

On top of all that, we have been planning this wedding. My only request was that it wasn't a huge wedding, and Dallas agreed. Landon insisted on paying for it as a way to make up for everything. He and Dallas fought a bit, but then, I said if it had been my parents he wouldn't have argued. He agreed, and Landon said he was doing it on behalf of my parents, and I cried my eyes out.

I turn back to face everyone and smile. "Let's get this wedding started," I say.

Landon heads out to get things in motion and let the wedding planner know. She has been a lifesaver, because there's no way I would have been able to plan this wedding without her. She has been great and also has kept the press in the dark, during our meetings, dress fittings, and tastings, too. I was so worried about my dress leaking out to the media that I even had a "dummy dress" set up just in case. Thankfully, we didn't have to use it.

Ivy, Belle, and Deanna all do last minute mirror checks. I asked them to be my bridesmaids. Ivy is my maid of honor, because she has been my secret keeper, and the one to keep me sane over the years. Dallas has my brother as his best man, and Dom and Mason as his groomsmen.

Yeah, our circle is small, but it's ours, and it's perfect.

I check my email one more time, before I turn off my phone. We finished up most of the major renovations, and now, it's smaller things like paint color and work on the property outside the house. Dallas insisted we be able to come home from our honeymoon to our house, and he made it happen.

"Okay, ladies, line up." The wedding planner calls, and then does a once over on me as well.

As we meet in the entryway, I notice Landon is nervous. He's walking me down the aisle today, but I think it's more than that.

His eyes soften, when he sees me, and then he shakes his head.

"What has you in a worse bundle of nerves than the bride on her wedding day?" I ask.

"I have some pretty big shoes to fill walking you down the aisle." He says.

"Landon," I say and hug him, because if I start talking about Mom and Dad, I'm going to cry.

"Let's get you down the aisle, so we can make Dallas a part of this family for real." He says, as I pull away.

That has to be the best part, since the engagement. Never once has he acted like he was losing me or giving me away. He sees this whole thing as legally making Dallas a part of our family, though, he's always been a part of it. This is just the final step.

When the doors open, and we start our trip up the aisle, I don't see the flashing lights, or the massive amounts of fairy lights making a canopy overhead, which was my one big request. All I see is Dallas at the end of the aisle with a huge smile on his face that matches mine.

Thank goodness Belle insisted I have someone video the wedding for us, because I don't remember much other than staring into Dallas's eyes the entire ceremony.

But that kiss. Wow. He kissed me like no one else was in the room.

Now, we're dancing at our reception. We have danced to five songs straight, and my feet are killing me, but I don't want to stop. This night is perfect.

"This is so much better than prom," I say and smile up at him.

"Well, there's much better food." He says.

"That and because you're mine, and I can do this." I reach down and squeeze his sexy ass. "Or this." I lean up and kiss him. "Any-time I want, and no one is going to bat an eye."

"I have to agree, and I also don't have to hide this." He leans for-ward, pressing his hard cock against me. "I was so hard all prom night and hiding it from you made it even worse."

"Well, we can do something about that now." I barely get the words out, before he's pulling me from the ballroom back to the room I got ready in.

He doesn't care that there are guests outside; he makes love to me thoroughly, before we head back and celebrate long into the night.

EPILOGUE 2

Dallas

Three years later

There's nothing like the roar of the crowd during a show. We just finished singing, *She's Still The One,* a song I wrote for Austin on our honeymoon. It broke so many records, and Landon and I both know there's no way we will top it. As I stand here and look out over the crowd screaming for just one more song on the last show of our goodbye tour, I know the next stage in my life is going to be so much better.

I look to the side stage where my wife stands. My wife. My pregnant wife. She nods, because she knows I'm asking if she's okay if we do one more song. I turn to Landon, and he gives the cue to the band. We play one of our first songs to ever get radio time, and even after all these years, the crowd knows it by heart.

Landon and I started the record label, and we signed some amazing talent. We put this goodbye tour on for our fans, but to also introduce the guys we signed. The tour has been great, and Austin has been at my side, and the fans love her coming on to sing with me, even more so, when her belly started to show.

The label is doing great. Milton has been helping a lot, and they did some great press with this tour, even had us doing a few back to backs with some of their guys, selling tickets to both shows, as a package.

Austin stopped taking graphic design clients and works just with the label now on album covers, the website, and plans to pull back and oversee the other designers, once our baby is born.

When we wrap up and head off stage, I wrap my arms around Austin. She doesn't care that I'm hot and sweaty from the show. She loves being in my arms as much as I love her being in them. Landon is there, when I finally pull back.

"Don't squish my niece!" He jokes and rubs Austin's belly. He's just as excited about this baby as we are.

"Come on, stud. Let them relax." His wife wraps an arm around his waist and pulls him to his dressing room.

Landon finally asked that girl on the charity board out to dinner again, and this time she said yes. They got married just before the tour six months ago. He did it the same way his dad proposed to his mom; the way I proposed to Austin. He bought her dream house and proposed inside of it. Austin got to help him with it, since he helped with our proposal.

He wears his father's wedding band, and every now and then, Austin will pick his hand up and rub her thumb over the band. I've seen Landon do the same to her ring.

Austin gets along with his wife, Opal, really well, so they went out to lunch and to get their nails done, before she brought her to the house. Their house had to have some renovations done too, so we convinced them to move into the guest house together, until after this tour and get the renovations done. They just got the call last week their place is ready to go. The best part they're only ten minutes up the road.

Our house renovations went well, and Landon moved in a month after we got back from our honeymoon. The big house sold pretty fast, once we gave the realtor the okay to say it was our old place.

Not much changed, once we sold the big house. Landon still insisted on cooking dinner every night, but he would go back to his place afterwards and give us the evening to ourselves. We carpooled to our label and worked hard there.

Many days, Austin would bring in lunch for us and spend Deanna's lunch break with her having girl time. Deanna didn't even hesitate, when we offered her the job. We offered her more than she was making, but she told us she would have done it for less, because she loves being close to Austin and helping new talent.

It's been a fun ride.

"Come on, I want to show you something," I tell her, as I lead her to my dressing room and lock the door.

"What is it?" She asks.

"It's the last show on the last tour. The last time I'll have a dressing room. I want my wife right here." I tell her.

Smiling, she shakes her head and pulls me in for a kiss.

When Austin told me she was pregnant, I cried like a baby. Our family was growing again. For three kids who had nobody but each other for the longest time, we're growing in the best possible ways. There will be five of us soon. Austin suspects Opal is pregnant, but hasn't said anything, so there will be six of us soon.

After making love to my wife in our dressing room, we go back to the bus for one last night on the road, before heading home. We got a new bus that has two bedrooms and six bunk beds. Even though it's our last tour, we plan to do many family vacations, and we figured we could use the bus with our kids and travel with Landon and Opal and their family, too.

Life as a family man is much different than one of a rock star, but it's one I like a whole lot more. I will pick Austin every time and know I will wake up, when we're old and gray and still be able to say she's still the one; she's still the love of my life.

✽ ✽ ✽

What to Read Next

If you loved *She's Still The One* and watching a playboy fall head over heels for his girl you don't want to miss **Sunrise from the Chasing the Sun Duet**.

Kade, a Hollywood playboy, goes to hide from the media in a small beach town. Add in a fake relationship, noisy townies, and a best friend who might as well be a bodyguard and Kade has his work cut out for him.

Looking for another friends to lovers' story?

Then make sure you check out **Texting Titan** and **The Cowboy and His Obsession.**

* * *

Join my newsletter and get two free books!

Join Kaci Rose's Newsletter

https://www.kacirose.com/KaciRoseBoB

* * *

Please Leave a Review!

I love to hear from my readers! Please leave a review on the platform you bought your book from!

OTHER BOOKS BY KACI ROSE

See all of Kaci Rose's Books

Oakside Military Heroes Series
Saving Noah – Lexi and Noah
Saving Easton – Easton and Paisley
Saving Teddy – Teddy and Mia

Chasing the Sun Duet
Sunrise
Sunset

Rock Springs Texas Series
The Cowboy and His Runaway – Blaze and Riley
The Cowboy and His Best Friend – Sage and Colt
The Cowboy and His Obsession – Megan and Hunter
The Cowboy and His Sweetheart – Jason and Ella
The Cowboy and His Secret – Mac and Sarah
Rock Springs Weddings Novella
Rock Springs Box Set 1-5 + Bonus Content
The Cowboy and His Mistletoe Kiss – Lilly and Mike

The Cowboy and His Valentine – Maggie and Nick

The Cowboy and His Vegas Wedding – Royce and Anna

The Cowboy and His Angel – Abby and Greg

The Cowboy and His Christmas Rockstar – Savannah and Ford

The Cowboy and His Billionaire – Brice and Kayla

Standalone Books

Stay With Me Now

Texting Titan

Accidental Sugar Daddy

She's Still The One

Take Me To The River